A MAN CALLED BRAVO

BEN CHEROT

Copyright © 2021 by Ben Cherot

All rights reserved. No part of this publication may be reproduced, distributed, or transmitted in any form or by any means, including photocopying, recording, or other electronic or mechanical methods, without the prior written permission of the publisher, except in the case brief quotations embodied in critical reviews and other noncommercial uses permitted by copyright law.

ISBN: 978-1-63945-108-1 (Paperback)
        978-1-63945-109-8 (Ebook)

The views expressed in this book are solely those of the author and do not necessarily reflect the views of the publisher, and the publisher hereby disclaims any responsibility for them.

Writers' Branding
1800-608-6550
www.writersbranding.com
orders@writersbranding.com

Contents

One	1
Two	4
Three	13
Four	17
Five	20
Six	28
Seven	35
Eight	44
Nine	50
Ten	58
Eleven	66
Twelve	73
Thirteen	80
Fourteen	88
Fifteen	93
Sixteen	95
Seventeen	103
Eighteen	111
Nineteen	120
Twenty	124
Twenty-One	130
Twenty-Two	139
Twenty-Three	145
Twenty-Four	152
Twenty-Five	157
Twenty-Six	164
Twenty-Seven	171
Twenty-Eight	175

Twenty-Nine 179
Thirty 184
Thirty-One...................................... 188
Thirty-Two 194
Thirty-Three 205
Thirty-Four 211
Thirty-Five 219
Thirty-Six 224
Thirty-Seven 228
Thirty-Eight 231
Thirty-Nine 234
Forty.. 242
Forty-One 245
Forty-Two 250
Forty-Three 255

ONE

The U. S. Marshal driving the black SUV gnashed his teeth, irritated for having to idle in the engine-pulsing tension of morning commuter traffic on Andrews Avenue in Fort Lauderdale. A line of cars and trucks preceding him in the right-turn lane delayed entrance onto busy Broward Boulevard; typical of morning traffic in South Florida.

The marshal alongside him in the passenger seat turned to the deputy assistant United States attorney on the bench behind them and shrugged to indicate their inability to relieve worrying whether they'd get to the courthouse on time. That concern etched all three of their faces. All wore flak jackets as a precaution against a possible attack by radical members of a Puerto Rican liberation movement because of their transporting the forlorn prisoner sharing the bench seat with the deputy assistant U. S. attorney.

The prisoner's limp black hair hung down the sides of his tawny face with its lack of expression for the usually daunting prospect of arraignment in federal court on a capital offense. He appeared equally indifferent to the possibility of an attack by his compatriots, though they'd tried and failed to kill him to prevent him sharing information with the authorities.

The driver gripped the wheel when the light blinked to green, eager to move forward. Both marshals then scowled when traffic only inched ahead. Seconds ticked off as one vehicle after the next crept around the corner—progress retarded by the choke of traffic backed up on the boulevard. The damned light went yellow just as they reached the intersection.

The car ahead of them turned fully onto the boulevard, permitting the marshal to nose around the corner just as the light flashed red. But only half of their long-ass Chevy Tahoe made it onto Broward Boulevard—a virtual canyon flanked by tall commercial buildings and high-rise condos. The vehicular glut finally crept forward permitting them to turn fully onto the thoroughfare while hemmed in the right lane, with a need to turn left at the next corner.

Denied options they inched along with traffic until the car on their left dawdled, allowing them to nose into the middle-lane. They still needed to get into the left lane before reaching the end of the block. Providentially the car on their left failed to keep pace leaving a space for them to dart into. But even after getting into the proper lane the marshals could only stare down the block and across the boulevard at the huge United States Court House with its majestic columns—so close and still so distant.

As they crept along in that vehicular crush the seemingly endless block to Northeast Third Avenue they anguished again until entering the left-turn lane. But relief evaporated when they saw that traffic headed in the opposite direction denied them an opportunity to cross those three lanes. Like most South Floridians, they tolerated that vehicular glut during the winter months. But by mid-April they expected most of the snowbirds and tourists to have returned north, reducing traffic. Not this morning.

"About damn time," the driver grouched when a break in the endless trail of cars and trucks permitted him to accomplish the turn. He didn't speed up even though Third Avenue had sparse traffic since he needed to go only one block before turning left onto the street behind the courthouse. Then he had only a few hundred feet to pass the concrete barriers positioned there since nine-eleven to prevent car- or truck-bombers getting close enough to damage the building by detonating their vehicles.

Beyond that he saw the down-ramp on his left, into which he needed to turn to park under the courthouse, but had to concede the right of way to a big-ass Lincoln sedan rolling down the street from the opposite direction. He scowled when the damned thing pulled into the garage down-ramp blocking them from entering.

So he pulled close behind it to avoid their tail end protruding into the street.

Then they resigned themselves to waiting while the two security guards checked the Lincoln driver's authorization to enter that parking area, plus inspect the interior of the car and its trunk, and finally surveil the underside with mirrors on long poles to ascertain that a bomb hadn't been attached to it. Rigid security had become a necessity with the rash of extremists of one persuasion or another inflicting pain and fear on society to publicize radical causes.

The marshals and the deputy assistant US attorney gasped when two delivery vans screeched to a stop behind them. Doors sprung open and three men in ski masks leapt out of each vehicle firing fusillades with stubby TEC-9 machinegun pistols into the front and back windows of the black Chevy Tahoe.

Denied time to react the two marshals collapsed with blood spurting out of their faces and necks. The deputy assistant US attorney convulsed when bullets tore into his head and neck. The prisoner screamed curses at the shooters in Spanish, but received twice as many bullets as the others, some shooting his eyes out.

The driver of the Lincoln clambered out, brandishing a semi-automatic pistol and shot the two unarmed security guards who stood frozen by the assault. "*Viva independencia de Puerto Rico!*" was shouted by several of the assailants while scampering back to their respective vans, joined by the driver of the Lincoln, who abandoned that vehicle. Both vans raced up the street to screech around the corner and disappear.

TWO

Ray Bravo climbed out of the taxi into the clatter and activity of downtown Fort Lauderdale, its march of tall buildings dominated by the federal courthouse diagonally across heavily trafficked Broward Boulevard. Attaché case in hand, he basked in the mid-April sun during the short walk to enter the towering office building with the number 500 decorating its modernistic glass façade.

Dressed in business attire like most in the spacious lobby, he joined those boarding the elevator. He hadn't bothered to consult the directory, having been informed that the office complex of the Assistant US Attorney would not be listed for security purposes. After exiting the elevator on the seventh floor he entered a small foyer where he encountered a metal detector. It preceded entrance to a reception booth, a half-round bubble of see-through bulletproof plastic.

Anticipating the metal detector to sound an alarm, he held aloft his credentials to be seen by the uniformed guard inside the enclosure. With his other hand, though burdened by his attaché case, he flapped open his suit jacket to reveal his black semi-automatic pistol strapped under his left arm.

The guard kept his hand on the butt of his holstered weapon as the visitor approached, then relaxed upon perusing the man's credentials identifying him as a federal agent with the Bureau of Alcohol, Tobacco and Firearms. The guard nodded acceptance that the visitor resembled his photograph: six feet tall and athletic looking for fifty-one years old, with black hair topping a mature face with dark eyes. His olive complexion fit the Hispanic name of Ramón Bravo.

"Who did you need to see, sir?" the guard asked.

"Not certain. It's about escorting a prisoner named Elizondo to Washington."

The guard gawked but quickly recovered his composure. "You need to wait a sec, sir." He punched in a few intercom numbers on a telephone console before speaking cryptically to someone.

Bravo didn't bother to listen, accustomed to guards requiring guidance. So he paced the limited reception area, harnessing patience for anyone superior to a security guard to accommodate him. It gratified him when almost immediately a door opened and a round-faced young man emerged.

A few inches shorter than Bravo, the curly-haired guy stared wide-eyed at him. "This for real? You're here to escort that prisoner, Gaspar Elizondo, somewhere?"

When Bravo nodded, the young man said: "Just a minute, sir," and disappeared. Bravo scowled at the closed door, then turned questioning eyes to the security guard, who shrugged and turned away. Bravo hunched acceptance of the man's reluctance to get involved in explanations.

After a minute or so of shuffling around he perked to the door opening again and the curly-headed young man waving him in. Without uttering a word he gestured Bravo to follow him down a hallway flanked by closed office doors, then into an executive office.

Bravo winced upon recognition of the mature man behind the commanding desk. A meticulously trimmed gray mustache with turned-up ends adorned the man's grim face. "Didn't expect *you*, of all people, Bravo."

Bravo tried not to grimace displeasure at the unexpected encounter and harsh greeting. The name Jerome Archison flashed into memory, along with related incidents he hadn't anticipated revisiting. Shrugging acceptance of the situation he thrust out his hand in an effort to appear congenial. "I take it you're prosecuting out of this office now, sir?"

"I'm the Assistant US Attorney in charge here."

Bravo nodded acceptance of the man having been promoted.

Jerome Archison half rose to grudgingly shake hands, then waved the visitor to a chair facing his desk while he dropped back into his leather throne. "What the hell is this with regard to your coming here to escort one of our prisoners to Washington?"

"I'm certain the bureau advised you of it, sir."

"We received a request without specifics regarding who they'd dispatch for the pick-up. However, we'd already decided to indict and try Elizondo from this office."

"If you informed my office of that decision why in hell did they send me here?"

"Explain your assignment," Archison said.

Bravo tried not to reveal being stung by the arrogance of the guy to disregard his question while having the audacity to demand he answer one. Exhaling he forced himself to remain cordial since he addressed a superior in the Department of Justice. Withdrawing a sheaf of papers from his attaché case he handed it to the assistant US attorney. "There a problem?" he asked while watching the man peruse them.

"Elizondo's dead," Archison said. "Gunned down this morning while being taken to the federal court house diagonally across the street."

When Bravo stared slack-jawed at him, Archison said, "Which is why I'm assembling a joint-agency taskforce, to take those ruthless assassins off the street."

A rap on the open door incited both men to turn to a barrel-chested man in tweedy sports-coat filling up the doorway. Close-cropped blond hair with a sprinkling of gray topped his square face. He plodded into the office followed by a mature blonde in a tight-fitting dark blue suit that emphasized her full-figure.

Archison introduced the visitors to each other. "Special Agent Bravo of ATF, this is Detective Peter Olecki of the Broward County Sheriff's Office, and his partner, Detective Cleo Broderick. They've been dispatched by their office in response to my request this morning for additional people to expand the taskforce so we can take those brazen assassins off our streets."

Bravo rose to shake hands with them, after which Archison waved everyone to seats. Fingering his pretentious mustache as he sat he directed: "I want those rotten-assed extremists that pulled the raid at the courthouse hunted down and captured—or killed— for brazenly murdering two US marshals and a deputy assistant US attorney, as well as two courthouse security guards—along with that prisoner."

"Any luck in identifying those cold-blooded bastards?" Detective Olecki asked.

Grim-facced Archison shook his head. "Sonsofbitches wore ski masks. And the two delivery vans they used were stolen and have been abandoned."

"You saying we have nothing to point us in the right direction?" Detective Olecki asked.

"The surveillance cameras recorded the event but gives us very little to go on," Archison said. "To view it you'll have to go to Miami since the film has been sent down to the FBI lab with hopes of identifying one or more of those heartless bastards."

"We sure as hell need those FBI folks to come up with something," Detective Olecki said, "to get us a heads-up so we can bring them down before they melt away."

"Our best hope is identifying the driver of the stolen Lincoln," Archison said, "even though a bushy gray beard concealed most of his face, with a mop of gray hair adding to the illusion of age."

"Let's hope so," Detective Olecki said, "to help us cleanse that brazen attack from the slate of Broward County."

Detective Cleo Broderick bobbed her head in agreement. Her blonde hair pulled tight against her head accented her toughness. However, Bravo considered her tight-fitting skirt-suit emphasizing her full figure as over the top . . . for his bureau anyway.

"Those bastards killed one of my deputy assistants," Archison growled. "Arthur Meyers was an astute and dependable prosecutor."

"Artie Meyers!" burst out of Bravo. "Artie Meyers—from New York?"

"You knew him?" Archison asked.

"We went to college together—at CCNY—while we were New York City cops." Bravo closed his eyes, stung by pain and disbelief. Shaking off emotions, he reopened them and said: "Artie went on to study law at NYU. I joined this bureau, which was then in the Treasury Department. ATF has since been transferred to Justice."

"Then you're feeling as much pain as we are," Archison said. "We need you to assist us in taking those rat-bastards off the streets."

"Yep," Bravo said. "Need to get transferred here." Then he blinked as memory struck. "Oh shit! Have to be back in Washington tonight. Can check with the bureau in the morning and request to be assigned to this case. Believe me, I want to be in on it and get the bastards killed Artie Meyers, a real good buddy in the old—"

"Clarify your coming here to escort Elizondo to Washington," Archison said.

Bravo frowned, baffled by the inquiry, as well by the man's abrupt change of subject. But he shrugged and replied: "Assignment—plain and simple."

"Why'd they send you particularly," Archison asked, "considering ATF has a staff here in town, not all that far down Broward Boulevard? Why not one of those agents?"

Bravo shrugged. "Was in Houston, waiting for a flight to return to DeeCee when instructed to alter my plans and stop-over in Fort Lauderdale to pick up and escort that prisoner to the capital."

"Why you particularly?" Archison asked.

"Don't know. Didn't they explain it in their request?"

"In their customary arrogance they disregarded sharing particulars."

"Then you know as much as I do."

"Probably dispatched you because you're Puerto Rican," Archison said.

"What the hell does being Puerto Rican have to do with anything?" Bravo asked. He clenched his teeth to suppress expressing resentment, having endured a lifetime of ethnic slights.

"That prisoner got killed was Puerto Rican," Detective Cleo Broderick said.

"Those who did the killings more'n likely also were Puerto Ricans," added Detective Olecki, "same as that bunch raided the airport."

Bravo frowned, perplexed by the airport reference. But before he could question it, Olecki said: "This whole thing is about Puerto Rican terrorists that call themselves *Independistas* or something like that."

"According to FBI information," Archison said, "they belong to a group referred to as LPR."

"Libertad Puerto Rico," Bravo said, "who advocate for independence from the U. S. Why was this Elizondo in custody?"

"He took part in a raid on the Fort Lauderdale Executive Airport two weeks ago," Archison said.

Bravo bobbed his head in acknowledgement of that incident at the sizeable airfield off Cypress Creek Road, separate of the busy and better-known Fort Lauderdale-Hollywood International Airport. He knew it accommodates cargo planes as well as corporate jets of all sizes, with long enough runways for some military aircraft. All government agents had been informed of that incident and alerted to be on the look-out for those offenders.

"What did they get?" Bravo asked.

"Combat weapons earmarked for a local army reserve unit," Archison said, "were stored at the Nininger US Army Reserve Center located on the perimeter of the airport at Fusion Boulevard and Northwest Fifty-Fifth Street."

"Left the care of those weapons to some clerks and a few sleepy guards," Detective Olecki said. "Guess those folks never anticipated a raid on that storehouse."

"Like nine-eleven," Detective Cleo Broderick said. "You'd think we'd wise up and stay alert."

"Too much concentration on Islamics," Olecki said, "while too little on all the other terrorist groups."

"Of which there are no end," Detective Broderick added.

"Received a report of that incident while in Houston," Bravo said. "How'd the raiders gain entrance to the airport grounds, considering the level of security most airports practice these days, especially those of the size and importance of that one?"

"They stole a truck from Amos Landscaping," Detective Olecki said. "That ole' boy contracts with most of the independently owned buildings on the perimeter of the airfield to maintain their small lawns and gardens."

"Consequently," Archison said, "appearance of that truck didn't raise an alarm. A number of armed men in ski masks surprised and overcame the warehouse personnel. Then they loaded weapons, ammunition and some explosives onto their stolen truck."

"A couple of security personnel eluded detection," Detective Olecki said, "and alerted the Broward County Sheriff's sub-Office on the far periphery of the airfield."

"Half a dozen deputies responded," Detective Cleo Broderick added, "and shot it out with those bad-asses, resulting in the wounding of several deputies and three terrorists."

"The raiders succeeded in carrying away two of their wounded," Olecki said. "Elizondo, who'd been shot in the thigh, was unable to hobble back to the truck quick enough so ended up getting shot by his *compadres* while they fled in that truck."

"Those heartless bastards," Archison said, "didn't intend to leave anyone behind to be questioned, but managed to put bullets only in his arm and leg."

"Hard to shoot someone from a lurching truck," Olecki said.

"Worse part," Archison said, "is that goddam truck evaded a dragnet, despite having AMOS LANDSCAPING emblazoned on it."

"And in spite of the Sheriff's Department immediately putting out an APB on it," Detective Cleo Broderick added.

"Took damn near two hours to find that sucker," Olecki said, "in the parking lot of an office complex off Cypress Creek Road and Northwest Twelfth Avenue . . . not all that far outside the airport."

"Learned from interviewing people who work in that complex," Detective Cleo Broderick said, "that Hispanic laborers transferred the cargo from that open truck to a closed rent-a-truck, which had been waiting there."

"Those folks didn't report it though until damn near two hours after the raid," Olecki said.

"Despite the bolo as well as repeated news reports on radio and TV about that daring robbery," Cleo Broderick added.

"Hard to believe," Olecki said, "that nobody in those buildings associated the transference of cargo from an Amos Landscaping vehicle to a rented truck as connected to that airport raid."

"Paid so little attention to that rent-a-truck," Cleo Broderick said, "that nobody remembered for sure the rental company name on it."

"Nor did it dawn on anyone to report the abandoning of a truck with Amos Landscaping painted in large letters on its sides," Archison said.

"Despite it blocking a number of parking spaces," Cleo Broderick added.

"Any of those landscapers see the hijackers up close and personal when their truck got stolen?" Bravo asked.

"Well enough to describe the vehicle they arrived in," Archison replied. He picked up and read from a file on his desk that the hijackers showed up in an aged and battered pick-up truck with a partially broken taillight. Most agreed to its color as green, though they disagreed whether they identified a Dodge, a Ford, a Chevy or a foreign brand. Some said it had half a rear fender missing—maybe rusted off. Others reported that it had no front bumper. Two of them noted that it had a spidery split in the upper right corner of the windshield. Most agreed that the license plate number ended with an 8 after three or four other numbers and letters . . . while disagreeing on those."

"What about physical identifications of the truckjackers," Bravo asked, "like ethnic make-up, height, weight, complexion, mustaches or beards, scars, and like that?"

"Most any of those ole' boys of Amos remembered," Cleo Broderick said, "were those damn guns in their faces. Anyway, doubtful those black laborers could tell a Puerto Rican from a Cuban or a Mexican. Hell, I can't."

"The landscaper boss recognize any of them?" Bravo asked. ". . . Maybe as former employees?"

Olecki shook his head. "Amos Robisson, an admired black man who's been in business in this part of Florida for a lot of years, hires mostly black folks. Says those truck-nappers were Hispanics, and only became aware of them as Puerto Ricans when they raced away, yelling: *Viva Puerto Rico*."

"Sure appears like they didn't want folks to mistake them for Cubans or something," Cleo Broderick said.

"They damn sure advertised themselves as Puerto Ricans," Olecki said.

"Any idea why they killed the prisoner instead of freeing him?" Bravo asked.

"We kept Elizondo under heavy guard while hospitalized," Archison said, "concerned that those extremists were daring enough to raid the hospital to spring him. Didn't know they wanted to kill him. Fortunately, the prisoner didn't have serious wounds so could be transferred to the security of the county jail."

"Which, like as not," Olecki said, "kept him from getting wasted."

"Why in a county jail instead of a federal facility?" Bravo asked.

"No federal facility in the area," Archison said, "so we utilize the county jail, with US Marshals overseeing federal prisoners."

When Bravo nodded acceptance of that, Archison said: "It would be helpful if you clarified why you were assigned to escort Elizondo to Washington, rather than by agents posted here in Fort Lauderdale."

Bravo gestured to have the telephone on the desk pushed to him. "I'll call my office and ask. Might just be relevant."

THREE

"Special Agent Ray Bravo here. Need to speak to Assistant Director Justin Ball. Yes, I'll hold."

He frowned when, a minute or so later, the female voice informed: "Assistant Director Ball isn't available to receive your call, sir."

"Did you inform Assistant Director Ball that Special Agent Ray Bravo called?"

"Yes, sir, but he said to tell you he's in conference with two congressmen and is unavailable at the moment, but will get back to you."

Bravo's brow furrowed, certain that the director had been informed about the courthouse shooting and knew Bravo had been dispatched there to escort that prisoner to Washington. But why, he wondered, hadn't they contacted him upon the demise of the prisoner to abort the mission? "Is Deputy Assistant Director Kermak available?" Clicked on hold again he inhaled patience for a minute or two, during which he was assailed with messages designed to guide the uninitiated to various services and departments. "Hey, Wally. Ray Bravo here—in Fort Lauderdale. What? How are you surprised that I'm here when you dispatched me to Fort Lauderdale? Remember?"

Bravo shook his head and rolled his eyes back while taking a breath. "Next thing you'll tell me you don't know what happened here this morning. Then why in hell wasn't I brought up to speed and advised not to bother picking up a prisoner who no longer existed?

"Too hectic to remember me? Yeah, I'll bet you're aghast. At least tell me why I was assigned to escort that guy to Washington instead of one of the resident agents already in Fort Lauderdale? You don't know? Can you at least tell me what that prisoner's value was. Of course you expected to get information from him. Why else would you want him transported there? I'd like a few specifics. Okay, I'll hold."

Bravo averted his eyes from the faces focused on him, embarrassed by his bureau treating him like a newbie, then parking him on hold and denying him the respect deserved by a veteran. Besides, he believed his bureau needed to share that intel with the US Attorney's office here, considering the losses these people suffered.

He perked to the voice on the phone. "What? You aren't able to convey any information? Know what: I need to talk to Justin Ball, to get some pertinent damn information. Why the hell isn't he available? Why the hell can't he be disturbed? This is important, goddam it! Yes, I'll hold."

Bravo kept his eyes averted, humiliated as well as chagrined by the short shrift he received from his own people. After a couple of minutes on hold, and incensed by a continual repeat of the intermittent messages, he concluded he'd been hung out to dry, so pulled out his cellphone and speed-dialed.

"Ball here."

"Justin, this is Ray Bravo."

"Jesus H, Ray, you're interrupting a conference with two congressmen."

"For a damned important reason, Jus."

"You, of all people, Ray, know I'm not to be called on my personal cellphone unless vital."

"This is vital . . . an extreme emergency. I'm here in Fort Lauderdale with a lot of angry people, their buddies shot up, five dead, plus the prisoner wasted. These people deserve to know why in hell you sent me here to baby-sit that Elizondo guy. Instead I'm getting sandbagged and parked on hold. What the hell is going on?"

"For the moment, Ray, this business is under wraps."

"The guy is dead. What the hell is so confidential now that it can't be shared with the US Attorney's office here in Lauderdale—who incidentally is also a member of the Department of Justice."

"They'll receive definitive explanations in due time."

"That's bullshit, Jus. These people don't deserve to be jerked around, any more than I do. Fact is they're threatening if they don't get answers real quick, they're going public to raise awareness of a possible bureau goof that resulted in the deaths of various law enforcement officers as well as the murder of a prisoner who just might have imparted vital information."

"Jesus H, back them off that play, Ray. This bureau has enough black-eyes over the years to contend with."

"All it takes is giving them the explanation they deserve."

"You work for us, remember, not them."

"I agree with them that they deserve answers . . . as do I."

"Don't go that route, Ray, and scuttle twenty-two years of advancements."

"Sounds like I've already been hung out to dry, with you guys treating me like an outsider. Might as well take the farm as be kicked in the face by my own guys."

"I hear you, Ray, and despite being antagonized by your attitude, I intend to render a detailed explanation in due time. Meanwhile you need to convince those folks to give us a few days before issuing any statements."

"That won't cut it, Jus, considering Assistant US Attorney Archison has a press conference scheduled in an hour, at which he intends to blame the brutal murder of that prisoner and those law enforcement people on the lack of cooperation by our bureau." It took effort not to mention Artie Meyers and his personal relationship with that man.

"Holy shit!" Justin Ball exclaimed. "We can't afford that kind of mud-slinging—have enough problems with congressional inquiries about past escapades."

"Stopping them is your call, Jus."

"Okay, tell them to give me ten minutes to wrap up this conference with the two congressmen and I'll call back to explain it to everyone's satisfaction."

"You got it, good buddy. This man is willing to give you fifteen minutes to get back to us before he paints the bureau with publicity it doesn't need." Bravo accepted the click as the conclusion of that discussion. He shrugged to the others, having no need to brief them about what transpired since they'd overheard most of it and could guess at what they didn't hear.

"You're as audacious as ever," Archison said, "resorting to extortion and intimidation, even when dealing with your bureau superiors."

"It's getting results, isn't it?"

"While flirting with insubordination."

"Long as he gets it done," Detective Olecki said. "We need straight answers and they obviously are sandbagging him—consequently us."

"I like his style," Detective Cleo Broderick said, batting her blue eyes at Bravo.

"Would you address superiors in that fashion?" Archison asked her.

"No, sir, don't have me no balls that big."

FOUR

Bravo tried not to cringe and expose feeling slighted by his own peoples while waiting for the return call. So he forced himself to converse with the others despite fretting that Ball didn't intend to call him back. Every few minutes he repeated to them the need for patience, assuring that the call would come. The lines tautening his face revealed a waning of optimism.

He exhaled relief when a secretary stuck her head in the door and announced: "Call for a Special Agent Bravo on line six from an Assistant Director Ball of ATF."

He picked up. "Hi, Jus. I've clicked the call onto conference speaker so everyone can hear."

"Jeezus H, why?"

"Because these people deserve to be privy to every facet of this case, so just lay it out."

After an audible sigh, Justin Ball informed that the prisoner, Elizondo, had a go-between contact them, ostensibly because that prisoner didn't speak English well enough to confer with them. That contact informed that Elizondo had valuable intel about a cell of Puerto Rican *Independistas* with a mad plan to publicize their agenda by blowing up an important building in the capital within the week. Those insurrectionists obtained the needed explosives in that raid on that Nininger US Army Reserve Center.

That caller, Assistant Director Ball, informed that Elizondo was in fear of being assassinated, so refused to divulge any specifics until under ATF protection in Washington. He didn't feel safe in that jail, or anywhere in Florida, so demanded to be put under wraps before divulging any information.

"And you believed him?" Bravo asked.

"Ruled on the side of caution," Assistant Director Ball said.

"Gullible," Archison said.

"I remind all," Assistant Director Ball replied, "that the man's extremist cohorts had already tried and failed to kill him."

"They finally succeeded," Bravo reminded.

"The bureau might have prevented that," Ball retorted, "had the assistant US attorney not insisted on arraigning the guy in court there rather than surrender him to the bureau as requested."

"Bullshit!" exploded out of Archison as he bounded out of his chair and looked about to jump onto the desk, his elaborate mustache quivering.

Bravo held up a hand to calm him while responding to his boss. "Did the guy give specifics why he didn't feel safe here?"

"The intermediary," Ball replied, "insisted that the *Independistas* had a wire into that jail, as well as into the Sheriffs' Office."

"Bullshit!" burst in unison out of Detectives Olecki and Broderick.

"Whether true or not," Ball growled back, "nothing convinced the prisoner he'd be safe there. He persisted he'd talk only if spirited off to the safety of Washington."

"Why'd you pick me in particular to escort him there?"

"Elizondo demanded his escort be ATF as well as someone who spoke his language—preferably a Puerto Rican, and with the capability to protect him."

"And you folks bought that trumped up story?" Archison asked.

"The bureau felt duty-bound to obtain that intelligence," Ball said, adamantly, "to prevent any buildings in the capital being detonated. The country has suffered enough traumas from terrorist strikes. Yes, and I don't deny the ATF relished the prospect of being publicized as the agency that saved America from another catastrophe."

"Did you share that intel with other agencies?" Archison asked.

"No, sir, since it might have been a ruse by Elizondo to have the ATF whisk his ass out of danger in Florida. Maybe there wasn't any bombing planned in the capital, influencing caution with respect to needlessly alarming folks in *the district*."

"That doesn't excuse not sharing with this office," Archison grouched.

"You're quite right, sir, but we needed to avoid looking like dupes if we were being conned. On the other hand, we couldn't take a chance, since the terrorists had gotten explosives from that raid on the Nininger Army Reserve Center."

"What's the identity of Elizondo's go-between?" Archison asked.

"The guy declined to identify himself," Ball said, "fearful of being targeted by the terrorists."

"Then how do you know he was genuine?" Detective Olecki asked.

"We refused to act on the request without proof that he'd actually been in touch with Elizondo and wasn't flim-flamming us. So the caller admitted his employment at the jail and alluded to things only insiders would know about, which testified to his having familiarity with the place. But he refused to identify himself further, having been convinced by Elizondo that the terrorists had tapped into law enforcement offices in the area—something we failed to convince him wasn't credible."

"Can you give us any description of the go-between?" Bravo asked.

"He had an Hispanic accent, but refused to identify himself, fearful of jeopardizing his family. He insisted we believe him or he'd bow out."

"Not a lot to go on," Detective Olecki said.

"Can't argue with that," Ball said. "But we were loathe to ignore the possibility of a terrorist attack and end up with a major goof on our record, so agreed to accommodate Elizondo even with the caller refusing to reveal his identity. That's the whole of it."

FIVE

Bravo signed off with his boss and was placing the telephone in its cradle when he flinched. He'd been unprepared for Archison to slam the tabletop with the palm of his hand.

"Goddam bureaucrats!" the assistant US attorney bellowed, the turned-up ends of his mustache quivering. "They play politics and publicity games at the cost of human lives."

Detective Cleo Broderick nodded. "Always said government agencies need to seriously consider their missions and work in concert instead of competing,"

"Especially," Olecki added, "during these trying times of national security."

"So let's get to work," Archison said, "and bring those rat-bastards to the bar of justice."

"Roger that," Olecki said. "I'll have the sheriff's office fax me all the Hispanic personnel employed in the county jail, especially guards."

"I've done that," Archison said, lifting sheets of paper from his desk, "having assumed the prisoner would seek someone Hispanic to converse with since he spoke little English." He cleared his throat while adjusting his reading glasses before reading that a couple of the jail guards are Mexican-born, one US-born of Mexican parents, two Brazilian-born, two Cuban-born, and two: Cortez and Botero, mainland-born of Puerto Rican parents. Only Teodoro Martinez had been born in the island of Puerto Rico.

"Sure sounds like we need to interview this Martinez," Olecki said. "Any idea if he's presently on duty?"

"I'll find out," Archison said as he lifted the phone. He talked to someone and signed off before addressing the three people in his office. "I'll have the FBI contingent assigned to this taskforce interview the lot of them."

"I'd like to be the one talks to this Martinez fellow," Olecki said. "Special Agent Bravo can accompany me to keep it a government investigation, if that's required."

"Need to catch a plane back to Washington," Bravo said. "My wife is depending on me to escort her to a ball at the Spanish Embassy tonight."

"Goddam!" burst out of Cleo Broderick.

"Personal affairs," Archison growled, "go to the back burner . . . especially balls at foreign embassies. We have a terrorist situation here. Maybe you've forgotten how they mowed down Arthur Meyers and two marshals."

"Plus two unarmed guards," Olecki added.

"No, I haven't, sir. But I do have a personal life. And this is important to my wife, who was born in Spain and has retained many social connections there."

"Are you telling me that's more important than apprehending terrorists wreaking havoc in America?" Archison asked. "Are you prioritizing personal issues over the pursuit of terrorists threatening America?"

"No, sir, I am not. But certain concessions to my wife are also important. As dedicated as we are, we need to indulge our families. Tomorrow I can arrange reassignment to this taskforce and spend full-time pursuing those radicals."

"I'd appreciate you spending a couple hours this afternoon with us on this thing," Olecki said. "Then you can go do whatever it is you need to do."

"Okay, but by five I'm flying out of here."

Before the Assistant US Attorney had a chance to vent frustration, his phone rang. Answering it he jotted down the information received and handed it to Detective Olecki. "That's the address of Martinez, the guard. He's off duty so might be at home."

Olecki nodded. "We'll pay him a visit. You coming, Special Agent Bravo?"

Bravo nodded and accompanied the two sheriff department detectives down a flight to the sixth floor garage. Olecki removed his tweedy jacket before climbing behind the wheel of a somber gray Chevrolet Impala, one of the unmarked four-door sedans used by the sheriff's department detectives. Cleo Broderick also removed her blue jacket before plopping herself in the front passenger seat.

So Bravo shucked his suit coat before sliding into the back, to sit on a standard upholstered bench. Most police cruisers replaced them with plywood or plastic that rendered the seats easy to hose off the urine of people frightened when taken into custody, and the vomit of drunks and the over-dosed or those needing a fix.

Olecki rested his elbow on the opened window as he tooled the Chevy into traffic on Broward Boulevard, flanked by high-rise office and apartment buildings. They headed west among the press of cars, trucks and buses polluting the environment with exhaust fumes. After a number of blocks they passed into a district of bargain- priced stores and inexpensive eateries, with a gas station at many of the cross streets.

After rumbling over railroad tracks, they passed through an area of grungy retail stores, followed by a residential neighborhood a few degrees above ramshackle, with mostly African-Americans on the street. Scrubby pines, black olive and palm trees, with occasional clusters of leafy arecas, burdened poorly tended lawns and gardens. A diversity of older pick-up trucks, outnumbered hard-used minivans, SUVs and sedans of the same vintage in driveways and along the curbs of both sides of the streets.

Cleo swiveled around to at Bravo. "I'm sure impressed 'bout you taking your wife to that embassy ball. Never ever even hoped to do something like that."

Bravo pretended not to notice her flirtatious fluttering of eyes, as well as the way her white blouse molded her full figure; involvement with her being the last thing he needed.

"You and Butch need to get you invited to one of those foreign shindigs," Olecki said and sniggered.

"Know damn well that won't ever happen," Cleo said. "But the som'bitch could take me out to a nice restaurant on occasion, not just to another noisy gin mill. Most times he plops his lazy ass in that big-ass easy chair in front of the tube and shovels take-out in his face, with no damn concern that I deserve to be indulged now and again."

"There's the difference," Olecki said. "Special Agent Bravo takes his wife to foxtrot at the Spanish Embassy."

"It's Ray. And truth be told, it's the only embassy affair I've ever been invited to as a guest, though I've served in a security capacity at a few. Besides, I'm not as eager as Yzabel to go."

"You saying she's hot to trot," Cleo asked, "and you're not?"

"Called me twice in the last two days to remind me to get home in time . . . obsessed with attending that damned thing."

"What if a case gets in the way?" Olecki asked.

"Don't even suggest that."

"Sounds like you don't have the gumption to stand up to her," Cleo said.

"Marriage is tough enough," Olecki said, "without making unnecessary waves."

Bravo nodded. "As it happens we're going through another rough spot. So I'm trying not to intensify things."

They crossed Interstate 95, a high-speed north-south highway linking the many regions of the Florida peninsula. Then they passed into an area of middle-class dwellings with a variety of tropical vegetation in neat gardens. After crossing the Florida Turnpike, another high-speed north-south highway they turned north onto a highway designated as US 441. While not as heavily trafficked as Broward Boulevard, it had its share of cars, and especially of trucks.

Olecki shook his head while chuckling ruefully. "Marriage ain't easy. I'm on my second, in spite of having more hell than I needed with the first." He turned east on moderately trafficked Oakland Park Boulevard for a few blocks, passing through a commercial area before swinging into an older development with small houses, their little yards overgrown with tropical bushes and trees. All had the unmistakable mark of self-tended as opposed to the manicured appearance of professional care.

A few more turns and Olecki pointed to a house that resembled all the other stucco-faced block homes in a variety of pastel colors with coral dominating and beige a close second; most of them mildew-streaked to varying degrees. Because a road-weary station wagon parked in front of the designated house, he pulled into the available spot across the street, in spite of parking in the wrong direction.

Cleo elected to wait in the car, remarking that two were enough to interview a jail guard. She sure didn't expect any trouble interviewing the man. Bravo and Olecki concurred as they climbed out and crossed the street. Both noticed the Hispanic-looking man behind the wheel of the parked vehicle. His flinty eyes followed them as they stepped onto the walkway to head for the front door.

"Sure looks hinkty," Olecki said.

Bravo's jaw rippled, irked by having to profile a Latino. But it also bothered him that the guy never took his eyes off them, a scowl on his ugly puss the whole time.

The front door opened while they were still twenty feet away and five people emerged in a tight group. Two scruffy guys flanked a mature woman and a teenager on each side of an older male with a bushy mustache. Those three in the center clutched each other as they trundled along with heads hung, appearing cowed by their escorts.

The two flankers gawked at the two men in shirts and neckties. Both went wild-eyed and brandished semi-automatic pistols. "Raise the hands!" one yelled.

Both law officers froze.

"Who you are?" one of the flankers demanded.

Olecki gestured to the badge on his gunbelt. "Best thing you boys can do is lower those weapons so's nobody gets hurt."

The two gunmen gaped, apparently hadn't noticed the badge, and now were uncertain how to react. One pulled the older female in front of him while continuing to threaten the lawmen with his weapon. The other one shielded himself with the younger female while also keeping his semi-automatic trained on the newcomers.

"Help us!" the older man begged. "Help us!"

One of the hoods shoved his gun against the older man's head, quieting him. Bravo and Olecki stared at them, aware of those two awesome pistols pointed at them—at close range—denying them confidence they had time to extract their weapons. Bravo's peripheral vision took in the man the station wagon climbing out on the far side of that vehicle and aiming a long-barreled revolver over its roof. Fearful of what might happen next he whispered hoarsely to Olecki: "We need to act."

"I'm with you," Olecki said. "On the count of—"

"Drop that damn weapon!" The shrill command jerked all eyes to Cleo who'd climbed out of the passenger side of the Impala and leveled her Glock semi-automatic across its roof. "Drop that damn weapon and throw up your damn hands!" she commanded.

Startled, the man at the station wagon froze; apparently hadn't noticed that someone remained in the Chevy. Suddenly he swiveled around while trying to bring his revolver to bear on her. Tat. Tat. She squeezed off two shots that knocked him backwards against the car. He tried to lift his weapon, but Cleo's semi-automatic barked again. He convulsed as he slid down the side of the car, his weapon clattering onto the macadam road.

Aware that the shooting momentarily stunned the two gunmen in front of them, Bravo and Olecki drew their pistols. At the same time Bravo squatted to reduce himself as a target while Olecki turned sideways to achieve the same effect. The two gunmen trained their weapons on the lawmen but wavered at shooting, confused by their antics.

The man closest to Bravo, using the mature woman as a shield, fired. Bravo winced as the bullet whizzed inches above his head. He knew another would follow—better aimed. So without taking too much time to aim above the woman's shoulder he squeezed off two shots. She'd flinched when her captor fired the gun in her ear, leaving him partially exposed. The man yelped and stumbled backwards when the two bullets tore into his shoulder. He struggled to retain his footing while losing possession of his weapon.

Released, the woman bolted away from him and into the protective arms of the older man with the bushy mustache—knocking both to the ground. Bravo rose to his full height, his nine-millimeter semi-automatic Beretta clenched in two hands and thrust toward the other hood.

Olecki held his forty-caliber Glock clutched in both hands, extended and aimed at the same third target, but held fire for fear of hitting the teenager—in spite of the guy obviously intending to shoot. The gunman blinked as his eyes danced from one gun aimed at him to the other, then to his cohort who'd dropped to his knees clutching his shoulder.

The teenager screamed, panicked by gunfire and flailed her hands around, throwing her captor off balance. Olecki fired three shots in a triangular pattern at the man's exposed body. The guy staggered backwards and toppled onto the lawn.

He struggled to his knees while trying to aim his gun. Bravo discharged two shots. The man's body jerked as the pistol fell from his hand. He clutched himself and stared in disbelief at the cops before crumpling onto his face.

The other assailant struggled to a sitting position and strained with both hands to raise his weapon. Olecki put a bullet between his eyes. The ruffian collapsed onto the walkway. Bravo quickly stepped forward, his pistol at the ready, and kicked away the hoodlum's gun.

Cleo hurried to the one she'd shot, her weapon clutched in both hands. He'd sunk to his knees and leaned against the car writhing. After kicking his revolver out of his reach she patted him down to make sure he had no other weapons. He flopped onto the roadway. She felt for a pulse in his neck, then shook her head as she called out in shrill voice: "This one's a goner."

Olecki hustled to the third one to ascertain that he'd been disabled and no longer had weapons. Feeling the carotid artery he concluded that man also had expired. Bravo called to them that the other assailant also was dead. With no further concern for bad-guys, the three law-enforcement officers tended to the three panic-stricken people. Despite panting from hypertension, as law officers generally do after a shoot-out, they tried to calm the man by convincing him that neither of the women nor himself had been harmed.

Olecki cradled the hysterical teenager. The older woman sobbed as she also hugged the youngster, then threw herself against her rescuer, embracing both.

"You Teodoro Martinez?" Bravo asked the bushy-mustached man.

"Sí. Sí. You are police? In truth? Gracias a Dios." He crossed himself.

"You know those men?" Bravo asked him.

Martinez stared wide-eyed at his questioner. "They came into my house with guns. They threaten my wife and daughter."

"Who were *they*?" Bravo asked.

"*Terroristas*. They call themselves *Independistas*."

Neighbors emerged, curious now that the shooting had terminated, some persistent they share the titillating revelations. A few sounded sincere when inquiring if the Martinez family was all right. Olecki instructed Cleo to take the three hostages into the house and try to settle them down. Then he called on his radio requesting backup at a shooting scene, adding that all bad guys had been subdued, but they needed help in preserving the crime scene. Oh yeah, send a morgue wagon for three dead skels.

While waiting for the back-up, the two law-enforcement officers pranced about, breathing deeply to dispel the effects of that shootout. They snapped at spectators not to trod on the crime scene. When two cruisers arrived they assigned those deputies to contain the curious. Then Bravo and Olecki went inside to join Cleo in interviewing the three victims.

SIX

Bravo and Olecki entered the house, after which Olecki approached the older man. "I'm Detective Olecki of the sheriff's department."

"Gracias a Dios!" the swarthy man crossed himself then rumpled his bushy mustache. "Gracias—thank you—for save us—myself with my wife and daughter."

"My associate here," Olecki said, "is Special Agent Bravo from the Bureau of Alcohol, Tobacco and Firearms. We know you're Teodoro Martinez."

Martinez gawked. "How the ATF know to come? And just in time. *Dios te bendiga*—God bless you."

"Because of one of your prisoners," Bravo said. "But I think you know that."

Martinez bowed his head and glanced askance at the two females, a gesture Bravo read as reluctance to divulge anything in the presence of his wife and daughter.

Olecki gestured Cleo to usher the two women into the kitchen, allowing them to interview the husband in the small living room, relieved of reluctance to be overheard by the females.

Cleo drew glasses of water for the two females and herself and suggested they brew coffee.

"You ready to explain it all now?" Bravo asked Martinez. Olecki had fetched the man a glass of water and he gulped it down.

Martinez wrinkled up his face, his dazed eyes blinking to dispel the horror of that escapade. "Those barbarians, they kill that poor bastard."

"Killed who?" Bravo asked, glancing around.

"The prisoner. You know, it was on the television news. Those animals—"

"How well did you know Elizondo?" Bravo asked.

"He—he was one of the prisoners I guarded."

"How well did you know those terrorists?" Olecki asked.

"How I know them? You joking?" He absently handed the emptied glass back to the detective.

"How is it then, that you knew they were terrorists?" Olecki asked.

"They announce themselves, proud of their evil organization. Every Puertoriqueño knows of them. Sí, I have fear of them. Of course I—"

"You must have liked that prisoner a lot," Bravo said.

"Why you say that? Why I like *malos*—bad people—prisoners at the jail?"

"Why else would you make those telephone calls for him to the ATF in Washington?" Bravo asked.

"Not me. No way, man, not me." He glanced guiltily toward his wife.

"We're sure going to prove you did," Olecki said, "by getting a record of phone calls made from your work and home."

"And your cellphone," Bravo said. "The lugs show any calls made to the ATF in Washington and you're in trouble."

"For what? I do nothing illegal."

"Lying to the police investigating a homicide," Olecki said, "is obstruction."

"Which will result in your getting time on the other side of those bars," Bravo added.

Martinez blinked repeatedly and shook his head as he muttered unintelligibly.

"Get out in front of this," Bravo said, "to save yourself and us time and trouble by telling us about those calls, so we don't have to come down hard on you."

"So far you haven't done anything criminal," Olecki said. "But if you answer our questions dishonestly it's going to go against you, maybe cost you that job."

"Hey, I got kids—a mortgage on this house. I need that job. My other daughter, she just start college at Central Florida. Gracias a Dios she is away in that place and did not suffer this business happen here today."

"Then come clean," Bravo said. "Save yourself grief."

Martinez shuffled about, bobbing his head as if in a quandary. His eyes mirrored guilt as he glanced to his wife, who strained to hear what he said.

Bravo ushered Martinez farther away from the kitchen. Even so, the man lowered his voice when he said: "That prisoner, he spoke little English, so I did him a favor. Is that criminal?"

"Why did he want to go to Washington?" Bravo asked.

"To survive," Martinez said in falsetto, as if surprised that they asked. He gestured to them to accompany him in into the small hallway accessing the bedrooms, distanced from the ears of his wife. "That one scared like hell. He have fear that his *compatriotos* put a hit out on him. But we keep him secluded to prevent them getting to him. And he scared like hell about going into that courthouse. Sure enough, it happen like he say."

Martinez wagged his bowed head side to side. "They almost got us also this day—myself, my wife and my sweet daughter. Gracias a Dios, you arrived." He again made the sign of the cross.

"Why didn't you come forward after Elizondo got iced," Olecki asked, "and inform us of your involvement with him?"

"I think to do that. It only happen a few hours ago."

"You should have come forward immediately," Olecki said.

"I no have time." Martinez glanced to his wife and daughter. "I need to do it without they know. No way I want to admit to them that maybe I cause those *terroristas* to threaten our lives." "You saying you expected them to come after you?" Olecki asked.

"No, man! I never think those *malos* track me down. How they know? The ATF, they tell them?"

"You know that's not true," Bravo said.

"That prisoner, he say those *Independistas* have wire into the sheriff's office."

"Nonsense," Olecki said.

"Tell us about your association with Elizondo," Bravo said.

"*Pobrecito* worry that one of the convicts kill him. It happen sometimes because gangbangers in there contract with people outside. Those—"

"So you made phone calls for him," Bravo said.

"He speak little English. How I deny him that small favor? Besides, he have information to take the terroristas off the streets to let decent Puertoriqueños live in peace."

"What information did he offer the government?" Bravo asked.

"To blow up a building in Washington. But he refuse to say which one until he safe in that place with those ATF."

"Why the ATF?" Olecki asked. "Why not the FBI or the sheriff's office?"

"And why Washington?" Bravo asked.

"Is what he insist. Many times I try to convince him to trust the sheriff's office or the FBI. But no, he say he only—"

"And what would *you* get out of it?" Bravo asked.

"Nothing. He had nothing. What could I get?"

"What did Elizondo expect to get?" Bravo asked.

"For that ATF to save his life," Martinez said.

"You share that information with any of your co-workers?" Olecki asked.

"He warn me to say nothing, to trust no one."

"How about to your superiors?" Bravo asked.

"You crazy? I say nothing to no one in event they corrupt. Elizondo say those terroristas have a line into the jail and other government offices. No, man, I say nothing to—"

"If you wanted to help the man," Bravo asked, "why did you report to the terrorists what he was planning?"

"What you say? You crazy? You think I want to commit suicide, get my family kill?"

"You certainly got involved with Elizondo by making phone calls for him," Bravo said.

"To arrange a deal for that man with you agency. Believe that I have no idea how the Independistas know Elizondo talk to me, and that I make those phone calls. You think I want to put my wife and sweet daughter in danger?"

"How'd they know he was being taken to court this morning?" Olecki asked.

"How I know? They supposed to have tight security because they worry that the *extremistas chalados* try to spring him."

Bravo nodded acknowledgement to the term: *lunatic fringe*, then cynically questioned: "And the US Attorney's office wasn't convinced?"

"How they do not know it dangerous? Why else they have him wear flak jacket? Elizondo say prayers and prepare for death when he learn he go to court here in—"

"So why did you make those calls?" Bravo asked.

"To make a favor. He have right to live. *Pobrecito patético*, he the last of what they call *jíbaros* in Puerto Rico."

When the two officers stared dumbly at him, Martinez explained: "They are call *jíbaros*, those who live in the countryside, in the mountains and in the rural areas, on the farms where they grow coffee and sugar cane, where they raise livestock, and in the forest where they cut lumber. They wander from job to job, employment decided by seasons. Those simple people disappearing now that the island changes, with the building of factories and military bases eliminating that way of life."

"Did the other Puerto Rican guards send messages for him also?" Olecki asked.

"*Dudoso*. Doubtful. He never trust them—call them *Nuyoricans* because they born and raised in New York and no understand the soul of real Puerto Ricans. I am born in Arecibo, on the island, so he trust—"

"You're lucky to be alive," Olecki said.

"Gracias a Dios." Martinez crossed himself again.

"I'm curious," Bravo said. "why they tried to take you away from the house."

"I can only thank God that they did," Martinez said. "If not, maybe—"

"When did they arrive?" Bravo asked.

"Less than one half-hour past. They ring the bell and when my daughter answer, they put guns in our face and demand I tell them what Elizondo told me about their *vasillo*."

"Their what?" Olecki asked.

"They announce themselves as soldiers of *El Vasillo Rojo*—The Red Cell—like that make us bow and kiss they rings. But we never hear of that *Vasillo Rojo*. And we know nothing to tell them."

"Then why didn't they kill you?" Olecki asked.

Martinez threw his hands out. "I can no say why. I fear they do that—worry that they kill my wife and sweet daughter. But they only slap us around." He glanced toward his wife in the kitchen, obviously lamenting having gotten them involved.

"Why'd they spend so much time with you?" Bravo asked. ". . . Hanging around a whole damn half-hour?"

Martinez twirled his hands. "They question us over and over to know what things that Elizondo tell me. They know my wife and daughter know nothing of that man. But they threaten to hurt them if I no tell—"

"And you told them what?" Bravo demanded.

"I have little to tell them—no more than I tell you. It is why they threaten to kill me. After one speak on cellphone they start to take us somewhere. I know not where."

"I'll have that call checked," Olecki said. "But it's probably to one of those disposables with its calls untraceable."

"My take on it," Bravo said, "is they intended to take you to where they can torture you. Couldn't risk doing it here and have the neighbors hearing your screams and calling the police."

"You know where that place is?" Olecki asked Martinez.

"How I know? Maybe you police they know."

"Wish the hell we did," Olecki said. "Killing those three in the shootout deprives us of a source to question with respect to their organization and location."

"Circumstances being what they were," Bravo said, "we either put them away or they'd have done us."

"Along with this guy and his wife and daughter," Olecki said, nodding agreement. Then, shaking his head in commiseration, he said to Martinez: "We're going to need you to come in and make a statement."

"Will that affect my job?" Martinez asked. "Madre de Dios, I no can afford to lose it—and those benefits."

"Not if you make a full and honest statement," Olecki replied, "making damned sure everything you tell us is gospel. You lie, you lose."

"I no lie." Then his eyes narrowed as he gazed from one to the other of them. "Will others of that *vasillo* try to kill us again?"

"Just might," Bravo admitted. "We'll keep you and your family in protective custody until this thing is over." He turned to Olecki. "Want to clear that with your superiors so they can set these people up in a safe house. My bunch is on a tight budget and will wriggle out of providing it."

"My bosses are not going to like it," Olecki said, "considering the manpower required and the cost. Our budget isn't any better than yours . . . maybe worse. Let's see if we can get the marshals or the FBI to shoulder the burden."

"You should have trusted the sheriff's department," Bravo said to Martinez, "and confided what you were doing right from the start."

"It might have prevented what happened to your family here today," Olecki added. "And just maybe Elizondo would still be alive."

"Along with Artie Meyers," Bravo added.

"I see now I make a bad decision," Martinez said. "But many experiences influence that. So how we can trust our lives to gringos who look over they noses at Puertoriqueños?"

SEVEN

Bravo exhaled after climbing into and flopping onto the back seat of the Impala, aware the other two also expelled the tension of the last half hour. With every breath came the realization of how close they'd been to injury . . . or death. The after-effects of shootouts remained with combatants long after echos of those shots fade into the past requiring days, sometime months, to expel residual trepidation . . . a condition referred to as post-traumatic stress disorder.

"Hope they don't bench us," Cleo said, "making us have to bullshit some shrink that the shoot-out didn't affect us."

Bravo nodded. "Tell the psychologist he needs to get shot at before he can advise you how to react."

Olecki chuckled. "Gotta' give you credit for the way you showing a lot of guts . . . not only in that shootout but the way you put it to your boss on the phone."

Bravo grimaced. "Hope to hell that wasn't a mistake."

"Ain't sure I'd be that mouthy," Cleo said, trying to sound jocular to disguise lingering hypertension.

"Reason I teamed up with you," Olecki said, "being ATF and not one of those superior-acting FBI smart-asses."

"The bureau generally recruits from among law or accounting graduates," Bravo said, "while many ATF agents have backgrounds with local police forces. I put eight years in the job in New York City."

"Why in the world you leave that to become a fed?" Cleo asked. "ATF pay that much more than local cops?"

"If it was for pay," Bravo said, "I'd probably have been better off staying with The Apple. Might even have moved up a lot faster there.

Guess I got seduced by the prospect of becoming a G-man. Damn few Puerto Ricans in my generation achieved something like that."

"How'd a polished guy like you come to be a cop anyway?" Cleo asked.

"Needed a job when I got out of the army, and there wasn't all that much available with any decent perks."

"What kind of education qualifications you needed in New York?" Olecki asked.

"High school diploma back then. Had that. Fact is, already had two years at Queens College before I went into the army."

"Ever get the other two?" Cleo asked.

"Sure did—while in the job. It took nearly four years with departmental time constraints to finish them up at City College of New York. Anyway, upon graduation the Treasury Department recruited me. It just seemed too good not to accept."

"But now your bureau's under the auspices of Justice?" Olecki said. "You have any particular specialty?"

"I head up a National Response Team investigating crime scenes when yahoos blow things up or burn them down."

"Any particular location?" Olecki asked.

"While generally consisting of agents in place throughout the country, the special agent in charge is dispatched from a central location, as I'd been to Houston from Washington. Trained forensic scientists and explosive technicians in the area assist at the crime scene."

"What happened for you to have to go to Texas?" Cleo asked.

"Abortion clinic got bombed. So they shuffled my butt down there to bust those who did it. Turned out to be a bunch of dumbheads who left a trail a blind man could follow—besides brag-assing to publicize what they considered an achievement."

"Different strokes," Cleo said. "Some of us think abortion is inhuman."

"And some don't," Olecki said.

"My objection," Bravo said, "is to yahoos who blow up a clinic, killing people, and claim they're doing it to save lives."

"Agree with that," Olecki said. "One life has the same value as the other."

"Pisses me off though," Bravo said, "to get stuck on this thing on my way home, with my wife eager to attend that ball."

"Hopefully," Cleo said, "it won't take all that much longer so's you can get on your way and cozy up to your old lady."

"Didn't I hear you say you were born here on the mainland?" Olecki asked.

"Yep, in New York City—Spanish Harlem, but grew up in an area called Jackson Heights—nicer than the barrios most Puerto Ricans lived in fifty years ago."

"How'd you get all that lucky?" Cleo asked.

"After emigrating here my father became a successful masonry contractor, providing us a nice home."

"Lucky you," Olecki said. "My old man was a millworker—when he worked. While born here he didn't have any more education than his immigrant father. We lived in a poor section of Detroit . . . the reason I quit high school and shipped out on a lake freighter at seventeen."

"Unusual start for a cop," Bravo said.

"Guess it was. But when I matured I realized I needed something better so got me a job on the docks in the maintenance department. Went to night school and got my high school diploma, after which I got me assigned to clerical work in the Maritime Division."

"And you transferred to the police from that?" Bravo asked.

"Nope. Needed a bad marriage to start me on that track. Jane worked for the Maritime Division too, which is how and where we met. That ball-busting bitch took me apart piece by piece. When she got pregnant and had to give up that income I got a second job to pay the bills. Landed one as a security cop at night in an office complex."

"That's one way to get into cop work," Bravo said.

"My marriage had been deteriorating, and all those hours spent away from home didn't help things. About when little Marilyn was three, Jane went back to work and not too long afterwards filed for divorce."

"You saying you got blind-sided?" Cleo asked.

"Sure should've seen it coming. We hadn't been on good terms for a long damn time. Wouldn't surprise me if she had hots for some stud who prompted her to file for that divorce."

"Y'all get to punching each other out?" Cleo asked.

"Close. But it didn't get that far. Anyway, once I'd shed that bitch, or been shed, as it were, I didn't want to go to work and see her mean ass every day. So I up and moved down here to Hollywood, light-miles from that ball-buster."

"That was quite a transformation," Bravo said.

"Lived with my cousin for a while, who's with the Sheriff's Department here in Broward. He tried to get me on board but they weren't hiring so I got a job as a security guard on the cruise ship docks."

"Ever get you a free cruise?" Cleo asked.

Olecki snickered while shaking his head. "Most a year later a couple spots opened in the Sheriff's Department. Guess I did good on the exam, resulting in getting accepted to attend the academy."

"Where we all start," Cleo said.

"Had the good sense to take courses in adult education at Broward County Community College after getting on the force," Olecki said. "Took me nearly six years to get assigned to the Major Crimes Division and work as a detective. Never regretted becoming a cop."

"None of us do," Cleo said.

"But you married again," Bravo said.

"Hell yeah. What man can live alone. But I got me a good one this time—a Polish girl—American born, of course. We got us two daughters: Stella's now eight and Jennifer's five."

"What about your daughter," Bravo asked, "from your first marriage?"

"Marilyn's fifteen now and one major pain in the ass. She came to me when she was thirteen, claiming her stepfather tried to sexually abuse her."

"Good reason for her to split," Cleo said.

"Still wondering if that was truth or bullshit," Olecki said. "Figured she and her mother didn't get along. Like as not, Jane was glad to palm that maverick off on me."

"You did what a dad does," Bravo said.

"Yeah, but I ended up with more trouble than I needed, especially with a new family started, and since Marilyn didn't make any effort to get along with anybody. She cuts classes regularly, hangs with the wrong types, got her a bunch of ugly tattoos, and probably messes around with dope. Don't know what to do with her."

"You have children?" Cleo asked Bravo.

"Two sons. Esteban's nineteen and a sophomore at Duke, while Romero is sixteen and attending Saint Francis High School in Rockville, Maryland."

"Gave your boys Spanish names," Olecki said.

"My wife's a stickler for traditional values."

"You don't have no trouble with your boys from the sound of it," Cleo said, "but I sure get vibes that you got you some problems with your old lady."

"We've always worked things out and will again." Bravo sighed appreciatively upon arrival at their office building on Broward Boulevard since it saved him from sharing more of his personal problems.

Upon exiting the elevator on the seventh floor and passing through the metal detector they encountered Archison in the office corridor. He escorted them into the conference room where a number of people gathered around an oblong table. "You'all know Detectives Olecki and Broderick of the sheriff's office. Everybody meet Special Agent Bravo of ATF."

After a flurry of waves and bantering of greetings the assistant US attorney identified the bureaucrats in their dark suits seated at the table. "These three are FBI, Special Agent Joe Lee Baggler along with his subordinates, Agent Ronald Loscalzo and Agent Boisey Epps."

Joe Lee Baggler, a pudgy dark-haired man, nodded though he didn't vocalize a greeting. Ronald Loscalzo, the younger man on his right waved while calling out a greeting. Boisey Epps, the tall and angular African-American to Baggler's left, threw the newcomers a lazy salute. Archison then introduced a chubby African-American with receding hair as Danly Coombs, a deputy assistant US attorney recently reassigned to this office from Baltimore, a blessing since they had to fill the vacuum left by Arthur Meyers.

Motioning to the short end of the table he presented an olivy-complexioned man as DEA agent Loreano Pedrazo, donated to the taskforce by Treasury to fill a need for someone who speaks Spanish.

Bravo riveted his attention on the African-American woman seated next to Pedrazo. Archison introduced her as Deputy Assistant US Attorney Maylene Galbreath Brown.

Ay Dios! Bravo hadn't expected to encounter her. He had to admit she was still one good-looking lady, and stylish as usual in a tailored blue suit. Conyo! First Archison, then this gal. Who else would pop up from his past in this office? And, no, it didn't surprise him that she didn't greet him with a beaming smile. Actually she pretty much glowered at him while nodding curtly. Okay, he had no right to expect her to convey delight to see him. Noting Archison's questioning expression, he explained: "We worked a case together in Atlanta."

"From where she's recently been transferred," Archison said, "and now serves as one of my top prosecutors."

Remembering her as ambitious, it didn't surprise him that she'd moved up the ladder. By his calculations she'd inched past forty, though she hadn't changed appreciably since he'd last seen her. Yep, one handsome woman with almond-shaped eyes, she still wore her black hair meticulously coifed. Oh yeah, she'd been divorced. Doubtful that comely lady remained unattached.

"Special Agent Bravo arrived today," Archison explained to the assembly, "dispatched to escort that prisoner, Elizondo, to ATF headquarters in Washington."

"Been a heap better had you come a day earlier," FBI Special Agent Joe Lee Baggler said. His two subordinates nodded while struggling not to snicker.

Before Bravo had a chance to respond, Archison said: "We have a number of people in the taskforce from diverse organizations, so I had cards typed up for each of us with everyone's cellphone numbers for all of us to stay in touch."

"Good looking out," Baggler said. "As the primary in this investigation I need ever'body kept in the loop at all times and available to each other."

Bravo nodded, remembering that inability to communicate cost a lot of lives on nine-eleven at those towers in New York as well as the Pentagon in Washington. He shuddered, recalling that day.

"Okay, let's get down to business," Archison said, "by reporting on what transpired today. Hopefully we've opened the door to taking those extremists off the street?"

"Martinez, the guard we interviewed admitted being the go-between with the ATF," Olecki informed. "But it's doubtful he wanted those wild-asses who raided the courthouse to visit him like they did today."

"Hell, they tried to take that ole' boy out," Cleo added.

"We got there in the nick of time," Bravo said, "to abort an attempted kidnapping by a bunch who called themselves the *Vasillo Rojo*, or Red Cell."

"That's a new name," Agent Loscalzo said. "Get any info about them?"

Bravo shook his head. "Martinez didn't know that much about them."

"But those bad boys sure had a line on Martinez," Cleo said. "Makes you wonder if the guy had it right about those radicals having a wire into officialdom."

"Won't be the first incidence of a leak from an official source," Olecki said.

Archison scowled and waved dismissively at that supposition. "Anybody with something substantial to contribute?"

"We took Agent Pedrazo with us so we'd have two teams of two to interview each of the two Puerto Rican guards," Baggler said. "Neither gave us anything about that courthouse shooting."

"Typical of that type," Pedrazo remarked.

"What the hell does that mean?" Bravo asked.

"Even though the guard named Botero has the name of a *Colombiano* famous for his paintings of fat people," Pedrazo said, "he has the brains of a burro."

"Unless he was smart enough to string you along," Olecki said.

"Not that one," Pedrazo said. "He might have trouble finding his way home."

"How dumb can he be," Bravo asked, "having passed a civil service exam?"

Pedrazo waved his hands about, but before he could reply, Agent Loscalzo reported: "We also got squat from that Cortez guy. Fact is, he wasn't particularly cooperative."

"Even if he had been," Agent Epps said, "doubt he had anything relevant to impart. Hear what I'm saying?"

"Difficult to believe that none of them knows anything," Maylene Brown said, "considering that somebody leaked Elizondo's court appearance to the terrorists."

"And we'd damn well better learn who," Archison said.

"Those extremist who call themselves *Independistas*," Loreano Pedrazo said, "make a nuisance of themselves all over the country, even to terrorizing decent people in their own island of Puerto Rico."

Bravo studied the man disparaging those guards, in spite of obviously being Latino. "I take it you're not Puerto Rican."

"A proud Cubano." Pedrazo said.

"Never understood," Baggler said, "why Puerto Ricans need to be terrorists."

"Just a small segment of the Puerto Rican population advocates independence," Bravo said, "as opposed to those supporting continuation of commonwealth or those seeking statehood."

"It's not new," Maylene Brown said. "They've been revolting for independence since before the Spanish-American War, while still a territory of Spain, consequently before they became a commonwealth of the United States."

"Wow!" Danly Coombs exclaimed. "That was more than a century ago."

Bravo nodded. "That faction has never given up the desire to be independent."

"They have them some real yahoos who don't mind dying for their cause," Boisey Epps said. "I'm not just talking your everyday activists. Hear what I'm saying?"

"Bad time for new martyrs," Baggler said, "what with all those Islamists ready to blow their damn fool selves up for some indefinable cause."

"Puerto Rican extremists," Maylene Brown said, "tried to assassinate President Truman back in the fifties."

"Not too long after that," Danly Coombs added, "a group of them yelling *viva Puerto Rico* sprayed bullets from the back of the house gallery, wounding five congressmen."

"Enough ancient history," Archison said. "And enough glorifying misguided political activism. Let's concentrate on strategizing how to round up those conscienceless bastards who slaughtered our people."

"May I suggest we run lugs on all jailhouse personnel," Bravo said, "to see what telephone calls any of them made during the past two weeks."

"Home, cell and work," Cleo added.

"Might be a good idea," Olecki said, "to run credit checks on all of that personnel to see if anyone got them some extra bucks for tipping the terrorists about everything occurring at that jailhouse."

"We didn't happen on any info suggesting an inside leak," Baggler said. "Anyway, ole' Ronnie boy has a talent for running down that kind of intel." Joe Lee Baggler pushed the telephone from the center of the table to in front of Agent Loscalzo.

"I never have no problem obtaining information," Epps said. "I'm as effective as anyone. Hear what I'm saying?"

But Loscalzo had already lifted the handset and dialed. Baggler's shrug to Epps conveyed that it was a fait accompli.

"I need to check on flights to Washington," Bravo said, "needing to get back there by seven or eight."

"Not today," Archison said. "Talked to your superiors while you were out and got you assigned here until we conclude this terrorist threat."

Bravo gaped. But he clamped his jaws to refrain from butting heads with an assistant US attorney who outranked him in the Justice Department and had the ability to strew roadblocks in future career advancement. "Need to talk to my office."

Archison gestured to Loscalzo utilizing the one phone in the conference room. "Avail yourself of any available phone in an empty office along the hallway, using whatever wiles to attempt to rescind that assignment."

EIGHT

Bravo's jaws rippled from being incensed by Archison arrogantly blocking his flying home tonight. The sonofabitch issued it as if it was a challenge. It took effort but Bravo suppressed objecting to the directive—butting heads with a superior in Justice. Accepting he'd been denied options he tromped out of the conference room to find a telephone. He entered the first office he found unoccupied. Its size, along with the impressive desk and leather swivel chair, as well as the two leather-padded visitor chairs, spelled executive.

There weren't any pictures around to indicate who worked there. But he inhaled a fragile musk that reminded him of that night two years ago when that ebon goddess in glorious nudity emitted that arresting scent. Ay Dios! That had been incredible. But he shook his head to erase that memory while punching the numbers on the telephone dial pad. Damn right it pissed him that his bureau had farmed him out without any concern for his personal life.

Conyo, he expected his wife to fume when learning he wasn't available to escort her to that ball. Fucking Archison! He breathed deeply to expel rancor while the phone droned four times. A female voice answered to inform him that he had reached the headquarters of the Bureau of Alcohol, Tobacco, and Firearms. "Special Agent Ray Bravo here. I have an urgent need to speak to Assistant Director Justin Ball." Then he nodded when she asked him to *wait one moment, please* —unconcerned that she couldn't see his gesture.

One moment turned into three minutes of assurances that Assistant Director Ball would be with him just as soon as he finished another call. He thought of again calling Jus on his cellphone, but decided against provoking the guy. In the bureau you followed protocol, went through channels—avoided interrupting important conferences by buzzing somebody at the wrong time, unless you had a really compelling reason. And you sure as hell didn't want to irritate superiors, considering that he or she influenced how and when your career with the bureau progressed . . . or didn't.

"What can I do for you, Bravo?"

He jerked to attentiveness upon hearing Justin Ball's gruff voice . . . and addressing him by his surname. He breathed deeply before asking: "Need to know why I'm being denied one night to go home, after three long weeks in Houston."

"A request of the assistant US attorney there. But I'm sure you know that."

"Shouldn't I get the opportunity to visit my family—for one night? I can be back here in the AM."

"Not my call, Ray. That decision came down from the top. Archison convinced somebody up there of the imperative for you to remain there during this emergency."

"He has FBI agents and local law enforcement people on the case."

"As you well know, Ray, the bureau is obligated to bolster national security and to protect against the threat to property and human life. The philosophy and the mission of the Bureau of Alcohol, Tobacco and Firearms, I remind you, is to serve in highly publicized areas, and to actively participate in organized task forces that target specific criminal activities."

"You getting back at me, Jus, because of that business earlier?"

"Case assignments are not determined by wounded egos or grudges, Ray, but by need for specific expertise. I remind you of your status as an explosives expert . . . the basis upon which Archison convinced the powers-that-be to assign you there. He claimed it as a high priority to keep you there since those terrorists obtained combustible material in that airport raid and have brayed their intent to detonate a government building."

"In Washington, not here in Florida."

"It's out of my hands, Ray."

"One night at home isn't going to affect the outcome of things."

"Stop kidding yourself, Ray. They're concerned with resultant media criticism if we fail to support that Fort Lauderdale taskforce.

Suppose those wild-assed radicals blow up a building there in Florida while you're gallivanting around in Washington?"

"Assign some agents from the staff here in town."

"None of those qualify as explosives experts. Besides, the assistant US attorney specifically requested you, and made it known that he'd reach as high as necessary in DOJ to accomplish that. The fucker has the connections to achieve his objective."

"Taking into account my longevity with the bureau, Jus, as well as my status, I deserve to be accorded consideration on occasion."

"Just accept, Ray, that the bureau considers this reassignment vital to national security. So if you have nothing else, I have other concerns that require my attention."

Bravo scowled, but accepted his fate and signed off, aware that the only way he could get out of the assignment was to resign. But he wasn't about to do that and screw up an impending promotion to an executive position in BATS, recently formed under the umbrella of Homeland Security.

They'd structured a Bomb Arson Tracking System to serve as an Arson and Explosives National Repository to develop comprehensive incident-based intelligence-sharing of real-time information in a nationally secure system to operate in concert with the nation's fire and post-blast investigative forces. His twenty-two years of service along with his expertise in that area made him a likely candidate for one of the top positions.

Equally important it earned him permanent placement in Washington, a condition he yearned to attain to alleviate some of the strain on his marriage. His constant absence had become a major bone of marital contention. Besides, he'd have the pride of being one of the first Puerto Ricans to achieve that lofty status.

Biting his lip he stared at the telephone while he fretted calling his wife. Shit! He knew she'd spew lava. Lately she objected to bureau business taking precedence. And he really didn't need to get into another row with her, with so many still to be reconciled. Their relationship needed a large infusion of solicitude to smooth over all of the bumps in the road.

Accepting his lack of options he inhaled resolve and dialed her office while mining his brain for words with which to allay her exasperation. "Hello, this is Mister Bravo. I'd like to speak to Mrs. Bravo."

"Sorry, sir," the woman who answered said, "but Doña Yzabel Zaraga is not presently in the office."

Bravo clamped his eyes closed for a moment, irritated by that reference to his wife, even though he expected that response. Yzabel had started the decorating business before he married her and continued to use her maiden name, insisting its continental connotation had more appeal than Mrs. Bravo. The increase in prominence of that firm justified her decision—or, at least, diminished counter-arguments.

Investigators of the various federal law enforcement agencies weren't all that highly paid, certainly not on the scale of a successful entrepreneur. Fact is, she earned three times what he did, which fueled the deterioration of their relationship. Promotion, with its attendant increase in salary, would go a long way in allaying that situation.

He breathed deeply and asked: "When is Mrs. Bravo expected?"

"There's no way of knowing, sir, since Doña Yzabel Zaraga left to meet with clients."

Without bothering to respond, he toggled off, then dialed her cellphone. He clenched his teeth when her voice mail answered. He knew she turned it on when engaged to avoid interruptions. No, he wasn't about to leave a message. No way he'd plead his case to a mechanical answering system.

Pushing himself up from the desk he plodded back to the conference room. Pausing at the door he breathed deeply to prepare himself to deal with the humiliation of admitting he'd been spurned by his bureau. There'd be endless wisecracks intended to assail his pride—a characteristic highly prized by Latinos.

So he sucked up intent and entered, to be confronted by an excited Olecki clicking off his radio. The detective breathlessly related that he'd just been informed that a patrolling deputy spotted a battered green Dodge pick-up truck answering the description of the one the Puerto Rican raiders used when they jacked that landscaper's truck. It was on the verge of exiting a supermarket parking lot on Federal Highway near Twenty-sixth Street, obviously waiting for a break in traffic to turn right, or south as it were.

Everyone in the conference room nodded as Olecki told how Broward County Sheriffs Office Deputy Kinzler spotted it and noticed the crack in its windshield. But being in the left lane he had to drive almost to the end of the block before traffic let up enough for him to pull over to the right and wait for the pick-up truck to pass so he'd get a better look to assure himself it was the fugitive vehicle they'd been instructed to search for.

However, the people in that green heap apparently spotted the cruiser pulling over, assumed it would scrutinize them, so instead of turning south they made a big-ass swing north. They'd cut across all four lanes of highway, darting between cars, trucks and busses headed in both directions. Brakes screeched all over the place and set off a tire-squealing and horn-blowing clamor.

Traffic delayed the deputy making a U-turn so he could pursue. But lacking certainty that he chased a criminal for anything more than reckless driving, he opted against endangering the citizenry by recklessly cutting into traffic. However, he felt certain the two he saw in the cab of that truck were Hispanics, so he requested back-up, evaluating it as A & D.

"What in hell are they basing armed-and-dangerous on?" Bravo demanded. "I didn't hear any mention of seeing weapons." He breathed deeply to resist commenting that it sounded like profiling.

"No sense taking chances," Baggler said, "with some wild-ass Hispanics."

"How about if they were wild-ass rednecks?" Bravo asked.

"They obviously are evading pursuit," Archison said.

"Besides," Baggler said, "nobody wants to risk their life with some wild-assed Hispanics speeding away in that damn pick-up truck resembling the one used in that airport robbery. Those old boys shot up that place. How the hell else they going to react?"

"I remind everyone," Archison said, "that our primary mission is to protect the citizenry from becoming the victims of a rain of devastation. If achieving that requires taking out a couple of Hispanics, Englishmen, Norwegians, or whatever, so be it."

Olecki hunched at that then continued relating how the pick-up truck raced up Federal Highway, swerving around vehicles and bouncing off cars—miraculously avoiding a devastating crash. The deputy slowed to avoid an accident, concerned with plowing into those cars skidding all over the road. He received a message that two Fort Lauderdale Police cruisers joined the pursuit.

The fugitive pick-up truck recklessly ran every light, sometimes swerving on two wheels around other vehicles, and scaring the hell out of drivers and pedestrians. The two Fort Lauderdale cruisers contacted the deputy to be instructed where and how to intercept— what with the erratic routing of the pursued, and the damned traffic. Another sheriff's department cruiser raced down from the north to join the chase.

Deputy Kinzler reported that the quarry rashly sped through the residential area of Wilton Manors, almost colliding with one of the Fort Lauderdale cruisers, forcing it to spin off onto the sidewalk. The sheriff's department cruiser from the north reported that they're about to converge with the other cruisers to box the fugitive, who's just run a light at Floranda Road. Cars skidded all over the place trying to avoid a collision, again temporarily blocking the cruisers.

Sirens and swirling lights got them through that congestion and back on the chase. But a stupefied Deputy Kinzler said the fugitive went off the radar. None of the law enforcement officers spotted hide nor hair of the quarry. Nobody had a notion where the som'bitches turned since that area is warehouses, supply yards, and factories. Vehicles parked every which way by workers and delivery trucks of all sizes. The pursuing police assumed that the fleeing pick-up probably ducked among that confusion or hid in one of the buildings.

"They searching those buildings?" Bravo asked.

Olecki shook his head. "Pointless. Sure they'd find them some Hispanics—half the workers in those factories and warehouses are Hispanic. Problem is, how would they identify the ones they're hunting?"

"The other half is some kind of blacks," Cleo said.

"Expected that," Epps remarked dourly.

NINE

"Goddammit!" Joe Lee Baggler slapped the table. "Almost had a couple of them."

"A couple of who?" Bravo asked. "Assuming they were Puerto Rican and not Mexican, Cuban, or something."

"Not enough description," Danly Coombs said, "to definitively identify them as the culprits."

"Som'bitches was running full-tilt," Baggler said. "That says they had something to hide."

"But it didn't have to be involved in the theft of that weaponry," Cleo said. "Shifties could have been hauling any kind of contraband. Maybe they had them some meth or joints."

"Or just be illegals," Olecki added.

"Might've been ripping stuff off cars in that supermarket parking lot," Epps said, "with no connection to the airport robbery. Hear what—"

Baggler glowered at his African American subordinate. "You against me too?"

Epps stammered, but before he had a chance to utter a denial, Loscalzo said: "Or were just plain frightened by the police."

"Frightened!" Baggler exclaimed. "What kind of candy-asses we talking about?"

"People of color are all too often victims of police injustice," Epps said. "Recent incidences verify that. Hear what I'm saying? Therefore they aren't all that eager to be pulled over."

"We need to eliminate speculations," Archison said, "and define things so we can attain definitive direction."

"Without profiling," Bravo said.

"Let's put aside sensitivities and personal attitudes," Archison said, "needing to prevent those terrorists from utilizing those stolen arms and munitions. It took two weeks of badgering but I finally received a list from the Army Reserve unit of everything taken."

He referred to the typed sheet handed him a moment ago by a clerk and read the list specifying they took sixty M4 automatic carbines, a shorter and lighter version of military rifles. They also took twelve thousand rounds of 5.56 millimeter ammunition as well as a quantity of Colt .45 semi-automatic pistols with a quantity of ammo. Last on the list is sixteen Bangalore Torpedoes.

"Anyone have familiarity with whatever they are?" he asked.

"Charges for clearing antipersonnel minefields," Bravo said, "as well as for blowing the underbelly out of tanks as well as blowing holes in concrete walls or destroying tank stops."

"Why would they take those?" Archison asked.

"Put enough of them together," Epps said, "and you have you one helluva bang. Hear what—"

"They're generally in five-foot lengths," Bravo said. "Connect sixteen of them and you can undermine a good-sized building."

"Easy as hell to conceal," Epps said, "being as they're small enough for each person to hide one or more sections on his person."

"Each five-foot tube is only two and one-eighth inches in diameter," Bravo said, "with a weight of thirteen pounds, nine of which is explosives—generally TNT. Once inside a building, in an area lacking surveillance, they can plug them into one humongous bomb."

"That's a scary prospect," Maylene Brown said, "with the possibility of creating another nine-eleven."

"Wonder if they got detonators too," Epps said. "In the army we used a blasting cap in the recessed end and ignited it with a time-delayed electric fuse."

"Can be done with a non-electric fuse also," Bravo said. "Consider ourselves blessed that they got those relics of World War Two. The army has new Antipersonnel Obstacle Breaching Systems with greater explosive power—babies that can take out sizeable buildings with ease."

"As primary of this taskforce, exactly how do you propose to terminate that threat?" Archison asked Baggler,

That man sputtered—apparently hadn't expected the question. Then he said: "Standard procedure." His eyes darted around seeking support from his colleagues.

"Drudging and doctrinaire," Archison said. "Typical bureaucratic response—lacking inventiveness—as has been most efforts this past two weeks."

Baggler continued to stammer. Loscalzo spoke up. "Investigations are sequential exercises. Results take time."

"Which is all you can ask from anybody," Epps added. "Hear what—"

"No," Archison said. "We can't put this community at risk while following foot-dragging procedures. We've already bumbled around for two weeks since that airport raid. Look at what occurred today at the courthouse. The vital nature of this threat demands innovative measures to counter and eliminate it."

"What exactly you suggesting?" Baggler asked.

"Getting creative," Archison said, "and moving this investigation past step one."

"Just might achieve that," Maylene Brown said, "by rooting out the person tipped off those terrorists that the marshals were taking Elizondo to court."

"Presumably an employee in the jail system," Danly Combs added.

"We interviewed the jail guards assigned to us," Baggler said, "and came up with zip. Actually, we took a long look at all personnel at the county jail as a matter of course and came across no one who knew all that much about Elizondo."

"Obviously one of them knows something," Maylene Brown said.

"No denying that," Epps said. He glanced admiringly at the deputy assistant US attorney.

Baggler again glowered at his lanky subordinate. "You going against me again?"

"No, man, I'm simply saying this lady is right, that some of them were in on it. Hear what—"

"In an environment riddled with grapevines," Olecki said, "somebody has to have heard something."

"Might be y'all need to let the sheriff's department detectives handle those interrogations," Cleo Broderick said.

Baggler thrust his jaw at her. "Nobody does this job better than FBI personnel."

"Like Detective Broderick suggests," Maylene Brown said, "now that we know one of those jail employees had the confidence of Elizondo, we need to pressure that person into leading us to others."

"That Elizondo fellow," Baggler said, "was kept out of the general population, so had no truck with other cons . . . eliminating the need to interrogate prisoners."

"We need a new direction," Archison said. "In the interest of expediting this investigation I'm appointing Special Agent Bravo to take over as the taskforce leader." The three FBI agents gawked at the assistant US attorney. Sucking in breaths they exchanged glances of disbelief. Baggler halfway rose from his seat. After dropping back into it he addressed Archison in cracking voice. "This team, sir, has been dispatched by the FBI Incident Command Center in Miami to handle this emergency, with me assigned as primary."

"You're still the primary of the FBI contingent," Archison said, "subordinated to Special Agent Bravo, since he's the explosives expert."

Bravo swallowed—as stunned as the others by the appointment.

"FBI always take precedence over ATF," Baggler said.

Epps nodded support. "Hear what this man—"

"Not this time," Archison said. "Bravo is an explosives expert, besides being conversant in Spanish, making him the best choice under the circumstances."

"I speak Spanish also," Pedrazo said. "Probably better than Special Agent Bravo, having been born in Cuba and speaking it all my life. He was born in New York and it's doubtful he's aware of all of the nuances of the language."

"You're right there," Bravo said. "I'm not up to date on a lot of idiomatic expressions. But I know how to catch bad guys, no matter what language they speak."

"But you're Puerto Rican like the skels," Baggler said, "and just might be empathetic toward yo' goombahs?"

"Expect me to come down on any skel," Bravo said, "whether Puerto Rican or any other Hispanic—even on your drawling redneck cousins."

"That's uncalled for," Baggler said.

"Enough contention," Archison said. "We're wasting valuable time better applied to the investigation. Bravo has more years in police work than any of the rest of you. He's also more resourceful, inventive, in fact."

Archison turned to Bravo. "I'm not going to deny he employs unorthodox methods that I don't always condone—find irritating in fact. But in this emergency I'm ruling on the side of prudence in appointing him to head up the taskforce. And I'd appreciate not hearing any further dissent."

"Works for me," Olecki said. "Ray sure as hell proved himself in that shootout this afternoon, showing he knows which end is up when it comes to cop work."

"I'd work with him any time," Cleo said. She grinned coyly at Bravo.

"That settled," Archison said, "I'm appointing Maylene Brown as the prosecutor of record, who will be in charge of making a case to indict those terrorists once we have them in custody. Coombs will take second chair. So keep them in the loop on all occurrences to assist in the preparation for an eventual day in court. Okay, what's our next move, taskforce-leader?"

Bravo winced, unprepared to respond, having not expected the promotion. Breathing deeply he accepted the need to exhibit leadership despite lacking time to formulate a strategy. "Put everything in perspective," he said as he glanced around at the others, affecting a stern visage to convey authority. "We can assume the terrorists obtained those arms and explosives with intention to publicize their cause by executing devastation of one type or another . . . as that dead prisoner, Elizondo, claimed."

"At least the field has been narrowed," Baggler said, "to searching for Puerto Ricans."

"With three million or so Puerto Ricans living on the mainland," Bravo said, "those statistics don't give us much to go on." He'd applied effort to keep his voice unemotional so as not to expose resentment.

"We can get the names from FBI files," Loscalzo said, "of Puerto Ricans living in this region and start interviewing those with records."

"What makes you think," Cleo asked, "that all political activists have records?"

"Besides," Olecki said, "with untold thousands of them in the area that procedure would be so time-consuming that the yahoos we're after will be long gone before we get an inkling of who they are."

"Besides," Bravo said, "we can't assume that the bad guys are locals." "What the hell else?" Baggler asked. "Why in hell out-of-towners want to come here to steal that stuff? Besides, how'd they know about those arms stored there if they weren't locals?"

"A renegade guardsman," Epps said. "They're not all true-blue patriots."

"I agree," Olecki said. "You can have any kind of scenario."

"Requiring," Maylene Brown added, "we keep open minds."

"Then where do we start," Archison asked, "mindful of the need to locate those terrorists in time to avert disaster?"

Bravo nodded to that as he rose to pace his side of the table, mining his brain for direction. "First, we need to learn specifically who we're after."

"A dozen or so wild-ass Hispanic skels," Baggler said, "with a mess of carbines."

Bravo nodded to that. "They made a daring raid to get them so be assured they intend to make hay with them."

"Therefore," Archison said, "let's apply our efforts to finding out who they are and relieve them of that destructive capability before they have an opportunity to do anything rash."

"Fine by me," Baggler said. "Have our experienced taskforce leader advise us how to accomplish that."

Bravo drew a breath to conceal intimidation and retain calmness while addressing the attentive faces. "The only people we know that possibly have any familiarity with the terrorists are prison personnel. We've established that Teodoro Martinez interceded for Elizondo in contacting the ATF office in Washington."

"And may not be the only one involved with Elizondo," Maylene Brown added.

"Sure sounds right to me," Olecki said. "Had to be another guard or someone working at the county jail that alerted the terrorists as to when Elizondo would be transported to the courthouse."

"Maybe a court clerk," Danly Coombs suggested.

Archison pointed a commendatory finger at that deputy assistant US attorney. "Look into it."

"Plus," Bravo said, "we need to interview everybody employed at the jail, especially Latinos, and more especially those three Puerto Ricans again."

"Don't overlook janitors and maintenance workers," Danly Coombs said, "as well as clerks, white, black, or Asian."

"Money," Archison said, "can be as compelling as political rhetoric or ethnic allegiance."

"Include commissary help," Maylene Brown said. "They have access to the grapevine . . . can inform those terrorists."

"We need to be given detailed direction," Epps said, "so we're each productive, not duplicating efforts." He exchanged glances with Baggler and Loscalzo, both of whom nodded approval.

Bravo tried not to reveal annoyance by their baiting to make him appear ineffective. "Maybe Agent Loscalzo can apply those talents that Special Agent Baggler applauds him for, by getting his office in Miami to do financial checks on everyone working in the jail, from the lowliest janitor to the top brass. A recent infusion of money in someone's account should alert us to investigate that person."

"Sheriff's office did that," Olecki said, "without uncovering anything."

"The FBI," Bravo said, "has deeper probes for locating accounts outside of Florida—even outside the country."

Loscalzo shrugged and reached for the telephone.

"Sounds like one big-ass game of chasing our damn tails," Baggler said. "But you instruct us, good buddy, as to where and how to start, and we'll sure as hell execute assignments."

Bravo ignored the appellation of *good buddy*, accepting their intent to set him up to fail, which reinforced his determination to succeed. "Deputy Assistant US Attorney Maylene Brown and her staff can interview the non-Hispanic employees there. This time we'll change around, with Pedrazo and Baggler interviewing Cortez. Loscalzo and Epps can take Botero. Olecki, Broderick and myself will have another session with Martinez, since we've already established rapport with him."

"Sounds like the way to go," Olecki said.

"Let's meet back here in two hours to discuss whatever we've extracted," Bravo said. "Hopefully we'll have gleaned enough information to formulate the next step."

"And hopefully," Cleo Broderick said, "we don't run into any more of those yahoos like the last time we visited those folks."

TEN

Archison gestured Bravo into his office as everyone shuffled off to execute their assignments. After shutting the door he twirled his mustache ends while clearing his throat, then growled: "Don't delude yourself that I'm optimistic of you having changed since Kansas City. You're a maverick, but I'm going to give you the opportunity to redeem yourself by proving you're the best choice to ramrod this joint agency taskforce."

Bravo nodded while keeping his mouth shut, anxious not to piss off a big wheel in the Justice Department. Advancement depended as much on how many superiors you didn't antagonize as on those you impressed.

"You enjoy an enviable record," Archison continued, a hard edge to his voice, "investigating complicated cases, besides being an explosives and arson expert. However, you don't produce and I'll bust you down and subordinate you to one of those FBI agents, just as quickly as I assigned you to lord it over them."

Bravo didn't doubt that Archison meant what he said. Okay, he had his work cut out for him, a challenge in fact to round up those terrorists before they utilized that destructive force they'd stolen—especially those Bangalore torpedoes.

Most daunting was the realization that to date law enforcement lacked a single clue as to who the bad guys were, where to find them and what they intended . . . in spite of having two weeks to investigate since that raid on the National Guard complex. They only knew they searched for Puerto Rican extremists, but weren't certain which group they sought . . . there being a number of off-shoot cells as well as parent organizations competing in that political arena.

Enjoying citizenship in the U.S.A. Puerto Ricans had free rein to enter or leave the mainland as well as freedom to travel across the country, making it difficult to keep track of them.

Dismissed by Archison, Bravo joined the two sheriff's department detectives in the garage, where he climbed into the back seat of the Impala. Cleo had already propped herself in the driver's seat and Olecki in the passenger seat.

"Never lets up," Cleo griped as she exited the garage and slipped into traffic. "We got us bumper-to-bumper cars, trucks, and buses on Broward Boulevard year round. Wasn't all that many years ago the snowbirds gave us back South Florida this time of year."

"Increase of *rounders*," Olecki said. "More and more folks from the north have moved down year-round, crowding the streets, restaurants and stores almost as much as during winter."

"Som'bitches need to learn to not dart from one lane to another," Cleo griped. "Oughtta' pull over some of those aggressive daredevils, but prosecuting this assignment is a whole bunch more important than ticketing a few traffic offenders."

Reaching Interstate 95, Cleo turned north onto that high-speed highway with its press of traffic, allowing her to drive considerably faster than on local thoroughfares, in spite of the increase of vehicles, especially of trailer-trucks. Twisting around to Bravo, she asked: "How's your wife reacting to your not getting home to take her to that Spanish Embassy ball?"

"Didn't get hold of her yet."

Cleo gasped. "You sure better . . . real soon."

"Sure glad it's not me having to face my old lady with tidings like that," Olecki said.

"Was me invited to a shindig like that," Cleo said, "and my old man didn't show up to take me there, I'd pitch me the loudest shitfit you ever heard."

"And she would," Olecki said.

Bravo grimaced. "She's not at her office or at home, and her cellphone isn't on. I'll just have to keep trying to reach her. But for now, I'm going to concentrate on taking those terrorists off the street." He blinked as he suppressed adding: and prove I'm worthy of taskforce leadership.

"My old man needs to get him a job," Cleo said, "that gets him invited to fancy dinners and such."

"What's he do?" Bravo asked.

"Drives one of them big-assed tandem-axel diesel rigs around the country. Som'bitch comes home after a week or so and ain't horny I know he's been boffing those gussied-up floozies at the truck stops."

"What do you do then?" Olecki asked. He appeared to clench his jaws to suppress snickering.

"One time I near beat on his burly ass 'til it turned to pulp. That som'bitch come home and ain't ready to perform, believe that I like to go ballistic."

"Lot of good that does," Olecki said, "big and rough as he is. Only thing you get besides painful knuckles is horny and neglected."

"Yeah, and I find me a stud to satisfy my needs. What about you, g-man, being away from home so much, you into getting you some side-action?"

Bravo winced, having not expected that direct question—wondered if it was a come-on. He shook his head to dismiss that consideration. "Most cases are too intense, with no time to even think about messing around."

Cleo slowed as they approached the Commercial Boulevard exit, where she left the highway and headed west into a residential community in Tamarack. While turning from one street to another she said to Bravo: "Archison sure pulled a sneaky by pressuring your bosses into reassigning you here."

"Wasn't the first time I got shafted."

"What surprised the hell out of me," Olecki said, "was his appointing you to head up the taskforce and supersede that FBI blowhard. Something about the way old stuff-shirt been treating you made me think you two had unfriendly history."

"Kansas City, a couple years ago," Bravo said. "He had a problem with the case I presented, having used street-smarts to expedite it, learned from my New York City cop days. Federal agents take longer to apprehend bad guys than local cops, because federal prosecutors painstakingly prepare cases before issuing indictments or even collaring the perps."

"Been through that," Olecki said, "more times than I care to remember."

"He demeaned the evidence I submitted," Bravo said, "as not worthy of presentation in court—practically accused me of creating it."

"Ooph!" Cleo exclaimed. "That's a blow can ruin your career."

"Might've been," Bravo said, "had I not bolstered it within the following week—made it indisputable. Guess he never got over the humiliation."

"So why," Olecki asked, "did he appoint you taskforce leader over that FBI puff-ass?"

"First time I ever saw ATF wield authority over FBI," Cleo said. She turned into a middle-income subdivision of cookie-cutter houses.

"Not the norm," Bravo said, nodding. "However, the FBI requisitions our expertise regularly, thereby conceding that ATF explosive and arson investigators are the best trained and most experienced to cover large-scale bombings and conflagrations."

"So do we," Olecki said. "You guys are the best."

"We also have the nation's most dependable weapons tracing center," Bravo said, "to assist every law enforcement group in the country. Most local cop forces consult with us."

"We sure as hell do here in Broward," Olecki said. "Its how I got familiar with your bureau. But that grump, Archison, had to have a lot of respect for what you do to appoint you to head up this group."

"Or getting heat," Bravo said, "for lacking lead one as to who the yahoos are that staged that daring robbery at the airport two weeks ago."

"As well as who-all blew away that prisoner this morning," Olecki said, "along with Assistant US Attorney Meyers and two marshals."

"Plus two courthouse guards," Cleo added.

"His superiors want answers," Bravo said, "which he's been unable to provide. So he appointed the Puerto Rican to ramrod the investigation. I fail and it gives him the built-in excuse that if an experienced Puerto Rican investigator can't get a line on Puerto Rican extremists, who can?"

"Means we need to grind our damn noses down, if that's what it takes," Olecki said, "to keep your ass from getting singed."

"Appreciate that," Bravo said. "I really do."

"I'd do most anything for you," Cleo said, swiveling around and batting her baby blues at him.

Bravo ignored her flirting. Last thing he needed was a fling with that audacious gal . . . not that he wasn't ripe for a burst of passion, considering that he and Yzabel hadn't enjoyed conjugal consummation for a few months. But over-anxious chicas usually end up a whole lot harder to terminate the affair with than it took to get their fannies into bed in the first place.

"This is the safe house," Cleo said as she pulled up to the front of the small house with its neat lawn and a small garden behind low hedges of dwarf ixoras ablaze with red blossoms. Similar medium-priced houses painted in pastel colors with traces of mildew surrounded it. They all had small lawns punctuated with a bottlebrush tree along with occasional queen palms. A few had spiky pin oaks at the front walk. The aroma of fried foods wafted on the soft breeze.

After parking in front of one of the small houses all three trod to the front door.

"Martinez is wary of his wife learning he'd brought that grief on his family," Olecki reminded as they brushed past an overgrown hedge of hibiscus with huge pink flowers. "We'll depend on you, Cleo, to keep her occupied, so's we'll have a better chance of opening him up without her hanging over his shoulder."

"Hell, I might just pump some goodies out of her," Cleo said, a pugnacious set to her jaw.

Olecki grinned admiration of her toughness, determination, and her pride as a cop. He was still smiling pridefully when two US marshals answered their knock on the front door. They scrutinized the visitors' credentials before waving them in. Cleo entered first, squeezing past piles of boxes while stepping over clothing and shoes scattered around the small living room.

Martinez, his wife and daughter, were busily sorting things to be put away. Mrs. Martinez glared at the visitors, incensed at their causing her family to have to move. But her husband expressed delight to see them. "Is hoped you are here to announce that you took those *extremistas* off the street, making it safe for us to return to our home."

"We're working real hard on doing just that," Olecki said as he gazed around at the scattered mess.

"Ain't easy," Cleo said, "moving in a hurry from one house to another. Been there, done that."

Mrs. Martinez nodded emphatically, irritation creasing her face. But Bravo spoke before she could. "The reason we're here is to get a run-down on Elizondo that can shed light on that lunatic movement, so we can help you folks get back to your home."

Martinez glanced to his wife and daughter, a tinge of guilt in his eyes. "I told you all I know. Yes, I made those telephone calls for him . . . foolishly. But that's all I did."

"Some background info," Bravo said, "that might lead us to his cohorts."

"I don't know all that much about him except he came from Puerto Rico." Martinez said it grouchily, obviously not anxious to discuss it further.

"From everything you've told us so far," Olecki said, "that prisoner pretty much knew those terrorists were out to kill him."

Cleo ushered Mrs. Martinez into the kitchen while chatting about female things. But the woman kept glancing over her shoulder, more concerned with what the men discussed, especially to what her husband admitted. It apparently provoked her that he had naively exposed them to harm.

"Let's get some fresh air," Bravo said as he ushered Martinez into the backyard. One of the marshals accompanied them, but stayed unobtrusively in the background. Martinez appeared less guarded distanced from his wife, where she couldn't hear his admission of bad judgment for his involvement with a high profile prisoner.

"Your sympathy for Elizondo," Bravo said, "motivated your helping him out."

Martinez scowled as he wagged his head, unwilling to concede the point. But after a moment he overrode reticence. "The man, he talk about the island and the bad conditions there for those without privilege. Conyo, I left a little over twenty years ago, but remember how bad it was. For that reason I understood his becoming an activist, though I don't agree with their methods."

"He the only one you felt sorry for?" Olecki asked.

Martinez frowned as he shuffled around on the scrubby lawn. "The guard, he must have the tough skin that the prisoners' complaints and troubles bounce off."

"But this guy somehow got under that layer of leather," Bravo said. He and Olecki nodded to each other, both having experienced moments when resistance weakened and they became susceptible to a sympathetic appeal.

"Yes, I have pity for Gaspar Elizondo," Martinez said, "a pathetic man in his late forties who looked to be sixty. He had weathered skin from a hard life and a yellowish complexion from eating junk foods and chain-smoking cigarettes. That one, he ignore a gargling sound when breathing. He laugh when told he was killing himself. Maybe he welcome the end to a sorry life."

"He ever tell you how he got involved with radicals?" Olecki asked.

"He tell me when he come to the mainland to live in The Bronx he join a cell to fight for the liberation of the island. The police they capture him during a bank robbery to finance political activism. When he get out of slammer he say he have no place to go except return to the barrio and his brothers fighting for independence."

Martinez breathed deeply before relating how a few years later, when the gang of Elizondo learned the police identified them as having taken part in a bank robbery in the Bronx, they fled to Chicago to lose themselves in the large Puerto Rican community there. It was there he was enlisted by the Vasillo Rojo. He believed in the liberation of Puerto Rico and condemned US exploiters for preventing his island home from growing and prospering. The more gringos he had run-ins with the more he became committed to separation from those who disdainfully abuse and stifle the ambitions of his people.

To extinguish that anger, Elizondo spent years as a revolutionary living in slums and surviving on slim pickings. He got his rocks off when he needed it with prostitutes and barflies. One gal he lived with for more than one year in New York had his daughter. Two in Chicago had his sons. But he had little communication with those children. He grew up without parents and saw no reason they couldn't.

"The never-ending extension of poverty," Olecki said. "Seen it among Slavic people back in the Midwest."

"While in the hospital," Martinez continued, "after he get shot in that raid on the Fort Lauderdale airfield he regret he have neglect those children. He worry he die so decide to make amends. He not want his daughter to become a prostitute, like his sister, nor his sons to end up as gangbangers and bleed out their lives in the gutter of a barrio."

"Got religion too late in life," Olecki said.

"He know that and expect to be convict. He also accept he be mark by those *compatriotos*. They fear he divulge the plans of the cell. That is why he seek to trade to the feds information about the movement in return for perks for those kids."

"What made him contact the ATF?" Bravo asked.

Martinez explained that years before ATF agents tracked him and others for transporting guns across state borders. Those agents scorned offers of money to be allowed to escape, in the way of some local police. So he reached out to the bureau that proved themselves honest.

"How 'bout other members of that gang," Olecki asked. "Has to be someone Elizondo contacted, or who contacted him."

Martinez shook his head. "Nobody contact him in that jail. And he never say anything about anyone except Abdulo."

Both detectives gawked—stunned by hearing the name.

"Who in hell is Abdulo?" Olecki asked in falsetto.

"All I ever learn from Elizondo," Martinez said, "is that Abdulo is leader of the Vasillo Rojo and that he bring it to South Florida from Chicago to steal those weapons. No, he never say how they come to know about the arms being stored at that airfield."

"Did he identify the building in Washington they intended to blow up?" Bravo asked.

"No, sir. The only thing he say is that *el caudillo*, the leader they call Abdulo, speak often of a raid to bring them fame. Even if they die in that effort they will write their names in history as martyrs, to be known and revered in the way of Bolivar, Che Guevara, José Marti and other Hispanic heroes."

ELEVEN

Joe Lee Baggler paced the conference room. "Eats my damn gut out to be superseded by a damn revenuer."

"Why do you call him that?" Pedrazo asked. Only he and the three FBI agents occupied the room.

"That agency started with agents hunting and collecting revenue on illegally distilled liquor by hillbillies," Loscalzo said.

"Moonshine they called it," Epps added. "Then they were expanded to hunting down tobacco products sold without federal stamps."

"Firearms," Baggler said, "became another addition to their mission, not that I understand why, considering every American has the right to bear arms."

"Whatever," Epps said, "that sucker's sure not up to your level. But then, you can't expect people of other agencies to operate as efficiently as we do. Hear—"

"Outrageous!" Pedrazo rose half out of his chair. "DEA is unparalleled in interdicting narcotics."

"We're talking running terrorists to ground," Baggler said. "Ain't no ATF agent nowhere that can teach FBI personnel how to do that."

"Perhaps not Puerto Ricans anyway," Pedrazo said, chortling. It set everyone except Epps to grinning.

"I don't play that shit," Epps grumbled. "Next thing you'all be whispering some shit behind *my* back."

"No, no. I never do that." Pedrazo looked and sounded sincere. "It is only that everyone knows that Cubans are the superior people in the Caribbean."

"You saying," Epps asked, "you'all are the only ones competent—that Jamaicans and other West Indians can't be?"

"No. No." Pedrazo swirled his hands.

"But if you had yo' druthers," Baggler asked, staring at Pedrazo, "would you or would you not prefer me to him to ramrod this taskforce?"

"To speak frankly," Pedrazo replied, "and without prejudice, I believe it a mistake to pick that one over myself to head up this taskforce."

"That wasn't the damn question," Baggler said.

"I'll go along with that," Loscalzo said. "No doubt in my mind that Loreano is a more capable group-leader than Bravo."

"Not better than me," Baggler said, then sucked in breath as he saw Bravo entering, along with Olecki and Cleo. A moment later Archison led Maylene Brown and Danly Coombs through the door. Everyone took seats around the table.

"Let's hear some reports" Bravo said.

"Interviewed just about every clerical employee at the county jail," Maylene Brown said, "without learning anything we didn't already know."

"Nor did we connect anyone to involvement with terrorists," Danly Coombs added.

"We were equally unsuccessful," Loscalzo said. "Didn't uncover any connection between the jail guard, Botero, and the terrorists."

"Even questioned his family and neighbors," Epps said. "He lives quietly and has a nice family. His finances are up and down at best. No windfalls."

"The FBI search turned up nothing with respect to any jail employee enjoying additional or unexplainable income," Loscalzo said. "Fact is, most are in debt."

"We sure didn't find the guard Cortez dirty," Baggler said, "and nary an indication that he connived with terrorists or anybody else."

"The man lacks intelligence for involvement in a conspiracy," Pedrazo added. "Why?" Bravo asked, "because he's Puerto Rican?"

"That's not what I inferred," Pedrazo said.

"Let's stay on point," Archison said, "and not go off on a tangent of sociological mumbo-jumbo."

Bravo breathed deeply to contain his emotions, not expose irritation that might reflect adversely on his leadership qualities.

Turning to Loscalzo he asked: "Can you trace gangs and criminals in Chicago through the National Crime Information Center, especially a guy called Abdulo?"

"Sure can try."

"Y'all inquiring about a Puerto Rican or a raghead?" Baggler asked.

"We don't use those prejudicial references," Archison snapped.

"Don't mean nothing demeaning or nothing," Baggler said. "Am simply trying to clarify the ethnic identity of the guy."

"It would be more productive," Pedrazo said, "to have both names."

"We got that much," Olecki said, "which is a whole bunch more than any of the rest of you got."

"As it happens," Loscalzo said, "I've consulted the NCIC on numerous occasions and learned that the list of Puerto Ricans with criminal records is countless, as are gang-related Latino names."

"Maybe it just might be more constructive to reach out to the Chicago police," Bravo said, "and see if they can tell us which gang leaders aren't in town presently. They just might be able to give us a heads-up on someone called Abdulo."

When Loscalzo pulled the phone to him and set about executing the task, Archison asked Bravo: "How does that particular information facilitate the investigation?"

"That dead prisoner, Elizondo," Bravo replied, "came down here from Chicago with a gang called Vasillo Rojo, or Red Cell, as we reported earlier. What we learned on this visit was it being ramrodded by someone called Abdulo. We learn who's not in town there we might get a line on him."

Baggler scowled. "Sounds like a wasted effort with half of those gangbangers like as not out of town, with the most of them in the slammer."

"And the rest on the lam," Epps added, then joined Baggler in snickering.

"Nothing wrong with giving it a try," Maylene said. "Sure beats simply criticizing others."

"You got my endorsement, sister lady," Epps said. His eyes swept her.

"You going against me again?" Baggler demanded of Epps.

"No, brother-man, just agreeing that we ought to be investigating every avenue of probability. Hear what I'm saying?"

"You come up with a suggestion," Baggler said to Epps, "and I'll be sure to shoot it down like you doing mine."

Loscalzo hung up the phone and held up a hand to forestall the bickering. Referring to notes scribbled on a yellow pad he explained that a lieutenant of detectives heading up an anti-gang squad in Chicago informed that the skel called Abdulo hasn't been around for a couple of weeks. A wild-ass whose real name is Clemente Galbos is believed to have adopted the handle of Abdulo when he became the *caudillo del Vasillo Rojo*, or leader of the Red Cell. That bunch is also believed to be members of the *Macheteros*, the most radical of the *Independistas*.

"Where in hell they come up with those funny names?" Baggler asked.

"What the difference?" Olecki asked. "Bringing them down is all that matters."

"Before they bring down a whole bunch of buildings," Cleo added.

"You saying," Baggler asked, "that what we got us is a Puerto Rican jihad?"

"Let's hope not," Cleo said. "We already got us more hell than we can handle with those Islamists."

"Then we'd better prepare ourselves for a rough task," Maylene Brown said.

"The guy has a reputation," Loscalzo said, "for not having any compunction about knocking off people who get in his way, including his own goombahs."

"Sounds like he's doing copy-cat on Islamic terrorism," Bravo said.

"Why a Puerto Rican need to adopt Muslim extremism?" Baggler asked.

"Who else offers them military training," Bravo asked, "as well as teaches them urban guerrilla tactics along with the rhetoric to enlist supporters and converts?"

"That's about how it goes," Olecki said. "You need you a friend, you grab onto whoever smiles at you."

"If those lobos tie in with groups like Isis or al-Qaida," Maylene Brown said, "we'll have a far more threatening situation."

"This business is beginning to sound more intense than anticipated," Archison said. "I'd better request additional staffing from Miami."

"Tried to request a couple more agents," Baggler said, "without success. Told us they have too many cases to spare any more agents."

"Which means," Bravo said, "we need to apply ourselves to uncovering that bunch before they can wreak havoc." He hoped that ended the discussion of additional staffers, concerned for his leadership being superseded if higher echelon FBI personnel joined the taskforce. Expecting media attention, he wanted to shine as one of the few Puerto Ricans who ever directed an investigation of this magnitude. Besides, he hoped his success offset the negativity of Puerto Rican activists wreaking havoc on America.

"While I'm not opposed to working around the clock when I think the effort is justified," Archison said, "its past eight o'clock, time to break for today."

"Considering the gravity of this thing," Bravo said, "it might be productive to keep at it for a few more hours." It irked him to have operations suspended this early after being denied returning to Washington for the night.

"I'm not sure we're going to accomplish anything with tired brains," Archison said. "You people are exhausted and it'll serve you best to rest rather than spin your wheels chasing slum rats in the dark. We'll resume when rejuvenated in the morning." "I agree," Loscalzo said, "that a break will invigorate us so we'll be ready to take out those badasses tomorrow."

"We damn sure better take them out," Maylene Brown said, "before this billows into massive terrorism and impacts on the country as a whole."

"You to have a drink with us, ATF-man?" Pedrazo asked.

Bravo shook his head. "Need to find a hotel room. Also need to call my wife."

When Danly Coombs gestured to the phone in the middle of the table, Bravo shook his head again. "Prefer to do this in privacy."

"Use my office again," Maylene offered. "You can even close the door so we won't be able to hear you begging for understanding why you have to stay over."

Bravo clenched his teeth, determined not to expose being irked by that jab.

"Was my old lady," Baggler said, "I'd just tell her to accept disappointments that go with the job."

"Your wife ditched your sorry ass two years ago," Epps said.

Bravo ignored the resultant needling and sniggering as he headed to Maylene's office. After closing the door he sat at her desk and dialed his home. Meanwhile he inhaled deeply but captured only the slightest suggestion of that arousing musk. Still, he inhaled enough to kindle memory of two years ago.

While the phone droned he glanced around and found interesting the way she kept everything in place, demonstrating a meticulous work ethic. He knew from association with her in Atlanta that she had a lot of smarts, and had earned a reputation for diligent performance.

After four rings the machine answered. That didn't surprise him since Esteban lived on campus at Duke University in North Carolina and Romero had gone on a three-day environmental field trip with his high school class into the mountains of Tennessee.

Unwilling to talk to something impersonal, he hung up, then called her office and got an answering service there also, so called her cellphone, to be transferred to a voice mail. Clicking off, he returned to the conference room.

"That was fast," Maylene said. "Y'all can't find things to chat about?"

"Nobody home," Bravo said. "I'm going to need transportation."

"Mind if he uses one of the bucars?" Archison asked Baggler. That man postured indignantly at the suggestion of an ATF agent borrowing an FBI bureau car.

"You each have a vehicle," Archison said, "while you generally ride around together. Giving Bravo the temporary use of one shouldn't place a burden on you."

Baggler scowled while hunching concession. "Give him your keys," he said to Epps.

The lanky African-American opened his mouth as if to object, but his change of expression indicated his awareness of it being futile. Accepting the keys, Bravo remarked: "Need to retrieve my luggage left in a locker at the airport, then find a hotel room."

"Want to crash on my couch?" Maylene asked.

His head snapped to her with disbelief widening his eyes. Glancing around, he deduced that everyone considered the offer as facetious rather than revealing. He hoped he hadn't blushed . . . hadn't exposed shock and disbelief.

"I never got me no offer like that," Epps complained.

"And won't," Maylene said.

"Try the Hotel Embassy on Southeast Seventeenth Street," Olecki suggested, then directed Bravo in how to find it.

TWELVE

Returning from the airport Bravo drove the black SUV east on Broward Boulevard engulfed in the emissions of engine throbbing vehicles. Then he turned south on Federal Highway, no less trafficked, but wider and faster moving. Following along in line, he whizzed down the ramp and through the tunnel under the New River. Ascending from it he arrived at the light to turn east onto Southeast Seventeenth Street, the access road to the coast.

Gazing around while waiting for the light he noticed the cozy motel tucked behind a shopping strip on the right side of the highway. But he dismissed it as an option, since he was in the left-turn lane, four lanes of traffic away.

Glancing ahead he spotted the Hotel Embassy a few blocks down Southeast Seventeenth Street. That four-lane thoroughfare took traffic across the Intracoastal Waterway Bridge to the beach, an area of luxury condominiums and high-priced hotels. The Embassy's twelve stories of bright coral walls and barrel-tiled roofs almost succeeded in achieving a semblance of Spanish mission architecture. It dwarfed the one- and two-storied buildings around it in that commercial area.

Considering that he'd have to use an elevator, with its associated delays, to get to and from his accommodation, especially during crises, Bravo elected for the motel across the street from him where he'd have direct access and egress. Since traffic headed in his direction had a red light, he hung a sharp right and darted across four lanes of traffic just as that light turned green. Pulling his neck into his collar he shrunk from the symphony of horns that regaled him.

A sign with the name Landed Gentry Motel adorned a two-story dwelling with wide wooden valances. Clumps of areca palms and tall ficus hedges all but concealed the chain link fence that separated it from the adjacent shopping plaza parking lot.

It disappointed him to find the lack of exterior entrances to individual rooms because the shopping mall parking hadn't left sufficient space. So all rooms opened off a central hallway accessed by the front door. But Bravo considered it preferable to waiting for elevators in a mid-rise hotel, especially at a time when his presence might be vital elsewhere. Despite it being on the brink of seedy he booked the one available room on the first floor.

Entering it he phoned home, to again get the answering machine. He grumbled that he'd call back shortly. After hanging his extra suit in the small closet and putting his other stuff in the bureau drawers, and the bathroom kit in the tiny bathroom lacking shelf space to lay anything out, he sat on the bed and again dialed the phone. It droned past the four times without the answer machine picking up, heartening him that she was home but away from the phone. So he let it ring, until he heard the click and then her voice.

"Hi, how's it going?"

A moment of silence followed by: "Please don't tell me you're still in Fort Lauderdale."

It wasn't the tone he'd hoped to hear, in her barely perceptible accent. "Don't have a choice. They reassigned me because—"

"You know how important attending this ball is to me."

"Yes, I do, but there are imperative things—"

"More important than escorting me to the ball?"

"The bureau doesn't assign me to unimportant cases."

"You can't get one night off to fly here?"

He grimaced, unwilling to reveal being denied that option; an admission that he lacked the influence he sometimes boasted having. So he grumbled: "What the hell is so important about a wingding at the Spanish Embassy?"

"It's everything!"

"Still nursing hots for that Nando guy after all these years?"

"Not hots . . . just a desire to revisit a by-gone life . . . to reminisce. Why is that wrong?"

"Because you're married. Your yearnings should be to see your husband, not your ex-lover."

"Where is my husband? He's never home. You spent the last three weeks in Houston. Now you're in Fort Lauderdale . . . for God knows how long. When do you come home?"

"It's what I do, Yzabel . . . what I did when we met. I've been doing this for the twenty-one years we've been married."

"Then it's time for a change—time to put me first."

"You've always been first. I've always indulged—"

"Then why not tonight—of all nights?"

"It's a big goddam case, Yzabel. Two US marshals and a deputy assistant US attorney have been killed. That assistant attorney, incidentally, was Artie Meyers. You remember Artie Meyers, a college buddy and one of my oldest friends."

"Who I've seen three times in my life . . . and not once during the past ten years. Didn't really know the man."

"Well I did. Served with him in the job in New York. He was my most important buddy in my early cop life. We—"

"All right. All right. Enough of Artie Meyers. He's dead. Bury him."

"That's unreasonably cold, Yzabel."

"Forgive me if it offends you. Meanwhile I have to get ready for tonight."

"You're joking. You're going to that ball alone?"

"Yes, Ramón, I'm not going to forego this opportunity to see Nando again, after twenty-two years."

"That's longer than we've been married."

"Of course. Met you at that ball at the Spanish Embassy the last time I saw Nando. It doesn't surprise me that you've forgotten."

"Doesn't marriage mean anything to you—have sanctity any longer?"

"What has this to do with marriage, Ramón?"

"Stop addressing me so formally. I'm still Ray—still your husband."

"Perhaps it's time to change that. You prefer your far-flung assignments to life at home. Let's end the marriage instead of wrangling about competing interests."

"This isn't the time to discuss something that drastic, Yzabel." He'd always used her full name since she had an aversion to it being shortened and objected ardently to being addressed by a nickname . . . sure as hell wasn't receptive to being called Izzy.

"Fine, we'll discuss it whenever you find time to come home. Meanwhile I need to get ready, to be pretty for Nando when he sees me after that long absence."

"Go ahead. Go to the goddam ball. Satisfy your compulsion to see an old lover. I'll be home as soon as I put this case to bed. It'll probably be another few—"

"Accepted." Click!

Clenching his jaws he thumped the phone in its cradle. Then he exhaled and stretched out on the bed, his depression deepening the more he thought about and accepted diminishing prospects of reconciling the dissolution of his marriage. Yes, they'd enjoyed bliss through the years but it had too often been interspersed with bitterness. Dios, he shook his head in commiseration at how many times during those unhappy lulls over the past twenty-one years he'd questioned his having married her . . . assumed she had also.

Reminiscence momentarily erased the gravity etched on his face. No way he'd deny he'd crash-dived into adoration the moment he laid eyes on that princess. The bureau had picked him and two others fluent in Spanish to work in concert with agents from the FBI and the Secret Service, along with a couple of US Marshals, to provide security at a diplomatic ball at the Embassy of Spain in Washington. They were assigned to prevent embarrassing incidents, such as assassination attempts by the Basque separatists who terrorize Spain.

He waggled his head, distressed to realize how many extremists around the world had no compunctions about resorting to the worst violence to underscore their lunatic agendas. Those fanatics callously wrote off human life and suffering as acceptable collateral damage for publicizing narrow-minded political perspectives.

Wearing tuxedos to assimilate all other attendees, they remained alert in that swirl of guests to any sign of aberrant behavior. While circulating he happened upon a lovely lady with black hair and beautiful Iberian features. Neural activity in his brain, stimulated by a rush of dopamine that suffused in the thalamus, rendered him *bocabierta*—gape-mouthed dumbstruck.

Trying to converse with her he hoped he didn't prattle like a juvenile while struggling to converse. Despite feeling like a dummy it took effort to overcome the paralysis of infatuation. Fascination intensified with every moment, like a mania, obsessing him to impress this lady. Only Dios knows how he managed to not exhibit dementia and turn her off. Everything about Yzabel Zaraga Ycaza fueled his yearning to establish a relationship.

Intoxicated by that beautiful and cultured lady, he feared he'd have no life without her. And he bubbled ecstatically when she included him in conversations with others that wandered over; even introduced him to many important people he never expected to have a social association with. A middle-class Puerto Rican boy from New York rarely rubs elbows with the upper class of Spain.

While chatting, he learned that Yzabel had been born in Valladolid, Spain, but now lived in New York City. He shrugged off that distance as merely an hour on the shuttle that flew back and forth daily. No force on earth could dissuade him from pursuing this Iberian princess.

Every once in a while he got the feeling that something disconcerted her, but he stifled the urge to question her about it, concerned with intimidating her and turning her off. Sure, he knew his family background didn't match hers. But they were in the good old US of A, an egalitarian society where that kind of snobbery supposedly didn't affect relationships. Yes, he determined to extend their encounter, despite lacking confidence that she'd be agreeable. Dios! That was an incredible moment in time.

The trill of his cellphone on the night table jerked him out of his ruminations. Scowling, he considered not answering it, not eager to abandon his joyful memories. He'd let the caller leave a message on the voicemail. But it occurred to him that it might be official and important—perhaps from headquarters in Washington or the U. S. Attorney's office here in town—with a lead about those terrorists.

Hell, it might be Yzabel calling back to make up. Yes, he wanted it to be her, so snatched it up and answered it. "Hello. Oh!" He tensed as the voice timbre rippling across the temporal lobe of his brain, stimulating memory.

"Thought you might like to reminisce."

Not anxious to deal with her at the moment he admonished himself for not having read the caller ID. It had been a long time and he wasn't in a mood to revisit the past . . . especially one that ended bitterly.

"Cat got your tongue?"

"Hadn't expected you to call."

"Surely you realized we'd have to talk about it."

Pulsing waves traversed the synapses of his cerebral cortex while searching for a response, but he failed to elicit a suitable reply.

"We could discuss it over supper," broke the short silence.

When he didn't respond she said: "You are planning to eat tonight?"

"Hadn't given it much thought." Hell, he really hadn't.

"Stomach acids suppressing your appetite, induced by squabbling with your wife for failing to be there to escort her to the ball?"

"Frankly it surprises me that you haven't remarried."

"If I had I wouldn't be available to help you climb out of that funk."

"I'm not in the mood to hang out, Maylene."

"Get real, guy. Pining over wifey doesn't mitigate your marital problems. A drink will help to dissolve your dismal mood."

"That isn't always the best remedy."

"I remember one heck of a remedy that night in Atlanta."

"We'll both be better off leaving that in the past."

"Fine, we'll talk about how we brought arsonists to the bar of justice. We did a hell of a job on that case when you look back on it."

"Aren't you satisfied with those lapdogs at the bar sniffing at your tail."

"As it happens, I didn't go with that bunch."

"Oh!" He felt stupid for vocalizing that accusatory supposition.

"Fact is, I'm at my apartment hoping you'll take me to dinner so I won't have to eat alone. We can talk about *old times*."

After a moment of silence since he didn't respond she said: "That was a hell of an *old times*. Don't tell me you're not receptive to a repeat of a dynamite one-nighter?"

"Frankly, Maylene, I'm concerned with where it'll lead."

"Only as far as we let it. At any rate, you owe me a dinner during which you must convince me that simply disappearing was the way to end it."

"You know the bureau whisked me off to Kansas City. Actually, that's where and when I encountered Archison. Now there's a—"

"I'd prefer discussing it face to face. Your sudden popping up here injected a new dimension into an old relationship, especially since we're going to see each other day after day for God knows how long. You owe me that much, Ray, to attain closure."

"Is that it, or are you nursing a two-year-old grudge because of the callous way you believe I ended that affair?"

"Thank you for that admission."

"That done, why do we have to meet?"

"To talk out face-to-face something that traumatically affected me. Is that too much to ask of you?"

"Okay. Where?"

THIRTEEN

Bravo dodged among the locals and tourists milling on the sidewalk of Las Olas Boulevard, a busy nighttime thoroughfare in Fort Lauderdale. Locals as well as visitors swarmed the upscale boutiques and art galleries, as well as the avant-garde cafes and upscale restaurants flanking the heavily trafficked street.

He had to shoulder his way through those clustered outside the door of Tangerine's, a popular bistro. That press of would-be diners waiting to be assigned tables amplified the decibel level, typifying the dash for Wednesday night fun, despite tomorrow being a workday.

Low barriers divided the large American-style bistro into several sections of tables crowded with diners. A large bar dominated the left rear corner, engulfed by happy-hour celebrants, most of which were men competing for the attention of the two alluring barmaids. The piped-in rock music pierced the drone of talking and laughter, as did the rattle of dishes and movement of patrons and servers, punctuated by the jingle and jangle of cellphones.

The hostess found the name he gave her crossed-off, so directed him to a center area. He applied agility to edge among, around and between that legion of prattling diners to where Maylene sat at a small table immersed among other small tables spilling over with animated people.

Her glowing greeting mystified him and ignited questions of why she'd dunned him for this meeting after the way their relationship concluded, especially considering the time lapse. Besides, this lady commanded attention without trying . . . sure as hell didn't need to beg for any . . . or carry a two-year torch for him or any other guy.

She exuded sensuality in her pink double-strap knit camisole and low-waisted denim jeans that fit her without a wrinkle. And, oh yes, it flaunted a tantalizing band of brown flesh. She'd relieved her hair to soften her beautiful features, transforming her from a proper business matron to a svelte ebon Circe.

He bobbed his head and mouthed a greeting while complying with her gesture to sit. A bustling waitress paused long enough to take his drink order. He decided on ale, wanting something that couldn't be construed as reunion or celebratory, in spite of awareness that she nursed a tall drink. Damn real he was reticent about diving back into that enthrallment at a time when his marriage demanded major attention.

But his recent telephone confrontation with Yzabel weakened resolve, even awakened contemplations of again wallowing in ecstasy with Maylene. Shaking his head, he wondered if this fox really pursued an encore, or jerked his chain as some kind of vengeance. Rejected females were renowned for retribution.

She leaned across the table to be heard in that din, exposing much of her breasts. "It's nice to talk to you without the inhibiting constraints of an office full of spectators."

He nodded, uncertain how else to respond. Her cleavage excited desire and evoked memories of that long-ago night. Blinking it off, he reproved himself for conceding to this meeting. Okay, so now he needed to apply discipline not to succumb . . . didn't allow himself to be swallowed up in a sexual abyss. Besides, he found it hard to believe this gorgeous creature carried a torch for him since that one-nighter of two years ago.

Dozens of guys sure as hell had to have pursued her . . . and a few sure as hell had to have scored. No way this chick could be horny. Amazing that she hadn't married again, except that she's probably too independent to make the concessions required. But there have to be guys competing for her attention.

Determined not to be vamped by her, he glanced at the menu to notice it offered simple American cuisine. Fine, he wasn't in the mood for fancy feasting. Hamburgers and fries obviously comprised seventy per cent of the food they served. He had to admit that they priced the food moderately, while not the drinks.

"Whenever you're ready."

His eyes jerked up to hers. He doubted she referred to ordering food.

"Let's talk about where we left off," she said.

He winced, then inhaled resolve to prepare himself to launch into an explanation —though unsure where to start and what to say. But before he got a word out the waitress placed the frosty stein of ale before him, then flitted away with drinks for other tables.

He raised it in a wordless toast, held it aloft while she raised and clinked her glass against his. He sipped it to delay responding. Truth is he was in a quandary as to how to approach the discomforting subject. Hell, he'd never expected to have to and hadn't prepared for that eventuality.

"We had a volcano that night," Maylene said. "Then, poof, you disappeared like a wisp of steam."

He shrugged, still uncertain how to respond . . . or why he needed to, considering she knew damn well he'd been dispatched to Kansas City.

"That extraordinary night," she said, "elevated you to the most exciting lover that ever came into my life. The following morning you dissolved into a memory."

He sipped his ale to conceal his surprise at her proclamation. And he groped for words to explain something he hadn't thought about for two years. But why did he need to? Hell, this knockout-gorgeous gal had to have terrific sex with any number of guys since then. And she'd probably been too occupied with admirers over that time to continue yearning for him. It simply wasn't credible.

"What was it, Ray? Why did you disappear from my life? You owe me an explanation."

"You damn well know that it wasn't a matter of choice. Duty called."

"Be that as it may, you never phoned, never answered my calls, or returned them. You never even wrote, or e-mailed, which would have been impersonal but at least shown interest."

"You knew I was married and had to know an affair couldn't have any future."

"True, you didn't conceal being married. But the way you plunged into that merging of our auras, no way you considered your marriage all that sacrosanct."

He grimaced, stung by that indictment.

"Yes, baby, you rocked the hell out of my boat, like no man before or since. Didn't it have meaning to you? If so, why did you avoid me thereafter?"

"Yzabel and I patched things up. We have two sons, you know. For their sake we need to continue to be a family."

"Man, you didn't exhibit any matrimonial dedication that night. Why did it suddenly come up the next day?"

Nah, he decided not to explain that he plunged into ecstasy that night because he believed his marriage irretrievable shattered that night. Besides, he knew she'd rebut whatever he said. And he didn't see any benefit to be derived from a contentious discussion . . . with a person trained in the art of verbal debate.

Maylene lifted her glass to her lips, but didn't drink, skepticism clouding the dark eyes she leveled on him. "Everything you said at the office this afternoon inferred that you have ongoing marital problems."

"That has nothing to do with you."

"Wrong, baby. I've been haunted these past two years, since you inserted yourself in my life. No way you can deny we had something really, really special."

"Frankly, I can't believe you haven't been immersed in other relationships, and gotten over a one-nighter by now."

"Tried, but couldn't find anyone to erase that night. Yeah, baby, I dove into deep water in search of obliteration of that memory."

"Hard to believe that a lady as beautiful and brilliant as you wasn't inundated in ardent pursuers."

"Then why aren't you attracted to me?"

"I wouldn't be human if I didn't find you stunning. But you need to accept that we had a one-night fling that ended the night it began—and get on with your life."

"Actually I had all but succeeded in picking up the pieces when you walked into that conference room this afternoon and shattered every building block of my new life."

"I find that hard to—"

"Every scintillating moment of that night surfaced when I saw you."

He averted his eyes, deciding not to respond to what he considered too far out to be feasible.

"Perhaps," she said, glancing coyly at him, "you're receptive to an experiment, to determine whether what happened that night was a phenomenon, or whether that magic was real and can be recaptured?"

"I'm human, for Christ's sake. I look at you and yearn for a replay. But I have a family—a wife and two sons—and am concerned with injuring those relationships."

"Are you saying there's no room for me in your life?"

He winced—stunned and stumped to find words delicate enough to answer honestly.

"Okay, ex-lover, you hung me out to dry. But I'm strong enough to go on."

"Then why this obsession to rehash a romance that ended the night it began?"

"To understand the motives that drove you to abruptly abandon me. I have a thing about closure."

"Or an ego-driven objection to being dropped. You wouldn't be so eager for this defining of motives if you'd dumped me."

"Screw you, Ray. You dropped off the radar to avoid the discomfort of calling it off face-to-face."

"It apparently didn't affect your career. You were an intern then, are now a prosecutor, occupying the first chair. Congratulations."

Before Maylene could respond, the waitress bustled over. "Ready to order?"

"Burger medium with spicy fries." Maylene grouched without glancing up.

"Dido that for me," Ray said. Then he nodded to the waitress's inquiry of whether they were ready for drink refills.

"Where were we?" Maylene asked when the waitress left. "Oh yes, I'm ambitious—admit that. I'm also sensitive, with the need to know why someone turns off on me so abruptly. Would you have dumped me that abruptly if I'd been white?"

"Get off that! You're bigger than that—know better."

"Okay, Ray baby, so there's no residual desire?"

He swallowed and again averted his eyes, determined not to let himself be induced into admissions he'd regret later. But accepting that the silence that prevailed provoked a response. He brought his eyes back to hers. "Surely by now you've met other guys. I'm surprised you aren't married again . . . at least, that you've taken up with a guy."

"Oh, I did. Even foolishly got involved with my boss."

"That antagonistic Assistant US Attorney in Atlanta?"

"It was antagonistic toward you, because you distracted me from being attentive to him. The guy leched for me from day one of going to work there. Blamed you for his failure to score. When you disappeared and left me despondent he consoled me and relieved the pain—ended up in my bed."

"Glad you shared that with me."

"You cut my damn heart out, left me vulnerable."

"Sure, my fault. But if you blame me for that, at least give me credit because it succeeded in getting you assigned as a prosecutor."

"I earned this, Ray . . . by studying and practicing law. This is not as a result of tumbling in the hay. I'm a damned good lawyer. And, yes, I'm ambitious and know how to play my advantages. But that doesn't excuse your insensitive abandoning me."

"Okay, guilty as charged. Can we now drop the subject of something that never got into orbit?"

Before Maylene had a chance to respond the waitress interrupted to serve their food, temporarily reducing conversation to groans of contentment.

"What's your take on Archison?" Ray asked after biting into his burger.

"A stickler for procedure," she replied, glancing askance at him; a glance he interpreted as awareness of his devious attempt to avoid discussing that long-ago tryst. "He runs a tight ship," she added. "But you know that, having worked a case with him."

Bravo snorted. "The guy exemplifies my indictment of prosecutors—too insecure to open a case until in possession of overwhelming evidence."

"Considering the cost of prosecuting it's the proper approach. Yes, he plays it close to the vest. And he's a taskmaster. Believe that he won't let up on any of us until those terrorists are brought to justice. Does that bother you because we're targeting Puerto Ricans?"

"No more than it affects you when we target African-American wrong-doers."

"How does it feel to lord it over the other agencies?"

"Love it. Don't get all that many opportunities to ramrod FBI guys."

"You know, of course, that you need to make headway to keep Archison from putting Baggler back in charge. He's mercurial, will shift primaries in a heart-beat."

"What makes him tick?"

"Same thing that impels most of us: ambition. It rankles him to still be an assistant US attorney, instead of heading up a region like most with his years in the system. My man expects his seniority to position him in line for the next large metropolitan area, where he'll be the US attorney, not a flunky in a sub-district."

"Meaning if he fails to put an end to this threat he'll be passed over."

"Hell, my man refuses to fail, which is why he'll be on your tail to clear the case."

"You drive here in your car?"

She jerked her head back, surprised at the question . . . then nodded.

"Then you don't need me to drive you home, so I'm going back to the motel and get a good night's sleep, needing to be chipper in the morning." He dropped a number of bills on the table to cover the check. "Shall I see you to your car?"

She shook her head, partially suppressed a grin. "Think I'll stay and have another drink. Have a good sleep." Watching him leave she winced, struck by the realization that she'd all but begged him to share her bed again . . . to resuscitate a long-dead affair. Okay, she accepted as a fault her clutching to extend a relationship that hadn't even gotten off to a real start. And, yes, he'd been correct when he commented that she might have reacted differently if she'd broken it off. Damn right it galled her to be dumped . . . by another white man!

Her daddy would have admonished her that you'd think the daughter of an automobile mechanic from Manasses, Virginia would know her place. Believe that's why she'd never informed daddy of encountering her first white lover while attending George Mason College in the neighboring city of Fairfax. Her escapades over the next three years with a number of white admirers earned her the resentment of many black students. She'd concealed those affairs from her parents.

After graduating she accepted recruitment by the Treasury Department, requiring she relocate to Washington. In spite of barely affording it, she rented a tiny apartment in the Adams-Morgan area not far from Dupont Circle, a trendy neighborhood with only a sprinkling of people of color. Sure enough, most of her friends, male and female, were white.

But despite a string of adventures with white men, she married Barnett Brown, a black executive at Treasury. Yes, that established her life in a less controversial manner than if she'd married out of her race . . . as well as earned her daddy's approval.

But hell, she needed to relegate all of that to the past, along with Ray Bravo. Yes, the time had come to move on. Assume some damn dignity, girl!

FOURTEEN

Yzabel glowed with pride when the limousine pulled up to the Embassy of Spain off Washington Circle at Pennsylvania Avenue. She'd engaged it determined to arrive in style. And yes she appreciated the uniformed doorman opening and holding the car door for her at the elaborate entrance of the large, square building with decorative windows dominating its façade.

An usher in red and black uniform, embellished with braid and a wide sash across his shoulder and chest, checked her invitation before escorting her through the spacious entrance alcove to double doors that opened into a huge ballroom festooned with banners draped from impressive crystal chandeliers. Thereupon, the usher announced in stentorian voice the attendance of Doña Yzabel Zaraga Ycaza.

She postured proudly despite being unescorted and in spite of her having omitted her husband's family name. Most importantly to her was making a grand entrance in her red and black gown, a mass of folds that accented the best features of her body. She'd artfully concealed some parts while accenting those that attracted praise. Having preserved her figure at forty-six, after having two children, she strutted proudly. Yes, she believed she competed favorably with any but the youngest of women.

Make-up, hair-do, and elaborate earrings masked whatever ravages age had imposed on her. Posturing confidently, she searched for familiar faces, to allow her to envelope herself among people she knew and liked, not stand about like a beacon of loneliness. Yes, she expected to have to make excuses for her husband's absence—as well as expose his middle-level station of government employment.

But that aside, she concentrated on encountering Nando. Breathing deeply, she invoked the patience required at a ball of that size with a virtual army of attendees. She responded to the hail of two older couples, friends of her parents in Spain. Her father, Lorenzo Zaraga, a renowned jeweler of Valladolid, enjoyed social prominence.

After hugging all around, one of the older women asked: "You are alone?"

"My husband had the bad luck to be called out of town . . . to a matter of importance, of course. With his position in government it's the norm rather than the exception in these times of national exigencies."

Both couples nodded, their acknowledgements indicating being impressed. Then they chattered happily, bringing Yzabel up to date about social events in Spain. Born there, she had been sent to The States at eighteen to attend Bryn Mawr, where she studied art and exhibited talent in the compatibility of colors.

Upon graduation she landed a job as an apprentice interior decorator with the firm of Maxwell Smythe in New York City, a renowned practitioner. She limited her involvement both socially and commercially to people of standing. Income required she share an apartment in the east sixties of Manhattan with another apprentice, French-born Fabienne Argonne of Nice, who had studied at the Sorbonne and the New York Academy of Art.

She and Fabienne, both gifted and determined, quickly made their mark in the world of decorators. That emergence led to their being invited to a soirée at the Waldorf-Astoria Hotel given by the Consul of Spain, where she met dashing Fernando Guijón Montoros, a scion of a prominent family of Barcelona. He served as a vice-consul, and was prophesied to have a promising career in the diplomatic corps.

His attentiveness flattered her, and she became so infatuated she disregarded his having a wife in Spain. *Dios en cielo!*—*God in heaven!*—she plunged with abandonment into a whirlwind romance and fell desperately in love. That intoxicating bubble burst when they recalled him to Spain for promotion and reappointment, resulting in a separation that thrust pain into her heart.

To her delight, Nando arranged at intervals for her to jet to various cities of Europe to extend their ecstatic relationship . . . but never in Spain. However she suffered excruciating pain when, after nearly five months of intermittent trysts, she received a letter from him informing that his superiors demanded he terminate those assignations to avoid scandal, consequently detriment to his career. The press had become aware of them. Crushed, she hibernated in her work and brooded over him for almost two years. During that time she and Fabienne started their own decorating business, catering to New York's upper crust.

She learned that the Embassy of Spain in Washington planned to fete Nando at a diplomatic ball so inveigled Arnold Goshen, a US Diplomat and recent widower, whose Fifth Avenue apartment she'd redecorated, to escort her to it. That sixty-one year old sycophant exalted in being seen with a young woman of her beauty.

But it aggravated her to learn that Nando brought his wife. Still, she determined to face him and make him tell her he no longer loved her, or—*con esperanza—hopefully*—that he never stopped loving her. But his greeting her impersonally devastated her.

Irate and vengeful, she set about to make the heartless bastard jealous by exaggerated attentiveness to one of the guests, dashing Ray Bravo. But Nando gave no indication of being affected, and returned to Spain within the week, with no further contact with her. During the following weeks she found solace in the attentiveness of Ray Bravo. That handsome, considerate, and charming man flew regularly to New York to dispel her loneliness and despondency.

A question from one of her lady friends jolted her out of her introspection. Yes, of course she found the hall and the affair impressive. They bubbled about the societal level of the attendees, and the wonderful gowns. The whole time she searched for a glimpse of Nando. But after two hours she accepted that the reunion with her prince was not to be. The romance had ended twenty-four years ago, with no hope of resurrection.

Dios en cielo! Just as she considered leaving she spotted Nando in a circle of people not too far away. *Por fin*! *Finally*! She wanted to rush to him, to throw herself into his arms, but constrained that insanity, aware that a social gaffe would destroy the slimmest chance of a revival. Yes, she yearned for some sign of affection from him.

Those long years of separation hadn't changed Nando appreciably. He still appeared rugged and handsome, in spite of maturity. Let him still find her attractive, even if it didn't culminate in a rebirth of romance . . . so long as he admired her. Hopefully he'd flatter her, assuage the dull ache of yearning she'd contained in a secret chamber of her heart.

Forcing herself to be patient, she chatted with those around her, confident he'd soon approach to reward her waiting . . . a moment she'd anticipated for so many years.

Glancing around, she spotted the group that had escorted Nando, but no sign of him. He'd simply vanished, injecting pain in her heart. No! She refused to believe that he'd left the area without speaking to her—didn't so much as endow her with a nod. Surely he'd seen her . . . had to have recognized her. Angry, she turned to leave when she spotted him socializing with people quite close. He'd retained that dashing manner that had seduced her and induced her sexual hunger.

Very well, she'd be patient, certain he'd approach in time. Surely he'd yearn, as she did, to revisit that love they'd shared. But he remained apart, making her wonder if he was unaware of her or avoiding her. Could she no longer mean anything to him?

She turned away and engrossed herself with her acquaintances in an effort to dismiss him from her mind and subdue the pain in her heart. *Dios*, she trembled when he ambled over and infiltrated her small circle. She'd yearned to hear his voice, after years of absence. But it disappointed her to see him with his arm linked in his wife's. Damn the woman! Why would Nando drag her along? Was this his way of telling her that no hope existed for them?

He greeted them affably, without any particular attention to any of them. No, she refused to let him know how much he wounded her. Damn him! He moved off with his entourage, his wife clutching him. Yzabel forced herself to continue smiling . . . refusing to reveal he'd gouged holes in her heart. Of course, he had to pay his respects to all the guests, the ball having been thrown in his honor. Still, she refused to accept that he needed to treat her so cavalierly.

When the two older couples invited her to accompany them to the huge tables that offered every variety of Spanish aliments she wavered, not certain she wanted to remain at the ball. But with nothing better to do, and no one waiting at home, she accompanied them and picked among the variety of tapas appealingly displayed and emitting arresting aromas. She accepted a glass of champagne from one of the waiters and waitresses circulating with trays of wines and aperitifs as well as hors d'oeuvres.

She felt her shoulder brushed, then froze at the words whispered in her ear: "You are as beautiful as I see you in memory."

That voice paralyzed her. It took effort to turn to him . . . even more to suppress the flush of vanity induced by his flattering admission.

"Can we meet?" His whispered entreaty softened her heart for him. "Tomorrow night at ten," he said, "in that lovely lounge at the Harvard Hall Hotel?"

She tried to respond but couldn't get words past a constricted throat and trembling lips. Her head quivered as seconds ticked away while she replayed his words and interpreted them as an invitation to tryst. Yes! She remembered that luxury hotel where they initiated passion.

Still, she couldn't emit words of reply. But her heart throbbed as she managed to bob her head up and down in acceptance. *Dios en cielo*, did he realize that she'd confirmed the meeting? She stood rooted, watching him melt back into the crowd. Did he interpret her restrictive reply as affirmative? *Ay, Dios*! She had no choice but to be there. Yes, she was going to be foolish, with no ability to do otherwise.

FIFTEEN

Ray rattled the key in his motel door, impatient to get inside and dial his home. He thumped his fingers on the lamp table while waiting through four drones until the machine answered, then slammed the phone into its cradle.

It defied credibility that she'd nursed a crush on that Iberian Casanova for more than twenty years despite being married. Had she taken that sacred vow and become his wife in spite of being in love with Montoros?

Clenching his jaws he called her cellphone, only to be immediately transferred to voice mail. Damn her! His eyes narrowed as it crossed his mind that during their years of matrimony she might have trysted with that bastard. Hell, she had endless opportunities while traveling for business to New York and other major cities. She'd even flown to Europe several times, as well as to Miami and the Caribbean. More often than not he was on the road on a case. Had he been cuckolded? He groaned, his Puerto Rican sensitivity wounded . . . though that suspicion lacked foundation. He tossed and turned after getting into bed, rankled by those nagging realizations denying him immediate sleep.

Jerking awake, his eyes shot to the digital clock on the night table. He blinked to clear mistiness, then noted the time as six: sixteen. It occurred to him that at some time during the long night his tortured mind had blacked out. Sighing heavily, he wrestled with whether to call Yzabel so early. Impulsiveness overcame prudence.

"What's so important that you're calling at this hour of the morning?"

Hearing the irritation in her groggy voice, he rued having awakened her. But he didn't know how to gracefully back off, so said: "Needed to talk with you." Dammit, he wished he'd waited another hour, hadn't surrendered to impetuosity.

"Are you all right? Have you been hurt?"

"No, I'm fine. Couldn't sleep, thinking about the anger of late."

"You've increased it, waking me from a deep sleep for no reason."

"It is for something—for who we are as a husband and wife."

"Are you sure you aren't calling to check on me, concerned that I might have slept with Nando last night? He's married you know, to a lovely lady who accompanied him to the ball."

"Thanks. I needed to know that."

"Is that the problem, Ray? You think I'm sleeping around?"

"No. No, of course not."

"Then I'm signing off so I can get a little more sleep before I go to the office for a long and demanding day."

SIXTEEN

"Fancy meeting you, and all that jive," Maylene said. She chuckled with the high pitch of forced frivolity. "Have a good night's sleep?"

He'd parked the bucar in the sixth floor garage and encountered her upon entering the elevator lobby, so assumed she'd parked there also. He pushed the up-button, despite it already being lit, then wondered why he acted so scatter-brained.

"I'm glad we didn't click last night," she said blithely. "Got a really good night's sleep after finally closing the door on that blunder."

He flinched, but swallowed his pride and reasoned that he gained by her concluding that misadventure. The elevator doors slid open and both boarded to join four other passengers, then rode the one floor without further repartee, neither anxious to air personal issues in public.

Entering the conference room they joined the others already sitting around the table chatting and sipping coffee. Boisey Epps leaned back in his chair and threw one lanky leg over the other before sarcastically remarking: "Sure doesn't surprise me to see you two show up together this morning."

Bravo winced, concerned that their arrival together set off rumors. He hoped to hell none of them knew he'd met Maylene for dinner last evening.

"What is your problem?" Maylene asked, cutting her eyes at the lanky African American.

"Y'all didn't join us at Murphy's last night," Epps said. "Did y'all have your own thing going?"

"We happened to meet at the elevator," Bravo said.

"Pay him no mind," Maylene said. "Fool has a screwed-up mind."

"That's unnecessary," Epps said. "Anyway, the word is out on you, girl. . . that you have eyes only for white men."

Loscalzo and Baggler jerked to attentiveness to assess Maylene from a different perspective.

"That's ridiculous!" burst out of Maylene. Hands on hips, her chin thrust forward, she glared at Epps. But her eyes rolled upward, as if to search her memory bank for the malicious person that outed her.

"Okay, woman," Epps said, "tell me why I never saw you go anywhere with any gentlemen of color."

"You monitoring every damn thing I do now, *brother man*?" She gave the ethnic expression a pejorative tone. "You don't know one damn thing about me, fool."

"No need to insult me. And I remind you that I invited you to lunch and dinner more than once and you always had an excuse to avoid going out with me."

"Did you get the message?"

"Yeah, I'm a black man."

"And you're not single, or have you forgotten?"

Archison entered with Danly Coombs. "Excuse me, but it's my belief that this meeting is to strategize preventative tactics to protect our citizenry from harm by those terrorists, as opposed to savaging each other's personal lives. Special Agent Bravo, have you a direction to share with us to achieve that purpose?"

"I have," Bravo said as he filled Styrofoam cups with coffee for himself and Maylene, then for Archison and Danly Coombs.

He directed everyone's attention to a large map of Fort Lauderdale on the wall opposite the windows, and passed a hand over the district that bordered Dixie Highway between Oakland Park Boulevard and Commercial Boulevard. "Our best lead is that green pick-up truck that escaped apprehension yesterday in this expanse of nearly eight square miles of warehouses, factories and storage yards. We find it we may locate its operators."

"Hopefully leading us to those arms and explosions looted from that airfield," Olecki added.

"Sounds real good," Boisey Epps said, "but could take days if not weeks to comb through that area. Hear what I'm saying?"

"That deputy that gave chase," Cleo reminded, "admitted he didn't get a good enough look at the vehicle to determine that it had a spidery crack in the windshield, a partially damaged fender, or lacked a front bumper."

"Nor was he able to read its license plate," Olecki added.

"More than likely changed the license plate by now," Loscalzo said. "Besides" Epps said, "they could have fixed the window and replaced the bumper, even repainted that sucker. Hear—"

"Let's put speculations aside" Bravo said, "and concentrate on finding the target vehicle by searching the prescribed area for a beat-up green pick-up truck. Then we'll determine if it's the one we're looking for."

"Makes sense," Olecki said. Cleo nodded with him.

"Considering that few of the buildings enjoy air conditioning," Bravo said, "the doors will be open in most. Expect unskilled employees there to be Hispanic and Haitian for the most part, and not particularly proficient in English. Some might have seen the truck. They may also be aware of Puerto Ricans in the area from whom information might be extracted."

"Pretty damn long shot," Baggler said. He appeared to stifle a snicker.

"Agreed," Bravo said, "but it's the best we have at the moment. It's possible that the terrorists stashed those weapons and explosives somewhere in that maze of narrow roads and closely constructed structures that are difficult to surveil. That junky vehicle just might lead us to them."

"Why then would that green truck go there when fleeing police pursuit?" Pedrazo asked.

"Last thing those ole' boys would do," Baggler said, "is lead us to their cache."

"Or to their hideout?" Epps added. "Hear what this man—"

"It just might be where they feel safe," Bravo said. "They're anything but geniuses. So we're going to poke through that area in hopes of locating that green pick-up truck, even if only to scratch it as the one involved in the airport raid."

"Let's be concerned with probable cause when searching," Archison grumbled.

"Of course." Bravo nodded but averted his eyes so as not to reveal having no intentions of abiding by every restriction. "Pedrazo and the three FBI agents can form two teams. I'll ride with the two sheriff's detectives, giving us three teams sweeping areas where we'll hopefully encounter those culprits."

"Sounds about like all we got to go on," Olecki said.

"Right as rain," Baggler said. "It's apparently all we have to go on."

Bravo ignored the sarcasm. "While your two teams sweep that area me and the sheriff's detectives will concentrate on industrial areas in western Broward, in the event they cached the weapons and explosives on that side of town. No telling in which direction the rental truck went after leaving that parking lot behind the office complex off Cypress Creek Road."

"Got us no end of those damned inconsistencies," Baggler said. He and Epps exchanged glances and suppressed snickers.

"We'll meet back here at one," Bravo said, refusing to expose being intimidated.

At the sixth floor entrance to the garage he sent Olecki and Cleo ahead while he cellphoned Yzabel at her office, hoping to patch up the earlier hostility. "Sorry, sir, Doña Yzabel Zaraga is at a breakfast meeting with a client. Would you like to leave a message?" He clicked off without responding and joined the two sheriff's detectives.

Olecki drove the Impala with Cleo in the passenger seat. Bravo settled into the back seat, relieved not to have the bucar, concerned with damaging it, which might happen in any kind of chase or encounter. He knew damned well that his superiors would have a shitfit if they had to reimburse the other bureau, contention between them being what it was. Besides, he wasn't in a driving mood, or any other kind except ugly.

Olecki headed west on Broward Boulevard, crossing Interstate 95 with its endless traffic. At Martin Luther King Junior Avenue he turned right, to pass between modest homes where they occasionally saw African-American children gamboling in small front yards and spilling onto the sidewalks. Turning into Northwest Twenty-Ninth Street they cruised between small and dingy warehouses while maneuvering around haphazardly parked cars and trucks that narrowed the roadway. Mildew, poverty and low-end labor infested the air.

Then they swung onto Northwest Twenty-First Avenue, with run-down stores on one side of the narrow macadam roadway and grungy warehouses on the other. The businesses ran the gamut from rebuilt auto parts to refurbished appliances, as well as cabinetry fabricators and upholstery shops. Most of the people they saw were black.

While tooling alongside an auto body shop Olecki gestured to three men working on a beat-up green pick-up truck that resembled the one they sought. Cleo agreed that it was worth a look-see so Olecki swung a U-turn and headed toward the auto body shop. One of the workers brought the attention of the other two to the approaching vehicle. All three fled into a crude block structure.

Olecki screeched to a stop a few feet from the entrance, where the three officers clambered out and took up positions on the far side of their vehicle to aim their guns at the crude opening. "Police!" Olecki yelled. "Come out of there with your hands on your heads."

Nothing stirred. Stagnancy infected the surrounding air.

"Policia!" Bravo yelled, translating the command to Spanish. "Salgan con manos arriba—a la cabeza."

Still no movement. Meanwhile Cleo called for back-up, explaining the situation as potential for A & D. Bravo sprinted over to the pick-up truck, stooping as low as possible to reduce himself as a target. Keeping it between himself and the crude building, he inspected it, only to be disappointed since it didn't conform to the description received from the landscape workers . . . not that what those people reported could be taken as gospel. Most eye-witness reports were unreliable.

Olecki left Cleo behind their car to guard the entrance while he darted to the vehicles parked on the opposite side from Bravo. He then sprinted along the side of the building to the rear of it. As he turned the corner he spotted a man slipping out of the rear door. "Halt!" he yelled as he aimed his semi-automatic weapon extended in both hands. "Manos arriba!"

But the man darted back into the rear entrance. Olecki caressed the side of his pistol with his trigger-finger, having resisted firing because he hadn't seen any weapons. He cursed the guy, the tension and the scary situation. Remaining in the cover of the building he gritted his teeth while communicating the occurrence with Cleo by radio.

Two police cruisers with lights and sirens arrived, each with two officers. Those from the second car hurried around to back up Olecki, while those from the first joined Cleo, who greeted them familiarly.

"We come out," came a voice from inside the building.

"With your damn hands in the air," Cleo yelled back.

"Throw out your guns first," one of the officers with her yelled.

"No guns," the voice from the structure replied. "No have guns."

"Then come on out," Cleo yelled to them, "one at a damn time."

Long seconds passed before one of the men hesitantly emerged, his hands on his head. His frightened eyes darted about as he obeyed directions to continue toward the car with the police officers. Then a second ventured out, and the third seconds later.

They lined up at the side of Olecki's car and abided by the command to place their palms flat on the vehicle. One of the officers kicked their feet apart and patted them down while Cleo and the other officer covered them with drawn pistols. The frisking officer hunched to indicate he hadn't encountered any weapons.

Cleo informed Olecki by radio that the three men had surrendered. Turning back to them, she asked: "Anyone remain inside?"

They looked blankly from one to the other.

Bravo had joined them and asked: "Alguna persona por dentro?"

"Nadie en chabola," one mumbled, shaking his head. He'd referred to the building as a shack, and claimed no one remained inside.

Bravo yelled that he was going in, then dashed to the side of the entrance. Cleo transmitted that information to Olecki as she watched Bravo probe the void with his weapon extended before him, crouched to reduce himself as a target.

Meanwhile Olecki and one of the other officers cautiously entered the rear door. They faced Bravo across a small shop with car parts and tools strewn around crude benches as well as on the cracked and broken concrete floor splashed with oil and grease. After nodding to each other they searched every nook and cranny.

Finding no one else, no weapons and nothing illegal, they went out front to question the three who'd surrendered. The one who spoke a modicum of English explained: "We run into chabola when approach the car with gringos because we think they are INS. No, señor, we know not that you are police. You no have the uniform." He gestured to the uniformed deputies to punctuate his statement. To Cleo's question he answered: "Sí, myself I have it the green card. Is inside. You want I get it?"

The other two averted their eyes and didn't say anything. "Where do you keep your guns?" Bravo asked.

"Why we need it guns for fix cars and trucks?" the spokesman asked.

"Who's damn truck is that?" Cleo asked, gesturing to the green pick-up.

"Contractor of carpentry work," the man replied. "It have problema in engine." He nodded emphatically when told the police wanted all of the information concerning said contractor.

"What country you from?" Olecki asked him.

"El Salvador, señor, as is my partner, Juan. Rogelio, he is from Honduras."

"Any Puerto Ricans working hereabouts?" Cleo asked.

When he shrugged, she remarked that they had nothing to hold them on, so released them to return to their work. The four troopers nodded as they returned to their cruisers. Cleo shook her head as she, Olecki and Bravo returned to the Chevy. She drove, continuing to cruise the grungy area. "Just never get used to scary situations."

"Thankfully," Olecki said, "it wasn't all that scary."

Cleo snorted. "Still got my damn adrenalin pumping. Oh shit! We never checked whether any of those mooks really had green cards."

Olecki shrugged. Cleo glanced back at Bravo in the seat behind Olecki. "How you feel about that, G-man?"

"ATF is not INS or ICE."

"But we, like all police forces, are part of Homeland Security," she said. "We need to protect our country—especially from all those damn illegals."

"That bunch didn't impress me as having terror on their agenda," Olecki said.

"Then why in hell'd they flee when they spotted us?" Cleo demanded.

"Caution is sometimes the better part of valor," Olecki said. "Ever pull over a black guy in work clothes driving a big expensive car?"

"That's a flag you just can't ignore," she replied.

"Ever pull over a white guy in work clothes," Olecki asked. "driving a big expensive car?"

"Whatever the hell for?"

"Ever think those black folks get a complex for getting pulled over for nothing?" Bravo asked.

"Why? We're doing our job," Cleo satd.

"Let's change the subject," Olecki said. "Anybody got any happy things on tap for tonight?"

Bravo shook his head, disinclined to discuss his situation.

Cleo broke into a grin. "Butch been on his run six days now. He just might get home tonight, tomorrow at the latest. Believe that those bedsprings going to squeal."

"If he's not tuckered," Olecki said—obviously suppressing a giggle.

Cleo's face lost its cheerful glow. "That som'bitch wasted himself with some skank before coming home, I'll hammer his big dumb head into the nighttable."

"And she would too," Olecki said to Bravo, "big as Butch is."

SEVENTEEN

"Y'all might've called us for back-up," Baggler said, glaring sulkily at Bravo and the two sheriff's department detectives when they entered the conference room. Epps, Loscalzo and Pedrazo also seated at the long table, nodded support.

"False alarm," Bravo said.

"Then why'd you call the locals for back-up?" Loscalzo asked.

"SOP," Cleo replied. "It's how we're trained."

Bravo gestured everyone to take seats, noting as he sat that none of the US attorney staff were present. Shrugging that off as not particularly important, he asked if anyone had anything to report.

Baggler snickered as he condescended to lead off, with intermittent quips by Loscalzo and Epps, detailing a long-winded report about having swept the area in two cars, which resulted in a waste of time, unless you find value in sight-seeing the slums. He concluded with: "We sure never had no reason to call for backup."

"The laborers we ran across," Loreano Pedrazo added, "were no more than burros—and none with the smarts to engage in a conspiracy."

"How many of them were Cuban?" Cleo asked.

Pedrazo snapped his eyes to her. His lips moved but no words emerged.

"Which leaves us on square one," Baggler said. He leaned back in his chair, appearing self-satisfied.

"Leaving us no options except to get out there and continue beating the rough," Bravo said.

"You don't mind, Special Agent, I'd as soon have lunch first," Cleo said. "This ole gal's body needs nourishment." When the three

FBI agents and Pedrazo concurred, Cleo said, "There's a real nice luncheonette 'bout a block away with tasty vittles at affordable prices."

"Right on," Epps said. He and the others rose from the table. "Joining us, bossman?"

"In a little," Bravo said. "Detective Olecki and I have something to confer on."

While filing out the others obliquely eyed the ATF agent and the Sheriff's Department detective. Cleo not only expressed surprise and curiosity but resentment as well for being left out of whatever they had going.

Bravo waited until they left before addressing Olecki. "Pedrazo's report about the guard, Botero, didn't cut it for me. While I'm not eager to accuse the guy of incompetence, I suspect he's prejudicial toward Puerto Ricans."

"You saying he's racially biased?" Olecki rolled his eyes back to recall the report. "I've partnered with a number of Cubans through the years, and all have been good guys and good cops—never exhibiting any more bad feelings or prejudice toward anyone than any other cop. The guy might have some personal concerns."

"Have to agree that matches my experiences with Cubans. Actually, most express an ethnic brotherhood. But I believe I've detected a bias in Pedrazo. That's why I'd like to go to the county jail and interview Botero, who's presently on duty. I'm having a hard time accepting that Martinez is the only guard had any interaction with Elizondo or any of the bad guys."

"Can't argue with that. Somebody in that jail had to know more than anybody's admitted. And we're desperate for a crack to illuminate a path of investigation."

#.

"Why come to me, man?" the chubby guard asked, cracking his knuckles while sitting tensely erect on the single visitor's chair of the tiny office in the county jailhouse.

"We need help," Bravo said as he sat behind the small desk.

Olecki perched on its corner and leaned toward the guard, close enough to intimidate him. "We'd sure appreciate if you'd help gather information with respect to how the Independistas learned the schedule of Elizondo being taken to court."

"What makes you think I know anything about that shit?"

"You're a guard here," Olecki said as he leaned just a bit closer. "We're hoping you heard something useful, in a place where everything that's said or happens circulates faster than the air in the ventilation system."

Botero appeared to shrink into his shoulders though he sneer. When he didn't respond verbally, Bravo said: "Give us a heads-up on who leaked Elizondo's scheduled court appearance."

"It goes no further than between us," Olecki said.

Botero scowled at one then the other. Bravo noted the flicker of concern in the man's dark eyes. "Hey guy," he said, "I'm Puertoriqueño, like you, and know about those ruthless badasses of Independistas and their reputation. Believe that I understand your concerns and reservations."

Botero scoffed at that, but shrunk into his shoulders while pretending interest in the far wall, bare except for a small calendar with the past days exed-out.

"Was born in New York, same as you," Bravo said, brandishing the man's file. "Experienced the gangs and understand your hesitancy to talk, not wanting those wild-asses coming down on you."

"Besides," Olecki said, "if your bosses learned you'd given out confidential information you'll be canned."

Botero's jaw hinged.

"But you cooperate," Olecki said, "and we'll keep your confidence—save you from losing your job."

"Accessory to murder is a tough charge," Bravo said.

"Carrying a penalty of a lot of hard years," Olecki added.

Botero blinked, swallowed, then averted his eyes.

"Stonewall us," Bravo said, "and the least you're looking at is obstruction, with a few years on the other side of those bars."

"Those cons," Olecki said, "got a whole lot of resentment toward guards. They get you on their side of the bars, they'll take a lot of that anger out on your ass . . . turn it into pulverized liver"

"Man, I ain't no Johnny-Come-Lately," Botero said. "Got fourteen years in here. Why you guys leaning on me like I'm some kind of skel?"

"Because you're uncooperative," Olecki said.

"But you deserve consideration," Bravo said. "Tell you what: you cooperate fully and I'll see you get immunity from prosecution."

"Nor will it affect your employment with the county," Olecki said.

"Better take that offer," Bravo said. "There won't be any better one on the table at any time."

"It's the only thing will keep your ass from ending up on the inside," Olecki added. "But it expires in five minutes."

Botero sneered at them, then looked away.

"Time's running out," Bravo said as he rose from his chair. Olecki stood also.

"Hold up!" Botero rubbed his face. "Immunity from prosecution. And you guarantee I don't get fired. Man, I got a family and need that salary and hospitalization and all."

"Talk to us then," Bravo growled. "We're out of patience."

"Okay! Okay, long as I get immunity and all."

"Start telling us about it all real quick," Olecki said, "before we get pissed and walk out of here."

"Those bad-asses barged into my house—four of them—threatened to kill my family—my wife—my two boys—my little girl."

"They demand that you keep them informed about Elizondo?" Bravo asked.

"One of those barbarians put his filthy hands on my wife." Botero's face contorted with repugnance as he cupped his hand to indicate how that animal touched her. Helplessness shone in wetted eyes. "They didn't give me any choice but to protect my family."

"So you told them that Elizondo spent hours talking to Martinez," Bravo said.

"They kept probing—threatening my family. *Maricones* promised not to harm Martinez, said they don't hurt *compatriotos*, their own kind. They laughed and—"

"What else you talk about with those *queer-assed cocksuckers?*" Bravo asked.

"They demanded I inform them of Elizondo's schedule to be taken to court. What could I do? I couldn't let my babies get hurt for some demented activist. Besides, I had no idea they'd do what they did."

"What'd you think they'd do?" Olecki asked.

"Bust him out." Botero waved his hands about.

"So you informed them when Elizondo was to be transported to the courthouse," Bravo said.

"No way I expected them to kill US marshals or nothing rash like that. Sure didn't think they'd pop their own man."

"Along with a deputy assistant US attorney," Bravo said, clenching his jaws.

"Plus two unarmed courthouse guards," Olecki added.

"I'm sorry! I didn't know!"

"Did you report that Elizondo planned to go to Washington?" Bravo asked.

"Go to Washington! What the hell you talking about? He was being taken to the federal courthouse on Broward Boulevard—right?"

"What did you tell the terrorists about Martinez?" Olecki asked.

Botero threw his hands out and fluttered them in dismay. "Only that him and Elizondo talked secretly all the time. Hey, those *malos* were in my home, night after night—had access to my family—could hurt them at any time—if not today then next week or next month. Still can."

"Identify them," Bravo said.

Botero made fists and cracked his knuckles. "*Malos*, man—bad-asses. Gangbangers like you see in any barrio."

"Maybe you remember the names of one or two," Bravo said, "from when you grew up in New York."

"No, man, not those guys. I never saw any of them before—not in the Bronx—not in Spanish Harlem. Yeah, all four were Puertoriqueños, but none of them was familiar—nobody I ever ran across." Botero shook his head. "And they never called each other by name, man, only *compatrioto*. I swear, that's—"

"Carefully trained," Bravo said, disappointment evident in his voice. "Describe them."

Botero rubbed his face. "The mulatto who did most of the talking had a bristly beard and a harsh voice. Scary, man, with those cold eyes. The other gorillas just stood around menacing us."

"That's not a description," Olecki said.

"Whatta' you want from me, man? I didn't dare take a hard look at any of them. Didn't want my throat cut, or my family harmed."

"They mention where they were from?" Bravo asked.

"No, man. But something about them said they're not from South Florida. They had that accent and the hip of the northern barrios. But I don't think it was New York."

"You can do better than that," Olecki said.

Botero grimaced, cracked his knuckles again. "They was husky and none of them mean-faced ghetto rats had any compassion, or any respect for women and girls. They had automatic pistols—you know, those gangbanger machineguns."

"Describe what they wore," Olecki said.

"Who paid attention, man? Oh yeah, one wore a bucket hat with a name of golf. Can't remember it right off. Don't play golf. Another one had a baseball cap from a Chicago team—Cubs, I think. Yeah, Cubs . . . a bunch that gets chewed up when they play the Mets. Why brag about being a fan for a team never gets into the play-offs?"

"How else were they dressed?" Olecki asked.

Botero blinked continually as he stared into space and tried to pierce the foggy wall of memory. "One wore a sweatshirt with the sleeves cut off—gray, I think. Another guy wore a blue tee shirt with a ferris wheel on it and something about a fair—in Chicago if I remember."

"Have you seen them since Elizondo was murdered?" Bravo asked.

"Thank God no!"

"You understand," Olecki said, "that you're going to be taken off direct contact with inmates."

Botero looked stressed. "You promised!—said I won't lose my job."

"You'll still be employed," Olecki said, "but not in direct contact with inmates."

# # #

Bravo and Olecki entered the conference room to be confronted by Epps. "Thought y'all were going to join us."

"Where the hell you'all been?" Baggler asked—all but demanded.

"Went to the jail," Bravo said, "to interview the guard, Botero."

The FBI agents gawked. DEA agent Pedrazo half rose out of his chair, his face a mask of shock and anger. But before he issued an objection, Bravo said: "You had your bite of the apple and came up empty."

"That's back-stabbing," Pedrazo said. "Does not show respect."

"Then do your job efficiently," Bravo said. "Don't report back here ridiculing people, then claiming a lack of intel when it's there for the taking. That goes for the rest of you."

"What in hell y'all saying?" Baggler demanded.

"That you went through the motions," Bravo said, "but failed to elicit info."

"We know to correctly interview them," Loscalzo said, posturing defiance.

"Believe that FBI agents are capable as any cinder-kicker," Epps said. "Hear—"

"Lose the inter-bureau rivalry," Bravo said. "We're all working for America and need to cooperate to save the streets from destruction and panic."

"We're working as diligently on that terrorist threat as you guys," Loscalzo said.

"Then concentrate," Bravo said, "on gleaning intel from interrogation that can lead us to that red cell, so we can take them out before they dispense terror."

"That—that *chistoso*," Pedrazo stammered. "That *wise guy* clammed up on me. Yes, of course he talked to you, one of his *compatricios*."

"His being properly interrogated is what impelled him to talk," Olecki said.

"That *zoquete* stonewalled me," Pedrazo said, his face twisted in anger. "He—"

"You should have respected him as a potential source of information," Bravo said, "not as a *blockhead* because he's Puerto Rican."

"I have prejudice toward no one," Pedrazo protested.

"Meanwhile," Baggler asked, "what exactly y'all get out of that guard?"

"As a result of intense questioning," Bravo said, "the man confessed that *Independistas* terrorized him in his home and coerced him into telling them the date Elizondo was taken to court."

"He identified those terrorists?" Baggler asked.

"He could only give sparse descriptions of them," Olecki said.

"I am incensed," Pedrazo said, "for being treated in this manner."

"Then bury your arrogance," Bravo said, "and do your job efficiently."

"You been in law enforcement long enough," Cleo said, "to know that everybody knows something."

"I try my best to do my job," Pedrazo said.

"Okay, it's behind us," Bravo said. "Everybody hit the streets to continue beating the rough."

"So what y'all reporting is y'all ended up with useless information," Baggler said. "But you ragged Loreano Pedrazo anyway."

"Everybody hit the street. Now!" Bravo said.

While gathering up his gear Baggler said: "Y'all watch your tails this time. We'd sure hate to hear harm came to our co-investigators because they didn't cover their asses by calling in backup . . . as secure FBI backup."

"We're in this as much as you are," Loscalzo said, "and as dedicated as you guys to take those skels off the street. We'd appreciate if something goes down, you don't leave us out of it next time."

"Promise," Bravo said. "Anything comes up and you guys will get called. It works both ways. You run into anything you call us."

"Let's hope we don't," Epps said. "I'm not anxious to get my ass shot up."

"You didn't expect to dodge some bullets," Baggler said, "you sure shouldn't have taken up cop work."

"I'm an investigator, not a combat specialist," Epps said. "I'd as soon arrive on the scene after the action concludes, to analyze what occurred and advise the best course of investigation. Hear what I'm saying."

EIGHTEEN

Bravo trudged along with Olecki and Cleo to the garage, aware that Cleo glared at him. He wasn't surprised when she irately asked: "Why'd y'all exclude me from interviewing that jail guard? Y'all don't consider me part of the team?"

"I apologize for not including you," Bravo said. "But that failing was not meant to criticize or demean you. It's just that I thought at the time that the least people involved, the better."

"That flimsy-ass excuse doesn't do it, special agent. I damn well deserve more respect from team-members—especially from my partner."

Olecki hung his head, looked contrite while steering the Chevy out of the garage to nose into heavy traffic just as the tropic shower inundated them. The windshield wipers had to be turned to their highest speed to swipe away the blinding downpour. But by the time they reached Dixie Highway the rain abated. And in a short time it passed off, returning the sky to clear and sunny with the temperature in the upper seventies.

With the faint musk of earth and vegetation pervading the air, Olecki cruised slowly through narrow streets between grimy warehouses and factories. Most kept their doors open to capture airflow since those buildings lacked air-conditioning. When the rain stopped the temperature steadily increased into the eighties.

They passed a lot of sweaty and dirt-streaked Hispanic workers, as well as blacks, which they assumed most to be Haitians. But without *probable cause* they had no reason to stop and interrogate any and couldn't search any buildings or vehicles. For the same reason they knew they had no chance of getting search warrants.

Pow! The windshield shattered. A bullet loudly embedded in the back of the rear seat—inches from Bravo. Olecki swerved the car as he hit the brake. It rocked to a halt. The three startled occupants scurried out to squat behind it. "Ten-seventy-eight," Olecki barked excitedly into his radio. "Shots fired! Officers need assistance! Shots fired!"

Two more gunshots rang out, with the bullets clunking into the Chevy. Bravo called Baggler on his cellphone for back-up, and told that man to relay that info to the others. Then all three huddled in the protection of their vehicle, their weapons at the ready, apprehensive as they searched for a target. But they saw only grimy buildings and chainlink fences closing off yards stacked with all manner of product. Scrubby bushes and trees backdropped some buildings.

The shot could have come from anywhere with cars and trucks parked helter skelter, filling up the area. The leaves of overgrown ficus and live oak trees festooned with beard-like moss concealed everything behind it. Sunlight sparkling off shiny surfaces further inhibited visibility.

"Sure sounded like a rifle," Olecki said. "High-powered sucker." The other two nodded and all three forced themselves to breathe as they peered into their surroundings, silent now. They noted that some workers in nearby buildings closed doors . . . probably after hearing gunshots. Since they were unable to determine the origin of the shots, the three law enforcement officers had no target at which to return fire . . . fusillades they itched to unleash.

A sheriff's cruiser arrived with sirens screaming, immediately followed by another. They parked at opposite ends of the narrow street. A third cruiser arrived to back up the others. While those deputies slipped out of and behind their vehicles, their weapons at the ready, the FBI guys drove up in two cars and skidded to a stop, followed by three more cruisers. Olecki directed the deputies in those vehicles to fan out and sweep the area.

Those on foot hugged the cover of buildings and vehicles while searching their surroundings. Long minutes of apprehension resulted only in disillusionment for a dozen and a half sweaty law enforcement people. Encountering no one with a rifle and no additional shots, they surmised that the shooter fled or went into hiding.

They conferred at the end of the street where the first cruiser had parked, out of the direct line of fire in case the sniping resumed. Olecki introduced two of the deputies to Bravo as Mac and Mac. Both huskies had mature faces; McGee the crew cut blond and Maguire, with retreating hairline and his brown hair peppered with specks of gray.

"Those suckers got them big balls to bring it to us," Baggler commented as he and Loscalzo joined them.

"Aggressive badasses," Bravo agreed, "assuming they're our perps."

"Who the hell else?" Loscalzo asked.

"Any angry sonofabitch," Olecki said, "with a long-time grudge."

"There are a whole lot of angry people in the world," Bravo said.

"What the hell's their problem?" Baggler asked as he continued to scan the area.

"Face some damned truths, man," Epps said as he ambled over to them. "Whitey been making enemies for years. Insensitivity and arrogance goes a long way in turning a relatively subdued person into a nut-case with a compulsion for retaliation."

"What in hell that means?" Baggler asked.

"All that shit y'all stacked on folks over the years been boiling in their guts. When it surfaces, watch out. Hear what I'm saying?"

"Instead of rationalizing," Bravo said, "let's get back to searching for those Independistas with the stolen weapons and explosives."

"Yeah," Olecki agreed. "We need to stop them before they hurt a lot of people."

"Word gets out," Maguire said, "and Fort Lauderdale will be in a panic."

"Hell, all of Broward County," McGee said. "Maybe all of South Florida."

"Half the United States," Loscalzo said.

Olecki grumbled to himself while glaring at his shattered windshield. He'd called on his radio for a replacement vehicle. When they brought a replacement, a three-year-old Ford Taurus, Olecki grouched that it was a goddam wreck before climbing in and driving it.

"Probably confiscated from drug peddlers," Cleo said. "Hopped-up suckers ran the thing into the ground."

Olecki scowled at his lack of choices, so continued sweeping the area. All three remained wary of the sniper having another try at them. Sunlight glinting off every shiny surface impeded clear sight, besides radiating heat. The air-conditioner clanked and groaned while expelling luke-warm air. Discomforted, the three occupants finally conceded to opening windows, in spite of dust from the roads and having to inhale a variety of emanations from the various shops, including over-worked cables and machinery to over-cooked food, as well as decaying vegetation and garbage discarded in weedy patches of open land.

Bravo breathed relief when the rest of the afternoon passed without incident, and five o'clock required they return to their office. After arriving in the garage and exiting the vehicle Olecki cursed while slamming the doors repeatedly to get the locks to work. Glaring at the hard-used vehicle he told Bravo and Cleo to go ahead; he'd catch up after calling to demand a better replacement car.

"Replacement car, my ass," Cleo whispered to Bravo as they headed into the hallway of the sixth floor toward the elevator. "Why'd he need privacy to do that? Ask me, ole' Peter's got him a squeeze on the side."

"You're jumping to conclusions."

"You can have you a squeeze, you want, and jump her conclusions," Cleo said. She sidled up alongside him and slid her arm in his.

He jerked his arm free as he turned shock-widened eyes to her. Sure she dressed so he couldn't help but be aware of her ample delights. And she flirted openly, even talked about having extra-marital activity. But her brazen play took him by surprise.

"I'm hot to trot with you, Ray baby." She rubbed against him and tried to hold his arm again.

Bravo jerked free. "Let's not lose control."

"What the hell's your problem?"

"No problem as long as we keep this relationship professional, and not screw up a good team."

"Screw is a real good choice of words, Ray baby. I promise you won't push this ole' gal out of bed."

"Can that stuff, Cleo. We have to work together without hanky-panky interfering with clear thinking."

"You saying you don't find me attractive?"

Bravo read the sensitivity displayed by her frown and in her flickering eyes and realized that the wrong words could prick her blustering armor and become detrimental to a working relationship. "Doubt there's a red-blooded man in America wouldn't drool over you. But sex and police partnering don't mix."

"Sure won't be the first time in this department, or any other for that matter."

"Then let's put it this way: nothing is going to happen between us, in spite of you being knock-out attractive."

Her eyes sparkled as they searched his face. "How 'bout if we weren't on a case together?"

"But we are and I'm adamant about keeping our relationship professional."

"At least you find me attractive. Okay, Ray baby, I'll put my yearning for you on hold until we put this case to bed. Then I'll put your sweet ass in that sack to teach you what a warm and loving woman is all about."

"What happened to Butch and marriage?"

"What the hell's that got to do with anything?"

The elevator door opened and he waved her on. Thankfully the presence of two people riding it put a hold on the subject for the one floor they had to go. When the door slid open they stepped into the small vestibule that led to the metal detector. Bravo disregarded courtesy and hurried ahead to display his creds and expose his weapon while passing into the entry alcove, without concern for how closely she followed.

Hurrying down the hallway he entered the conference room to be hailed by Loscalzo. "Hey, leader-man, you think it's time to break for the day and imbibe a little of that thank-God juice to dilute all that adrenaline pumping through our veins."

"Y'all better believe," Epps said, "I had enough excitement for one—"

"Hell, you didn't even get shot at," Baggler ribbed the lanky African-American. "We got there when the thing was over and damn near forgotten."

"That's the right time to arrive at a shooting," Epps said. "You know it's not your day if you arrive in time to get shot. Hear what I'm saying?"

"Breaking for the day is a good idea," Bravo said. "We all need to let off steam. See you guys in the morning when we'll plan our strategy for the day."

"You saying you not taking a drink with us?" Epps asked.

Bravo shook his head. "Need to make some phone calls. Another time." He returned to the garage and drove the borrowed bucar to his motel. Trudging into his room he hung up his suitcoat and removed his necktie. Then he sat on the bed and stared at the phone for long minutes before picking it up and dialing. He breathed deeply, lacking confidence, while waiting. The click elated him. "Hi. It's me."

"Are we going to put each other through another anger session?" Yzabel asked.

"Hopefully not. Let's accept that we both acted outrageously. I'm sorry I couldn't get home for you last night, appreciating how much it meant to you. Sorry, but that's the nature of my job."

"Why don't we hold this conversation in abeyance," Yzabel said, "until we're together. Then we'll decide how we're going to relate to each other in the future. But let's do it face to face, not over the phone."

"No argument."

"Good. Then I'll see you whenever you get back." Click.

Sonofabitch! He squeezed the phone in anger. But, as he thought about it he couldn't find fault with her rationale. Besides, he lacked optimism of the damage being repairable. He hoped to hell a break-up didn't adversely affect their relationships with their sons. The boys had matured and had to be aware that he and their mother had progressed to the verge of marital dissolution; far more so than at any of the previous times.

His cellphone jingled and he grabbed for it, hoping that Yzabel called back to mitigate the acrimony. Then he cringed upon recognizing Maylene's voice. Again he reproached himself for not checking caller ID first.

"Dinner tonight?"

He clamped his eyes closed.

"You need to eat."

Sighing, he replayed in his mind his conversation with Yzabel, a daunting reminder that he probably no longer had a working marriage. So, exhaling concession, he said: "Not at that noisy bistro again."

"I know a really nice steakhouse on the water. I'll pick you up within the hour."

# # #

Bravo grinned approval when Maylene drove up in her late model Beemer convertible, a dash of class in silver gray metallic crowned by ebon pride. He climbed into the passenger seat of lush gray leather to be greeted by a cheek proffered to him to kiss. Shrugging concession he pecked her silken skin, its glow exuding promise.

His eyes swept her adoringly while she drove. From the day he met her in Atlanta he'd become aware of her impressive attire. Demure while stylish during business hours, it changed to svelte after work. Everything about Maylene beguiled him then as well as now. Her creamy brown neck he remembered as succulent.

This lady exhibited class, in her beige skirt that had been tailored to fit her perfectly and to complement her silky white blouse cut to teasingly display cleavage and to showcase a delicate gold necklace. Expensive pendant earrings matched the two bracelets on her left wrist. A wide ring on the middle finger of her right hand completed the outfit, its dazzling marine blue enamel decorated with golden royal insignias.

"The sparkle in your eyes," Maylene said, "suggests you like what you see."

Bravo chortled, remembering that Maylene had always been audacious as well as vain. "Can't find anything about you I don't like."

"That's more promising than our last meeting."

"Things change, even attitudes."

"Right on! Can I assume I'm in for a really satisfying evening?"

"Let's not buy a saddle before we pick out a horse."

He viewed their surroundings as Maylene barreled along Southeast Seventeenth Street to *Markland's*, a trendy steakhouse on the west bank of the Intracoastal. After leaving the car with the valet they were ushered to a table where they lounged in the lazy breeze off the broad waterway. They enjoyed a panoramic view of boats of different sizes and levels of luxury. The moonlight reflecting off the water cast a romantic aura.

Remembering that she liked full-bodied red wine, he selected a pricey claret. While sipping that nectar, which proved velvet to the palate and exquisitely mordant, he recalled that Maylene preferred never to rush into anything. So they delayed ordering dinner. Actually he suspected she liked to vamp and tease. Damn real, she had every attribute to do just that.

"How's your investigation going?" she asked.

"Not as well as I'd like, but I'll get it going."

"Yes, Ray Bravo will emerge successful and save Fort Lauderdale additional pain and suffering."

"Can't deny that I'm driven. But so are you."

"True, I'm compelled by something inside me that won't let me not be successful, no matter how much I have to apply myself to achieve it."

"Similar to the aggressiveness you exhibit with men. How many have you gone through in the past two years?"

"That's mean, Ray. I'm not promiscuous, as I suspect you are."

"Wrong guy. Yeah, Atlanta happened, but that's the exception. Actually, I've been applying myself to making my marriage work."

"How's that going?"

"Not as well as I'd wanted."

"That makes it even nicer to have you here." She placed a hand over his.

"Frankly, it puzzles me that you respond so readily to this revival, considering how our Atlanta affair ended—if, indeed, it ever started."

"It started—for me at least."

"You're saying you fell deeply in love from that one sensual eruption?"

"Surprises me too, lover, especially since you disappeared immediately afterward. For a long time I hated you intensely. But don't fret it, baby. The moment you walked into the conference room I knew I wanted you back in my life. All is forgiven."

"Why, considering the circumstances?"

"You rocked my body and my soul more than any other man. Believe it or not, that one dynamite encounter made me want a relationship as never before."

"How could that be? You'd had other lovers—were once married. You certainly weren't a virgin—or naïve."

"Yes, I'd enjoyed a number of alliances, as well as a husband, but none of them rocked my soul the way you did. Probably why you hurt me by disappearing. I'm eager to renew and extend what almost started that night."

"I'm finding that difficult to believe."

"I can expound on the law, baby, but I can't explain the ramifications of love. Besides, let's face it, your marriage isn't about to enjoy longevity. And considering the ages of your boys, they're no longer the glue that's going to hold it together."

He grimaced his inability to refute that condemnation.

The smiling waiter appeared at their table. "Are we ready to order?"

# # #

After finishing their salads and steaks, they both eschewed dessert but lingered over espresso with sambuca. "That's great music, Ray. Feel like dancing?"

He didn't need coaxing to snuggle her into his arms and shuffle to the super-cool jazz from a by-gone era. A trio of black musicians who'd survived a number of generational changes in musical style produced the warm feeling that inspired a number of couples to sway together on the dance floor—most also veterans of those past eras. One of the gray-haired men in the band seductively crooned: *You're my everything*.

Ray and Mayline snuggled closer. "You ready?" she asked.

NINETEEN

Yzabel climbed out of the taxi at the entrance to the Harvard Hall Hotel on E Street and New Jersey Avenue, another of Washington's busily trafficked areas. Well-dressed people with the trappings of affluence swirled about the posh lobby, with everyone animated and chatting, apparently eager for a night on the town.

Misgivings denied her adopting their festive mood. Besides admonishing herself for what she intended to do she suffered apprehension about encountering anyone she knew. *Dios en cielo*! *God in heaven*! How would she explain being seen there in the company of Nando? But despite uncertainty she throbbed with anticipation of the encounter. She'd yearned for this rendezvous over the years, aware that it very probably would result in engaging in infidelity. And she harbored no delusions that it was wrong.

She'd never cheated on her husband nor shared any kind of intimacy with any other man since meeting Ray, much less since marrying him. True, their marriage had degenerated to the brink of divorce. Still she suffered guilt for groping at that excuse for considering intimacy with another man.

But she knew Nando as impulsive and demanding. He'd scoff at deferral of amorous satisfaction, be unreceptive to any excuse that denied him immediate gratification. Besides, she'd come this far, driven by a yearning to once again have Nando in her loins. Dios! Those had been scintillating times—the most exhilarating in her life—until he callously discarded her.

Through the years she'd persisted in believing he'd miss her and seek to remedy that insensitive severance. But it never happened. Nando never indicated a desire to once again become immersed in their special ecstasy—until last night. She snorted, scornful of her weakness—of her receptivity when he'd reached out in his arrogant way to invite her to tryst. She doubted it might occur to him that she'd resist succumbing to his lust.

Gritting her teeth, she determined to demand retribution by having the egotist beg her for forgiveness. Nodding to that determination, she strode into the bar crowded with celebrants. Failing to spot him she frowned disappointment.

Damn him!—for not extending the courtesy of being there to greet her when she arrived. She turned to stomp out, but that yearning welling up within her tempered that impetuosity. Bien. She would wait, but merely to talk. Only if he convinced her that he truly loved her would she consider sexual participation.

She took the only unoccupied stool at the bar, certain he'd soon appear. Wasn't it he who initiated the meeting? Okay, a man of his importance had justification for being delayed. She nodded to the bartender. "Yes, a dry martini with an olive."

She savored it as she did her memories, as if time evaporated the passing years, and they were once again together during that glorious spring in New York. It had become their playground, with him assigned to the consulate there—and his wife in Barcelona. Those blissful days were followed by a series of ecstatic rendezvous in various capitals of Europe—until that day her bubble of joy burst—when learning he'd discarded her.

A nice guy consoled her, made her feel wanted and beautiful. Yes, she married Ramón, then moved to Washington. And it took all of her powers of persuasion to convince Fabienne Argonne that it benefited them to have a branch there, to service the transient politicians, bureaucrats and businessmen eager to glorify their temporary residences . . . which, benevolently, changed hands every few years. The new owners invariably redecorated to satisfy personal tastes, as well to impress colleagues, visitors and constituents. Business flourished.

She jerked to alertness when the bartender inquired whether she wanted a refill, and realized she'd drained her glass. She nodded, then wondered why. She rarely had more than one. Dios! She never drank them quickly. Her eyes popped with a second surprise when she glanced at her watch and realized she'd been there more than half an hour. Where was Nando?

She searched the crowd, to no avail. A man at each end of the bar grinned at her. One raised his glass to her. She scowled at them, irritated by their lascivious attention. Did they think of her as some slut who frequented bars in search of companionship?

Grimacing, she conceded that sitting there alone gave them reason for their presumption. How could she convey to them that she waited for someone? When the bartender set her drink before her she checked her watch again and muttered aloud: "He's late."

But the bartender either didn't hear or didn't care, further irritating her. Perhaps he also considered her a barfly. Or her announcement had drowned in that cacophony of celebrants. If only Nando would arrive so all could see that she had a man.

She closed her eyes to suppress the anguish as it dawned on her that Nando might stand her up, disappoint her again—anger her, like that time when she refused to break off their affair—had, in fact, threatened to fly to Barcelona.

He'd changed his tone from overbearing to solicitous while begging her not to ruin his life and career. And when she remained adamant in her intention to publicize their relationship, he confessed that his family had gone through most of their money, though they retained social standing. Marrying Elena Teresa Montoya Vargas assured him of the backing of the Montoya millions. But his wife was possessive and unforgiving. He didn't dare provoke her to divorcing him . . . risk losing that wealth and the influence it provided . . . needing it to achieve his ambitions.

She'd slammed the phone into its cradle, swallowing the bitter realization that her dream had been shattered because he valued more the trappings of wealth and social status than their love. It took months to recover from that dejection. She suffered melancholy and spent long months before she accepted that she'd been discarded like a plastic bag stuffed with garbage and left at the curb to be tossed into a stinking truck.

Two depressing years had passed when she read the announcement that the Embassy of Spain in Washington intended to fete Fernando

Guijón Montoros. Determined to attend she'd enticed diplomat Arnold Goshen into escorting her to it.

But Nando treated her like a stranger. However, a nice guy became attentive. And she used him to make Nando jealous. But that conceited *hidalgo*, playboy of the nobility, remained oblivious to her. However, that nice guy, Ray Bravo, ardently pursued her and relieved her anguish. Within a year of dating, she married him. She needed him then—needed someone to love and someone to make her feel wanted.

Despite many rough spots in their marriage there had been many happy times, and two blessings. She loved Esteban and Romero more than anything in the world. She knew she should love Ray. She really tried to through the years, in spite of differences caused by his bureaucratic employment and lack of social status, plus the long separation because of case assignments.

Glancing at her glass, it shocked her to see it half empty. So she checked the time again. Ten after eleven. No! How could he have demeaned her again?

Pushing her drink away, she paid the bartender and left. While waiting for the doorman to hail her a taxi, she promised herself to never again be a fool. Why would she? She had a husband, a good man with whom she had a beautiful family. Yes, she needed to preserve it.

TWENTY

Bravo scrutinized Maylene as she drove back up Southeast Seventeenth Street in light traffic. He pondered how revival of their relationship will affect his marriage? Hell, the one-nighter didn't because he had the good sense not to extend it. This time, however, he feared it might blossom into a full-blown affair. So what? He doubted enough of his marriage remained to be saved. Wasn't Yzabel trysting with that Iberian? No, he didn't want to believe that—but couldn't suppress that conclusion.

Upon arrival at his motel she scowled. "This the best you could do?"

When he shrugged she parked within the low-wall enclosure of the motel. He climbed out to open her door and hand her out. She leaned into him, resting herself in his arms and captured his lips with hers . . . sucking hungrily and moaning ecstatically as his hands caressed her. "Let's get inside," she moaned.

Both chuckled as Ray led the way through the inner hallway to his door. She paused while entering to take in the mundane furnishings of a double bed with a lamp on a nighttable at each side of the headboard, and the matching bureau topped by a tall mirror alongside a chunky television set. The place lacked any semblance of luxury; in fact had the look and smell of overuse.

He swung the door closed behind them and sidled close to her. She responded as he'd expected, with no reservations about letting him know she relished the way he caressed her body. He remembered her laid-back approach to sexual encounter, and her ability to extend it to excruciating delight. Acceding to her unhurried approach, he took his time unbuttoning and removing her blouse, then her lacey brassiere.

God! He gawked as the sepia goddess stood there nude. Memory of the passion they shared a couple of years ago in Atlanta enveloped him. He kissed her neck and across her shoulders, then her breasts. She undressed him, garment by garment. When both were naked she shuffled him to the bed and prompted him to sit. Then she pressed her breasts in his face, and beamed when he sucked them with uninhibited passion.

She pushed him down on his back and mounted him, high on his stomach so he could continue suckling her. She slithered up so his lips whispered across her stomach, and finally into her pubic area. Undulating against his face she screeled her delight.

Having been brought to culmination, she rolled off him, then assisted him in mounting and penetrating her. He saw the satisfaction in her face, accepted that she had enjoyed retribution by dominating him and inducing him to bring her to the pinnacle of sexual satisfaction from a position of subservience. Okay, by rendering him submissive she'd been gratified.

Fine, he condoned her need for retaliation, accepting that he owed her that after abandoning her in Atlanta. Frankly, he'd enjoyed it as much as she. Her groans of delight increased his arousal while telegraphing her surrendering herself now to mutual delight.

# # #

"Hope you don't have a problem with my going back to my digs, lover."

Ray looked dejected as he watched Maylene sit up and thrust her legs out of the bed. "Anticipated waking up in the morning with you at my side."

"That's really sweet, Ray. It makes me want to climb back in with you. But this isn't inspiring ambiance." Her lip curled as she glanced around at the bleak room. "Let's do it tomorrow night at my place . . . where we'll be comfortable and make it last all night."

He blushed as he stammered to explain his reason for having chosen this place. But she placed a finger over his lips. "I understand budgets, darling. However, this kind of place is way behind me. Am not willing to slip back."

He nodded. "We'll sleep at your digs hereafter."

Then he blinked repeatedly when she finished dressing, finding it hard to believe that nothing about her testified to her having disrobed and engaged in sex.

"Soon it'll be our day, unless you have reservations about coalescing with a black woman."

"What kind of thing is that to say?"

"An honest one."

"Accepted, but unnecessary. You realize, of course, you'll have to be patient until we clear this case so I can go back to Washington to settle things with Yzabel."

"I'm patient, baby. You know I'm patient."

"Meantime we can be together."

"But at my place, baby. Not in this grungy room."

She pulled the door closed behind her and beamed confidently as she traversed the empty hallway, then the stuffy vestibule with its unattended desk, and exited the motel, causing a bell to jingle when she opened the door. Snickering at that cheap substitute for security, she went to and climbed into her car, her mind tumbling with all that had been discussed, all that had been finally brought into the open. She and Ray were a thing.

Remembering Ray's dazed expression when she announced she loved him made her chortle. Men never ceased to amuse her and make her wonder how they grew older without maturing. Those juveniles back in Manasses, Virginia had groped her, but none had the persistence to score. It wasn't until she attended college that she encountered a man with the courage and confidence to light her up to where she succumbed.

And the next two men she shared intimacy with were also white. A few black fellow-students half-assedly courted her but failed to seduce her. They were prodigies of new wealth and societal standing, had been steeped in proper conduct.

The white guys pursued and flattered her, romanced her and treated her as special while persistent in culminating sensual delight, as if it was their right of passage. To this day she wondered if white guys were naturally cavalierly, or were they arrogant and dominant, guided by a sense of superiority . . . especially when dealing with women of color.

Even after graduation and moving to the nation's capital to work at Treasury she dated white men more often than blacks. But concerns of marriage and children inhibited her marrying white. Lord, she knew her parents would never approve. Her good luck, a black executive in the department had eyes for her, and the courage to pursue her.

Less than a year later they married. But she and Barnett Brown weren't ready to interrupt their careers to have children. Just as well, she realized in retrospect, because Barnett lacked commitment to marital devotion. His brazen affair with that blousy blonde contributed to the dissolution of a seven-year marriage. Funny how she felt more betrayed because he cheated with a white woman.

Since he enjoyed superior rank in that *old boy* environment, he piled insult on injury upon finality of their divorce by having her exiled by transfer to Atlanta. But it was a city she quickly learned to like, and two years later she enrolled at Emory University to study law. She managed to graduate in three years despite having to integrate employment and education.

Yes! she passed the bar on her first attempt, a feat only exceptional students accomplished. As a result the US Attorney's office in Atlanta recruited her as an intern. Man, they clamored to hire both women and blacks, consequently welcomed her, a double response to progressiveness, and placed her under an expert prosecutor.

Assistant US Attorney Owen Howley, twelve years her senior, leched after her from day one. But she resisted . . . having too much self-respect to let that married white guy amuse himself with her. He pursued her persistently but made it plain that he only wanted her for a play-thing.

Encountering Ray Bravo, dispatched to Atlanta to work a case, saved her from caving to Owen. Having overheard Ray on the phone with his wife, she knew his marriage was rocky at best. Attracted to him and optimistic that he'd be available, motivated her to lay her mojo on him. They celebrated the night they cleared the case, with champagne that culminated in volcanic intimacy.

But the next morning Ray's office whisked him off to Kansas City to cover an arson case. She tried countless times to contact him and keep their flame burning but he didn't respond. In time every vestige of relationship evaporated, conveying the realization that Ray had no intention of extending the affair.

Vulnerable and in a state of despondency, she succumbed to Owen Howley. Yeah, baby, he let her know from the git-go that he didn't intend to let their affair affect his marriage. It made her wonder why she succumbed to become his mistress. And why did she always end up with white men? But once involved, she disregarded Owen's marital status and aspired for a definitive role in his life, in spite of the odds against it in the heart of the Deep South.

Why, she wondered, did she latch onto guys then resist their attempts to break free? What made her cloying and possessive? Did she suffer insecurity? Did she need a man in her life as living proof of her attractiveness and desirability?

Owen Howley decided to shake free of her after two years. When she resisted, he had her transferred to the US Attorney's office in Miami. Believe that pissed her off. She liked Atlanta—never warmed to Miami. But he had the juice to pull the strings that got her extricated from his life. And she lacked recourse in a government agency dominated by male power brokers.

Hardened, embittered, and calloused by the incidents in her life, she showed her tough side to guys and kept them at arms length, unless she wanted to dally with them. Actually, she wasn't anxious to remarry since she didn't want children to distract from her career. So why burden herself with a husband?

The prosecutor in the Fort Lauderdale office needed an assistant, so she inveigled the US Attorney in Miami to reassign her. She considered that appointment a benediction since she felt her ambitions stifled in the city of Latinos. In Fort Lauderdale she set her sights on achieving the first chair, though she hadn't anticipated Arthur Meyers being killed. However, since it happened and she took over first chair, she aspired to succeed Archison, who was rumored to be in line for promotion.

She already had a reputation for racking up convictions. Yes, and she had a ton of confidence. Maylene Brown walked with pride—a tall and svelte brown-skinned woman with arresting eyes who flaunted her legacy from the dark continent.

TWENTY-ONE

Bravo glanced up when the three FBI agents and Pedrazo, the T-man, bustled in. He'd been pouring coffee for Olecki and Cleo as well as for himself and became attentive to Loscalzo excitedly announcing that he'd gotten intel from FBI sources, relative to Puerto Rican activists in Chicago.

He read from his notes that the FBI had compiled a dossier on the man called Abdulo because the guy assumed a Muslim name. Obviously it triggered them to suspect him of collusion with Islamic terrorists. He had been born Clemente Galbos in Ponce in Puerto Rico and brought to Chicago when seven or eight by his parents. Like most who grew up in those Hispanic barrios he ran with the gangs from an early age.

He first came to the attention of law enforcement when a member of one of the most troublesome gangs in Chicago called Brigada Jalda Arriba. The FBI didn't understand the significance of that name which translated as Up The Hill Brigade, but knew them as a wild bunch clamoring for independence for the island of Puerto Rico.

Three years ago they robbed a bank, in which two of them ended up killed. Another couple bit the dust during shoot-outs at subsequent round-ups. But Galbos fled, turning up in the Middle East, where it's believed he spent more than a year training in guerrilla and terrorist camps in Pakistan and Afghanistan. Yes, they suspect he trained with an al-Qaida-affiliated group, but can't prove it. However a warrant has been out for his arrest since they learned through informants of his return to the U. S. and to Chicago.

Intelligence sources reported that he joined a master organization of Puerto Rican gangs known as Los Comanderos, overlorded by a thug who calls himself Julio Cesar, a handle he probably adopted to increase esteem. Galbos took on the name of Abdulo and formed his own brigade, which he called Vasillo Rojo.

The supposition is that in the Middle East he'd adopted Muslim Extremism but they were unable to corroborate whether or not he'd converted to the Islamic faith. According to informants, he flagrantly contested Julio Cesar for overlordship of Los Comanderos, decrying that commander as lacking the daring to publicize and promote the cause of Puerto Rican independence.

Julio Cesar responded by demeaning Galbos as having never done anything to merit leadership. He challenged Abdulo to prove himself by leading a raid in the nation's capital and blowing up one of the government office buildings. When Galbos questioned where he'd get the explosives to accomplish that, Julio Cesar criticized him for his lack of resourcefulness, thereby decrying his leadership potential.

Soon after, Abdulo and his bunch robbed a bank in Chicago, ostensibly to finance the intended operation. All law-enforcement agencies have since had a dragnet out for those lobos, which to date the bad guys have evaded. It didn't surprise the FBI to learn that Abdulo ended up in Florida, though they continued searching for him in the areas around Chicago as well as the nation's capital.

Yes, Loscalzo had been assured they'd keep the US Attorney's office in Fort Lauderdale posted of any new intelligence. In return they'd appreciate if the Fort Lauderdale taskforce kept them up to snuff on whatever intel they happened upon.

"Okay," Loscalzo said, beaming with the pride of accomplishment, "we now know who we're hunting."

"One genuine badass," Epps chimed in. "Hear what—"

"Sniffing out bad guys." Baggler said, posturing superiorly, "takes FBI expertise."

"Good work," Bravo said to Loscalzo, ignoring Baggler's remark. "But in spite of all that info we still need to bird-dog slummy areas in hopes of locating those yahoos and recovering those weapons and explosives."

"Then don't you think we need to confine our searches to neighborhoods predominantly Hispanic?" Baggler asked,

"There's no defined sections, like in the old days," Olecki said. "You'll find working class Puerto Ricans and other Hispanics on both sides of Oakland Park Boulevard and Commercial Boulevard, mixed in with working-class whites and blacks."

"Plus middle-income Puerto Ricans in upscale neighborhoods," Bravo added.

"Hispanics are moving into every neighborhood," Epps said.

"With rich Cubans and South Americans buying up those high-priced condos on the beach," Cleo said, smirking as she glanced to Pedrazo.

"It's called integration," Epps said. "Hear what I'm—"

"Considering the scum we're after," Baggler said, "we just ought to concentrate on the poorest areas."

"What makes you think those wildasses are only in the slums?" Epps asked.

"Because," Baggler retorted, "po'asses like that can't afford anything better."

"Terrorists and extremists come out of the middle classes as well," Cleo said. "Take that wildass McVey for an instance. His family was decent working-class folks and that yahoo blew up a federal building in Oklahoma City."

"Or that mad bomber—the college professor with the Polish name," Maylene said. Danly Coombs and Jerome Archison sitting alongside her nodded.

"Doesn't sound all that promising," Boisey Epps said, "with respect to narrowing the search. Hear what I'm—"

"Let's get back to combing warehouse areas where they might have secreted that hooch taken from the airfield," Bravo said, "especially since the green pick-up truck disappeared there."

"Keep in mind," Archison warned, "that search warrants are required if you don't have probable cause to poke around in buildings or vehicles."

"We sure could use a whole lot more manpower," Olecki said, "to sweep that area thorough like. Talked to my boss but they don't have anyone to spare."

"I'm available," Danly Coombs said.

Baggler snickered. "Lawyers doing cop work?"

"I've been through the training program at Glenco," Coombs said. "I can handle myself."

The others nodded acceptance since he'd attended the Federal Law Enforcement Training Center at Glenco, Georgia, thus acquired policing expertise, as did many federal and military law enforcement officers.

"Okay," Bravo said to Coombs, "partner up with Loreano Pedrazo. Hopefully this search mission doesn't deteriorate into sniper-attacks and shoot-outs this time. Anyway, Cleo can partner with Loscalzo, leaving Epps and Baggler to work together. With me and Pete Olecki, that puts four teams in the field."

"Burdened," Epps said, "with the task requiring a dozen. Hear what I'm saying?"

"Comb the commercial areas on both sides of Dixie Highway between Oakland Park and Commercial Boulevards," Bravo said, disregarding the lanky African-American's remark. "Olecki and I will poke around in that neighborhood west of Andrews Avenue in case they cached that stuff north of here."

"Makes sense," Olecki said, "being its closer to the airport."

"We'll meet back here at five," Bravo instructed.

"You forgetting about the taskforce prosecutor," Boisey Epps said. "Who is she partnering with?"

"Not me, brother-man," Maylene said. "I went through Glenco, but I'm ordained to administer my skills in a courtroom, not on any mean streets."

Bravo flagged his hand to eliminate her as one of the searchers as he led the way to the garage, relieved not to expose her to hazards. While Olecki started up the rattletrap Ford, Bravo called Yzabel on his cellphone.

"Sorry, sir, Doña Yzabel Zaraga is presently out of the office." He clenched his jaws to keep from grouching at the woman to call his wife Mrs. Bravo. And he decided against trying to reach Yzabel on her cellphone, concerned with pissing her off by interrupting her during an important meeting . . . if indeed she answered it instead of automatically switching calls to voice mail.

While climbing into the car he asked Olecki: "Cleo ever come on to you?"

Olecki jerked astonished eyes to the questioner, then chuckled. "Couple of times." His blue eyes sparkled with mirth. "Until I told her I'd put in for a different partner if she kept it up. Guess she didn't want the embarrassment, so stopped."

He drove west on Broward Boulevard, then turned into the lighter traffic on Andrews Avenue. He focused on his surroundings as they passed through a commercial area with offices and stores occasionally intermingled with restaurants on the ground floor of low-rise buildings. "She come onto you?"

Bravo nodded and made a face. "Put her off, but I can't say as I believe she accepted that as permanent."

Olecki chuckled. "She's thick-headed, but one hell of a cop, who makes a good partner. Got more guts than most men. Indomitable, I think they call that type. Wags her horny tail at a lot of guys. Lot of talk around about how forward she is. Wouldn't surprise me if a few of the guys boffed her. Problem is she's cloying, can drive a guy batty. Must wear her old man out."

"When he's home," Bravo reminded. And they chuckled.

"What?" Bravo asked when Olecki's head jerked around.

Olecki gestured to a weed-choked cul de sac. "Swear I spotted a battered green pick-up truck." He drove for two blocks before making a U-turn, so as to avoid alerting anyone of their interest.

While returning at a leisurely pace both men peered hard at the weedy cul de sac. Both saw the truck partially concealed in the clusters of pinnate leaves of an overgrowth of areca palms.

"Could be our baby," Bravo said.

Olecki nodded as he drove to the next intersection and made another U-turn. Along the way he called for back-up on his radio, pointedly informing that he may have happened upon the fugitive green pick-up truck they sought. If this turned out to be the one then he expected the situation to degenerate to A and D. Meanwhile Bravo contacted Baggler by cellphone to inform of the situation and the possibility of trouble.

Turning into the weedy cul de sac, they pulled up behind the target vehicle. Both men remained in the car and swept the area around them, prudence invoked by memory of yesterday's sniper attack as well as countless incidents during their careers. Law enforcement people often shivered from memory of scary events. Shaking that off they surveyed the dilapidated two-storied frame houses from almost a century past on the other side of the unkempt hedge.

"Has a broken windshield," Bravo said, "like the one we're after."

"But not a spidery crack," Olecki said.

"Eye-witness descriptions are often undependable," Bravo reminded. "But why else would somebody conceal that aging heap in those bushes?"

"Let's get us a closer look," Olecki suggested as he reached for his door handle.

Bravo peered around at the overgrowth of bushy ficus hedges that hadn't been trimmed recently. Interspersed with weedy growth, it formed a wall that induced hesitancy. "Think we'd be wise to wait for back-up?"

"This isn't where we got sniped," Olecki said.

"Doesn't mean we can't. Snipers don't have to stay in one place. And that yahoo may be itching to get another shot at us."

Olecki snickered. "Ask me, that more'n likely was some yahoo who'd acquired a rifle and couldn't resist the compulsion to shoot at something."

"Might've been a cop-hater," Bravo said.

"They'd have no way of knowing we were cops in civies and an unmarked car. Maybe we ought to let you go out there by yourself. If they recognize the ethnic similarity you'll be treated with less hostility."

"I'm law enforcement," Bravo said, "and they see me as the enemy now, same as they do you."

"Know what you mean. Had occasion to respond to domestic disturbances at Polish homes—Polish-American, of course. The husband always had a hard time accepting that a fellow Pollack intended to throw his ass in the can."

Bravo nodded to that rationale while continuing to search around.

"Just doesn't strike me as all that threatening," Olecki said as he tightened his grip on the door latch. "We just need to be real careful like."

Bravo hunched concession as they climbed out, their hands on their holstered pistols as they searched around, alert to the smallest movement. The music coming from somewhere beyond the hedge had the unmistakable rhythm of rural Mexico, languid while sonorous, as opposed to the frenetic beat of most Caribbean music.

They browsed one side of the pick-up truck, keeping the vehicle between them and the hedges that walled off the houses. Hearing the car pull into the cul-de-sac, they turned to see a cruiser. Recognizing Mac and Mac they waited for those two to back them up.

"Got something hinkty?" Maguire called as he clomped over, followed by his partner who warily scanned his surroundings.

"Nothing yet," Olecki said. "Just checking out this green pick-up truck. It's got a broken windshield, though not a spidery crack, and isn't missing any bumpers."

"Enough of those thing around," McGee said. "Anything incriminating in it?"

Olecki shrugged as he probed in it.

Bravo spotted an opening in the overgrown hedge and edged toward it while Olecki and the two Macs rooted around in the truck-bed. As he neared that breach in the shaggy brush, he saw it opened to a rickety dwelling encumbered by a number of haphazard extensions. Obviously those various increments had been built at different times, with little regard for compatible architecture. A paunchy guy in an undershirt appeared in the doorway to glower at him. Bravo noted his long black hair, olivy complexion and Pancho Villa mustache.

The squeal of tires turning into the cul de sac distracted Bravo. He turned to see Pedrazo and Coombs exit the bucar. After waving to them Bravo turned back to the guy in the doorway. "That green truck yours?"

The man rolled his eyes and made a face. Bravo couldn't interpret that as yes or no, nor whether or not the guy understood English. Then a chubby little woman emerged from inside the dwelling to posture pugnaciously in support of her man.

"For why?" she asked, scowling at Bravo.

Attracted by the voices, the other law enforcement officers became attentive. Olecki moved to Bravo's side while the others hung back a few paces, all with hands close to their weapons.

"Why is it parked like that?" Bravo asked, "like it's abandoned or something?"

The guy shrugged. "Motor no—" He turned to the woman. "Como se llama—no lo conduzca."

She glanced upward while apparently searching her brain for the translation of *the motor doesn't work*.

"Cuanto tiempo motor no lo conduzca?" Bravo asked to learn how long it hasn't worked.

The guy's eyes lit up at hearing the question in Spanish. "One months." Then he held up two fingers. "Quezá dos. Hay problema con esa camioneta?"

"No problema," Bravo said as he waved to the man and turned back to his guys.

"Thing doesn't even work. Been laid up for one or two months."

"So he says," McGee scoffed.

"No wheel tracks around it," Olecki said. "Looks to me like it's been parked there for a spell, certainly since before the last couple of heavy rains."

"Meaning it was put there before that raid on the airfield," Maguire said.

"They sure have a menacing appearance," Danly Coombs said.

"Scared," Bravo said. "Probably feel victimized."

"Or have something to hide," Pedrazo said, sneering. He used his cellphone to inform Baggler that no emergency existed and they didn't need any additional back-up.

"They look more like Mexicans than Puerto Ricans," Olecki said.

Bravo nodded. "Most of the Mexican laborers that come to this country are mixed with Indian, like those two."

"Unlike Cubans," Pedrazo said. "who are either white or black."

"You kidding?" Maguire said. "Half the Cubans I run into are bi-racial."

"Some perhaps," Pedrazo conceded. "Not half."

"Damned if I can tell a Cuban from a Colombian," McGee said.

"Hispanics in this hemisphere are dissimilar," Bravo said, "because they descend from different regions of Spain and diverse racial intermixes." He went on to explain that Puerto Ricans run the gamut from white to black, often within the same family. It's one of the confusions they struggle with when they come to the mainland, where they're generally regarded as less than white even when they're Caucasian. Not burdened with that problem at home they have difficulty understanding those racial attitudes here.

"Cubans any different?" McGee asked Pedrazo.

The Cuban stammered, but before he could reply, Maguire said: "Those people brought a whole lot more to this country than any other Hispanics."

Pedrazo nodded emphatically. But again before he could remark, Bravo said: "No other group of immigrants of any nationality arrived in one huge wave with their intellectual, professional, and business elite."

"Thanks to Fidel," Danly Coombs said, "who kicked out the rich and educated."

"I'm beginning to understand," Olecki said. "What we got with Puerto Ricans is a bunch of non-English-speaking immigrants that ain't really foreigners, but stubbornly refuse to give up their Spanish culture, despite wanting to be considered American."

Bravo nodded. "Simple as that."

Mac and Mac looked askance at Bravo and Olecki, then glanced at each other and shrugged, conveying that they didn't need to understand it.

TWENTY-TWO

"Glad we didn't have to tangle with those folks," Bravo said as they drove away.

Olecki nodded. "They have enough problems without us unnecessarily leaning on them. Believe me, I know. Not all that long ago Slavic people bore the brunt of being treated as inferior, especially by those from Western Europe. It took me years when a kid to realize I had a right to poke out my chest and be proud of being a Pollack."

"Had similar experiences because of people disdaining Puerto Ricans," Bravo said. "Amazing part is that prejudicial attitudes didn't come from only whites but from blacks and other Latinos as well. I've been condemned to carry that burden regardless of career achievements, level of education, talents and abilities. It took application to retain pride, resist being convinced of inferiority."

Olecki nodded as he drove up the ramp of their office building to park on the sixth floor. Then he and Bravo took the elevator to the seventh. Waving the detective into the conference room Bravo slipped into one of the empty offices and dialed Yzabel's office. Identifying himself as Mister Bravo he asked for his wife, Mrs. Bravo. The gal responded: "Doña Yzabel Zaraga is with a client. Can you hold, sir?"

She'd clicked off before he could express resentment for not referring to his wife as Mrs. Bravo. And he sure as hell didn't like being clicked on hold and being subjected to listening to continually repeated recorded promotional messages. Then he jerked to attentiveness at the sound of his wife's voice.

"I hope this call is meaningful, having pulled me away from important clients."

Bravo scowled, irritated by the annoyed and unfriendly tone of Yzabel's voice. "That stung—is not the greeting I expected—considering I called with hopes of mollifying antagonism."

"Isn't it a bit late for that?"

"Is it ever too late to attempt to save our marriage?"

"Not if you're sincere, Ramón, which would have required you to be here for me a couple of days ago."

"You know damn well I was ordered to remain here."

"Just as well since I thoroughly enjoyed attending a social event with diplomats —cultured people—instead of police types and middle-level bureaucrats."

He winced, stung by the put-down. But before he found words with which to retort she snappishly remarked: "No, I didn't dance with Nando, hardly spoke to him. Yes, his wife accompanied him."

Bravo winced again, chastised by answers to things he hadn't inquired about, though he wanted to—knew he deserved the rebuke.

"Is there anything else you need to know?" she asked. "I have clients waiting."

"Then I take it that your old flame didn't offer a renewal of a past relationship."

"Unfortunately, he did not."

"That's a hell of a thing to admit to your husband."

"Absentee husband most of the time."

"It's what I am, Yzabel. It's what I was when you married me."

"Thanks for continually reminding me what a gigantic mistake I made."

"If that's how you feel about it then you're correct in suggesting we end it."

"Believe, Ramón, that it has been on my mind for a long time, and is now on my agenda of things to attend to."

"What about the boys?"

"They're old enough to understand that we don't get along any longer. Divorce isn't exactly anomalous to teenagers in these times."

"Can we at least wait until I get home to discuss it further?"

"Whatever you wish." Click.

Bravo entered the conference room swallowing to conceal the bubbling of irritation in his gut. He also suffered frustration from his lack of success as taskforce boss. Not a bit of progress had been made in learning about the yahoos who raided the repo-depo at the airport. Yes, he knew if he didn't provide a semblance of accomplishment soon he'd be demoted . . . humiliated.

Nevertheless, he forced himself to be attentive to the various reports . . . none of which suggested accomplishment or hinted at any kind of success. After Olecki reported the incident in the cul-de-sac, Bravo called it a day and said he'd see everyone in the morning.

He drove the bucar to his motel with hands clenched on the wheel, cursing under his breath at slow motorists who refused to keep to the right, a situation endemic in South Florida. Entering the room, he hung up his jacket and removed his necktie before sprawling out on the bed, tired but too incensed to doze.

Another angst beside his eroding marriage and lack of success with his investigation wore on him. He'd been edgy since this morning when Loscalzo identified the caudillo, or leader, of the Puerto Rican extremists as deriving from a family with the name of Galbos. During his growing up years he'd questioned his parents on numerous occasions why they didn't visit the family in Puerto Rico, as did many middle-class families from the island. Hell, his parents took vacations in the Americas and Europe.

Because of his pestering them with questions about family there, they sent him on his twelfth birthday to visit his Tio Rico, his father's younger brother, Enrique, in the metropolis of Mayaguez on the west coast of the island.

A chubby and jolly man, Tio Rico lived in a big house befitting the manager of a business supplying concrete to construction sites. After dinner, Tio Rico lounged in a big easy chair and sipped cognac on crushed ice while he boasted how his progenitors migrated from Bilbao in the province of Asturias, on the northwest coast of Spain.

The immigrant great-grandfather, a brick mason, founded a contracting company in Mayaguez. His sons inherited the business and expanded it to supplying concrete to construction sites. And their children, with the exception of Ray's father, followed in the family tradition increasing that inherited wealth by becoming major wholesale dealers of pre-mixed cement as well as a variety of masonry products.

Naturally Ray wondered why his father hadn't remained in Mayaguez to share that bounty and its attendant social rewards. Whenever he raised the subject at home papá bragged of his success as a contractor in The States, reminding that he'd made his own way without handouts by the family.

No denying his father had provided a pleasant middle-class life-style. And papá and mamá lived comfortably until age took its toll, injecting illness, pain, and incompetence in their lives. After his mother died and his father lost his ability to perform normal activities, he put papá in a nursing home.

It went against the grain for Ray, as it did for many Latinos, to not personally care for their elderly. But the constant traveling connected to his job, and Yzabel's refusal to take time away from her business to care for the demented octogenarian, denied him options.

Several years ago, after papá died, Ray again visited Puerto Rico to learn more about his family. An old man by then, Tio Rico prattled one night about Ray's father having migrated to the mainland after being ostracized by the family for marrying the maid's daughter. Some of her family, like the Galbos and Panderas, had mixed blood.

Ray absorbed that shock and stored it, with intent to never share it with Yzabel or his sons. Whenever he could, he investigated that lineage, but found no evidence of dark blood in his mother's line of descendants.

Cognizant of the history of Spain, he accepted that her family might have had infusions of dark blood from the Moros, as Spaniards referred to the North African moors. His family migrated from Cartegena in Murcia on the southern coast. That area had been under Arab occupation for eight centuries. So if dark blood had been infused it probably would have been Semitic rather than African.

Yes, black blood from African slaves brought to Puerto Rico may well have infiltrated the family but didn't necessarily mean his mother's direct lineage had to be affected. True, obviously some of her relatives had mixed with blacks, a situation common in the island. However, while olivy complexioned, like most Mediterranean people, with black hair and dark eyes, she had no Negroid features.

Bravo always expressed gratitude for his father's success, allowing he and his sister, Maria Teresa, to grow up in the middle-class environment of Jackson Heights in Queens, a suburb of New York City. No doubt in his mind it saved him from the peer pressure of gangs that were rampant in Spanish Harlem and the South Bronx, where the majority of Hispanics resided.

Through all those years of public elementary and high schools, as well as at Queens College and CCNY, everyone accepted Ray as white—Hispanic actually. After the fact he regretted referring to himself as of Spanish descent rather than sticking his chest out and proclaiming his pride of his progenitors by representing himself as Puerto Rican.

Disenchanted with college, he enlisted in the army. He'd served as a battalion clerk during his first three years, then transferred to the Military Police for his last, which served as his introduction to the police universe.

When discharged, he passed the exam for the New York City Police Department and became a patrolman. Yes, he had been characterized as Hispanic in the cops, indicating they considered him neither white nor other than white.

That income allowed him to live in a small apartment in lower Manhattan, and a year later he enrolled at CCNY to get his college diploma. Graduating at twenty-nine, he responded to recruitment by the Treasury Department, even though he had passed the sergeant's exam in the NYPD and stood a good chance of getting that promotion. The Department Of Treasury assigned him to ATF because of his police experience and posted him in DC, where they trained him to become an explosives expert.

Thinking back, he conceded that he'd had a pretty good life overall. Only that specter of racial pollution haunted and discomfited him. He wondered how his boys would react if they learned they weren't pure white . . . not that it was a given.

Once when talking by phone to his oldest son at Duke he asked Esteban whether he had any chance of making the basketball team, aware of the zeal of his son to compete in that sport. Esteban despondently replied that the black kids get all the spots on the team—then asked why they are stronger and faster.

Ray didn't know how to explain it. And he wasn't about to shock Esteban by telling him that he might have strains of black blood, since no evidence existed and *might* was as close as he could get. Besides, he didn't want to traumatize the young man and have him questioning whether he belonged in white society.

Even more, he dreaded what Yzabel's reaction would be if he revealed that possible infusion. She detested blacks resulting from an experience with a black intruder. Thereafter she never felt comfortable among blacks, and avoided the slummy neighborhoods surrounding and threatening to intrude on downtown Washington.

TWENTY-THREE

Bravo climbed out of the bucar in the sixth floor garage, shaking his head to dispel the weariness resulting from a restless night. "Morning," he greeted upon entering the elevator concourse and encountering Danly Coombs, the chubby black deputy assistant US attorney. "Enjoy being on the street with cops?"

Coombs bobbed his head about for a few seconds before replying. "Yes and no." After a deep breath he added: "It's sometimes exciting and sometimes boring. Yesterday with y'all it was real scary, though it turned out to be a false alarm."

"Typical for police work. Most important thing to remember out there is to back up your partner. He'll back you up. Both of you have a better chance of surviving then." The elevator door opened and they stepped into it. Coombs averted his eyes as he said: "That's the consensus, I know." Then he appeared to search for words before grimacing and adding in lowered voice: "Pedrazo makes me dubious he's got my back . . . strikes me as uncomfortable around black folks."

Bravo blinked, taken aback by that unexpected indictment. He still wasn't sure how to respond when they disembarked on the seventh floor. He'd found fault with the Cuban, but wasn't ready to condemn the man of racial abhorrence.

"Didn't mean to put you on the spot," Coombs said.

"Since you have, enlarge on the condemnation."

"Pedrazo reminds me of some crackers I worked with in Baltimore. He isn't outright hostile, while his emanations send the message that he's not happy about our proximity and would rather not share space with me."

Bravo waved the younger man through the metal detector first, then joined him as both presented their credentials to the guard in the bulletproof glass booth. "If there's a problem it's Pedrazo's. Humor him."

Coombs nodded concession as they traversed the hall and entered the conference room, to be greeted by Boisey Epps whining about having to beat the rough in the rain.

"Let's give it a few minutes," Bravo said as he glanced to the precipitation dappling the windows. "Those showers come and go here in Florida."

Olecki and Cleo entered, both wearing rain gear, followed a moment later by Pedrazo. He rounded the table to sit with the three FBI agents.

"We've decided to wait out the rain," Bravo informed.

"Sure beats the hell out of having to deal with a whole bunch of soaked wetbacks," Baggler said, chortling.

"Don't let Archison hear you dissin' foks," Epps warned.

"It's worse in the most poor-ass neighborhoods," Cleo commented, "where dampness increases the stench and the misery of poverty."

"Believe that," Epps said. "Being wet is a whole lot worse in shanties and scruffy tenements. Hear what I'm saying?"

"At the risk of sounding anti-immigration," Baggler said, "I'm trying to understand why these folks come here and revolt against the government that succors them."

"Who you referring to?" Olecki asked. "I haven't run across any Mexicans or Central Americans revolting."

"He sure as hell don't mean those rich Cubans living in hi-rises on the beach," Cleo said, snickering as she glanced at Pedrazo.

He scowled, but before he had a chance to retort, Baggler said: "Y'all sure as hell can't deny that Puerto Rican wetbacks are waging war against us and threatening to blow our asses up."

"Puerto Ricans are American citizens, not foreigner-born wetbacks," Bravo said. "FYI, there are less Puerto Ricans involved in terrorism and armed dissent than there are good-old-boys in the back-country militias threatening to overthrow the U. S. Government."

"Another thing to remember," Olecki said, "is that the Puerto Rican activists are trying to make a statement, get some attention for their political ambitions."

Baggler sniggered. "Sure don't appear like anybody's listening."

"Damn shame," Danly Coombs said, "considering all they want is equality with other Americans."

"Don't they have that?" Loscalzo asked.

Epps laughed. "Where you been, man?"

"While they're generally considered citizens," Bravo said, "those who reside in the island can't vote on a national level, like for the president of the United States. They don't have national representatives like congressmen or US senators and can only vote for people running for office in Puerto Rico, or in the presidential primaries."

"You saying you can't vote for the president?" Baggler asked Bravo.

"I was born here, not in the island. I enjoy full citizenship privileges, same as you."

"Why," Loscalzo asked, "are so many of them migrating here if they dislike us and our way of life?"

"The financial situation in that island is crumbling," Olecki said. "The government of Puerto Rico is bankrupt."

"So why have they been coming here for years?" Baggler asked.

"Puerto Ricans were drafted to serve in the military at the outbreak of World War Two," Bravo said. "Many trained on the mainland and became aware of the difference in life here than in their neglected island that wallowed in poverty. After the war some refused to return to the indigence they had known all their lives. They settled in mainland metropolitan centers to seek employment and a better standard of living. And like most immigrants, they brought their families as soon as they could afford to."

"What the hell they expect to accomplish here?" Baggler asked, his face contorted with aversion.

"Like all forefathers who migrated to our shores," Olecki said, "they seek jobs, decent housing, and a chance to educate their children and give them a future."

"They sure didn't make out all that well," Epps said. "If those folks also had a dream, they're not singing *Free At Last*. Hear what I'm saying?"

"Ask me," Cleo said, "I'd say they got left in the shuffle."

"Not entirely," Bravo said. "Remember, the original migrants were uneducated and unskilled, so qualified only for low-end jobs. Many of their children born here enjoyed opportunities for education. Quite a few graduated high school, and some, like myself, from college."

"But in the same way as most black folks," Danly Coombs said, "they never achieved per capita income on a par with most whites, degree or no degree."

"True to a large extent," Bravo admitted. "But it's changing. Second and third generation Puerto Ricans born on the mainland are achieving equal to whites."

"Then why," Baggler asked, "those folks rebelling?"

"The Puerto Rican migrant is unique," Bravo said, "in that he is treated as a foreigner when in fact he is an American. All too often they are lumped in with other Caribbean immigrants, with an arrogant disregard of their having their own heritage, separate even of Dominicans and Cubans."

"And they keep on coming," Loscalzo said.

"True," Bravo said as he nodded. "That growth has exploded to approximately three million people, close to the population in their Caribbean homeland. The problem is that they've been scorned, spurned and disdained, which embitters them and reinforces their opposition to assimilating."

"My grandparents came over from Italy," Loscalzo said, "and grandpa worked as a laborer. My father went to high school but quit to work in a factory and rose to foreman. We lived comfortably. I'm not doing so bad, went to college and have a wide-open future, considering I'm only twenty-seven years old."

"That's what I call progress," Baggler said, "the American way."

"Moving on up," Epps quipped.

"For years," Bravo said, "social scientists defamed Puerto Ricans as the most downtrodden minority in the United States. But the Census Bureau refutes that by reporting that among Hispanics in the United States Puerto Rican workers overall are the second highest salaried. Fact is, they rate higher in education than all other Hispanics in this country. Almost sixty percent of mainland-born Puerto Ricans below the age of twenty-five have high school diplomas."

"So where do all these gangbangers come from?" Baggler asked.

"A large percentage of those mired in ghetto life have been indoctrinated into gang-life," Bravo said. "It serves as their lifeline to survival in those mean streets. Hence, they share a mutual bitterness against the society that disparages them. Those who are uneducated and unskilled resent being discarded to exploitation as low-end workers, consequently become willing candidates for activists enlisting recruits."

"Plus," Olecki added, "they have to compete with waves of illegals."

"Now that's a whole 'nother subject," Epps said. "Hear what I'm saying?"

Bravo nodded. "The military has become an escape for many, where they learn confidence and self-esteem, besides earning educational opportunities. That helped more than a few to become gainfully employed and escape the barrios with its oppressive mentality. Quite a lot of those are in civil service jobs, working for local governments. Some enjoy the ranks of middle management in industry. They are a people on the march."

"But those achievements," Epps said, "are unpublicized because the lifestyle of that successful group, similar to that of those in the black communities, doesn't offer the sensationalism the media uses to sell newspapers and air-time. Hear what—"

"Since they've accomplished all you claim," Baggler asked, "why can't they become Americans like the children of all other immigrants—mine, Loscalzo's, even yours?"

"Unlike other immigrants," Bravo said, "especially those from Europe, Puerto Ricans resist losing their culture through assimilation."

"European immigrants," Olecki said, "considered it a blessing to escape the oppressive regimes that harassed them in their homelands, so discarded old-country ways and strove to assimilate when they arrived here."

"Puerto Ricans on the other hand," Bravo said, "resist giving up their language, which is the essence of their ethnicity. They consider that, as well as music, foods, and other traditions, as valued legacies."

"What's so terrible about conforming to American customs?" Baggler asked. "Other immigrants have done it."

"What makes you think," Cleo asked, "that you're the same as every other American?"

"No question," Loscalzo said, "that there's diversity . . . especially in different parts of the country."

"Based on necessity," Olecki added.

"Rural and metropolitan," Epps said, "are two different worlds. Hear what—"

"Plus the sentimental attachment," Loscalzo said, "to the legacy of our parents. I'm proud to descend from Italians."

"What I'm asking," Baggler growled, "is how this condition with Puerto Ricans got started."

"The US military abused and subjugated the island of Puerto Rico to a slave-like status," Bravo said, "establishing firing ranges for naval artillery and air force bombing targets that resulted in widespread cancer. Besides, it forced people off the land they were born on to make space for military installations. The military occupies thirteen per cent of the arable land in the island, displacing a lot of farmers. Taxes are levied on the island residents by congressmen in Washington, while Puerto Ricans are denied representation in that body . . . defying the concept that led to the American Revolution."

"Didn't know about all that," Olecki said.

"Consequently," Bravo said, "many Puerto Ricans see self-rule as their only salvation. But like politics everywhere in the world, there is dissention, with those who favor continued commonwealth status versus those who aspire for statehood. And those two groups are opposed by that minority clamoring for liberation from U. S. domination and exploitation."

"Aye, there's the rub," Danly Coombs said. "Those who demonstrate for independence are regarded as radicals."

"Because they resort to terrorism," Loscalzo said.

"So much for polemics," Bravo said. "The damn rain is letting up, so let's get back to rooting out those bad guys and recover those weapons and explosives. We need to deny that bunch of yahoos publicizing their cause at the cost of human lives."

"I'm ready when you are, leader man," Epps said. "Am tired of hanging around here doing nothing but gabbing about a situation that won't change because we want it to. Hear what I'm saying?"

Bravo nodded while announcing: "While most of you return to sweeping the warehouse areas, me and Peter are going over to the jail to pump that other Puerto Rican jailer, Luis Cortez. Hopefully we'll elicit information that will help achieve our mission."

"It is I, not the detective," Pedrazo said, "who should accompany you."

"Why is that?" Bravo asked.

"You cast shame on me when you interviewed Botero without me. You owe me the opportunity to prove I am as good an interrogator as anyone."

"No skin off my nose," Olecki said. "I'd as soon get out on the streets."

Bravo shrugged. "Okay, Loreano, you and I will visit Cortez. Meanwhile, Peter, do me a favor and see if you can get us that small office over at the jail to interview him. Danly Coombs can team with you for the morning. See everybody back here at noon."

TWENTY-FOUR

While driving the black SUV Bravo glanced intermittently at Loreano Pedrazo who sulked in the passenger seat. Arriving at the Broward County Jail, a massive concrete building off Southeast Sixth Street and Third Avenue, he jockeyed with countless other vehicles for entrance right of way into the parking area, then competed with them in the narrow aisles while searching for a parking spot.

"I have not received the respect I deserve or consideration of rank I have earned," Pedrazo complained while they wound through the maze of parked vehicles. When Bravo glanced at him the Cuban said: "We are fellow Latinos but you ignore my experience and expertise . . . never consult me when planning strategy."

Bravo hunched, lost for a reply. Pedrazo continued carping. "Have been doing this work for fifteen years, since graduating FIU, so should get more respect."

Bravo had to think for a moment before identifying those initials as Florida International University, a highly accredited institution in Miami. "You get recruited upon graduation?"

"The four years experience I had serving in the Air Force before I attended college impressed on my résumé. My background qualifies me to be your immediate lieutenant and second in command of this taskforce . . . if not command."

"I certainly will depend on you more now that I know your background," Bravo said, forcing himself to sound sincere,

Spotting a space being vacated he pulled up to it and waited for the other car to leave. After parking they strode together to the jailhouse to pass through checkpoints before being shown into the small office in which Olecki had arranged for them to interview Luis Cortez, a robust man of obvious mixed-races.

"What the hell you two want from me?" the stocky jailer demanded.

"Why are you belligerent?" Bravo asked.

"Protecting my ass, man, from you *rabiblancos* dumping on me."

Bravo winced at that demeaning reference, accusing them of being white bigots who snubbed non-whites and the working class. "We haven't accused you of anything."

"Sure," the stocky mixed-breed said, "but you going to make me a scapegoat like you did Botero."

"Botero got victimized by the radicals," Bravo said.

"So he told me. Glad those gangbangers never visited me to get my ass in trouble. Through no fault of his own Botero got shunted to clerking in the stockroom with no hope of ever getting a promotion. That what you planning for me?"

"We're not out to railroad you or anyone else," Bravo said. "Our purpose is—"

"So why you here, busting my hump for the third time? Admit that you trying to make me another fall guy because you can't get a line on those *atrevimientos* who killed that prisoner, Elizondo."

"We have many leads," Pedrazo said. ". . . Are not without intelligence about those *outrageous people*."

"Then why you harassing me? Is that the Cubano way? Like you guys don't know you act all superior. You're *criollos Caribbeanos* like the rest of us but act like you shit don't stink."

"Let's not get into an ethnic row," Bravo said.

"Hey, I don't see you trying to lay this on any Cubano working in this jail. But you ready and willing to dump on Puertoriqueños."

"We're not dumping on anyone," Bravo said. "I'm Puerto Rican and I'm sure not against my own people."

"Then you, of all people, should know that being Puertoriqueño doesn't make a person a terrorist or a sympathizer of those radicals."

"Depends on the individual," Pedrazo said, scowling at the jailer.

"The man is right," Bravo said to Pedrazo. "All Puertoriqueños do not support that radicalism." Turning back to Cortez he asked: "What part of New York are you from?"

"The Bronx, man. Where else?"

"You still have gang affiliations?" Bravo asked.

"Get real, man. I'm a law enforcement officer now. That's why I booked from The Apple, to split from all that shit—the drive-bys and jugging brothers on the street for imagined slights."

"Then let's talk about associations with *extremistas Puertoriqueñas* here in Florida."

"I have nothing to offer on that subject of Puerto Rican extremists, bro'."

"Your job will be in jeopardy if you are uncooperative," Pedrazo said. "The sheriff will terminate you when he learns that you aided and abetted criminals."

"You have no basis for claiming that shit, man. Fact is, it never happened. I got no truck with bad-asses and gang-bangers."

"Help us out here," Bravo said, patting the guard's shoulder. "You're Puerto Rican, and know the importance of stopping those insane *disidentes*."

"Or face sanctions," Pedrazo added.

"Get this motherfucking rafter off my case," Cortez demanded. "Those *balseros* paddle their inner-tubes to get here because they can't afford the fare on a real boat. Then they have the gall to assume some kind of haughty-ass superiority around other Latinos. But they quick to pucker up and kiss gringo ass."

"I don't have to listen to bullshit!" Pedrazo said.

Bravo patted Pedrazo's shoulder to calm him. "You have to be less strident." Then he addressed the guard. "It's our responsibility—yours and mine as law-enforcement officers—to root out those bad guys by working in concert, not against each other."

Cortez threw his hands out in front of him in a gesture of dismay. "How can you lean on me when you know I'm clean? You been through my records, my finances, everything. You see I'm poor-assed, barely make my mortgage payments on time. Got more credit-card bills than brains. If I was into something you think I be dead broke?"

"But you're aware of the scuttlebutt," Bravo said. "Every prison has it. Tell us something that will help us find those *atrevimientos*."

"Believe that I would if I could give up those *outrageous people* to get you hard-asses off my case. But I close my eyes and ears to all the shit going in here. Been trying real hard to live a clean life—don't want to know anything ain't on the up and up."

"You expect us to believe you never hear anything?" Pedrazo asked.

"I shut my eyes and ears, man . . . don't want to know nothing."

"I'm going to ask you a favor," Bravo said. "Open your ears to anything relative to the Elizondo or Independista matters. Call us when you hear something. Help society take those bad guys off the street. Help decent Puertoriqueños live with less fear in their lives. Prove you support the rule of law."

Cortez shuffled around before hunching what Bravo interpreted as concession.

# # #

"Why did you give up on that hard-ass?" Pedrazzo asked as he and Bravo made their way through peopled hallways toward the exit to the parking lot.

"He clammed up because of what happened to Botero, and wasn't about to admit anything could negatively affect his job."

"Loreano!" A female voice brought the attention of both men to a bi-racial woman with her arms full of documents. She hurried to them, grinning widely.

Bravo noted that Pedrazo turned pale while stammering a greeting to the woman. "This is a wonderful surprise," she said, eyes glimmering, "to encounter you here in Fort Lauderdale. Don't you generally work out of Miami?"

"Nice to see you, Nina," Pedrazo replied, "but we're too busy to chat."

"Of course, Loreano. I understand. Anyway we'll talk when we meet at Pedro's house next week for the monthly family get-together."

Pedrazo winced, then waved to her as he distanced himself from her. When beyond her hearing he stammered: "A cousin married her."

Bravo decided against commenting. Interracial intermarriage was not unusual among Caribbean Hispanics . . . common actually.

They exited the building and traipsed across the parking lot. "There is none of that blood in my immediate family," Pedrazo said. "But some men become blinded by sex and end up married to women of inferior races."

Bravo snickered as they reached the car. He stored what had been said in his data bank, in the event he ever needed it.

TWENTY-FIVE

Bravo hurried to the conference room, concerned with being late for the taskforce meeting. FBI agent Loscalzo greeted him by waving a multi-page transmission. "Fax from the FBI information office," he said. "It's a dossier of Abdulo, including a photograph taken a few years ago by a surveillance team. The guy is a shrewd operator who plays the system and continues to works it to his own advantage."

Bravo read it, then studied the blurred and grainy photograph of the light-skinned mixed-breed with kinky hair. He gritted his teeth as he scanned facial features behind a wiry beard for similarities that might reveal Abdulo as a relative.

"Now we know what the guy looks like," Loscalzo said, obviously pleased with himself for his accomplishment.

"What we still need though" Baggler said, "is direction from our leader as to how to utilize this intel."

Bravo pretended concentration on the picture and the dossier while ignoring the barb. Then he shifted his attention to a smiling Olecki entering the conference room, wagging a sheet of paper. "The Major Crimes Division of the Sheriff's Office provided a list of suspected Puerto Rican activists in Broward County."

Bravo accepted it. "This is something that should have been obtained by the taskforce two weeks ago." The inference caused all eyes to flick to a red-faced Baggler, who sputtered but failed to verbalize excuses for his omission.

Bravo divided the names among the four search teams to find and interrogate them. "I advise everyone to be wary when confronting those people. Expect them to be belligerent as well as armed and dangerous, with women no less confrontational than men."

Receiving no questions, objections or other remarks, he assigned Pedrazo to partner with Baggler, Loscalzo with Epps, and Cleo with Danly Coombs, leaving Olecki to partner with him. He'd switched Coombs away from Pedrazo as a result of their earlier conversation, as well as because of his own observations. Neither Pedrazo nor Coombs voiced objection.

Olecki drove the rattletrap Ford in medium to heavy traffic to Oakland Park Boulevard near Thirty-third Avenue, en route to confront the first person on their list. The area consisted mostly of shanty-like mobile homes in various stages of disrepair, surrounded by scrubby bushes. Older cars as well as jalopy-like pick-up trucks and hard-used vans, many of them dented and scratched, had been parked haphazardly where lawns or gardens might have been. None of the houses had driveways, garages or breeze-ways.

While the majority of those vehicles needed repairs and painting none had a spidery crack in the windshield. Loud music vibrated from multiple sources. Caribbean rhythms, turbid and full of licentious promises, competed with Mexican and Central American ballads.

Finding the address they sought, one of the shanty-like trailer homes, Bravo knocked on the rickety door while Olecki backed him up from a few feet behind, his hand near, but not on, the butt of his pistol. A woman with her hair in disarray appeared in the doorway to scowl at the strangers and scoff at the proffered credentials.

"Need to talk to Juan Batista Perez," Bravo said.

She hunched skinny shoulders while clutching the door, as if ready to slam it closed.

"He lives here, yes?" Bravo asked. When the woman looked at him blankly, he asked: "Lo vida aquí, no?"

"Sí, pero es afuera."

"Adonde?" Bravo asked, inquiring as to where he went.

"Trabajando," the woman said curtly. And to Bravo's request for an address of where he worked she demanded in Spanish to know why they wanted her husband.

"Questioning about a pick-up truck that's been stolen," Bravo said in Spanish.

She snickered contemptuously. "Juanito no roba camioneta."

"Still," Bravo said in Spanish, "we need to speak with him."

"You make mistake . . . seek the wrong man," she snarled in Spanish.

"Perhaps you can tell us who is the right one," Bravo said.

"¿Por qué?" The woman sneered at him. ". . .Aunque si me conosco."

Bravo suppressed scowling at her remarking: *even if she knew.* He explained in Spanish that her husband is a suspect, and would be put in prison if he did not clear himself. The woman continued to smirk, but condescended to tell him that her esposo worked in a junkyard and gave him the address. Then she added, "Juanito no roba camioneta."

The woman continued to glower at Bravo after he thanked her and turned away. OLecki accompanied him in returning to their car. After a short drive they turned onto Northwest Twenty-First Avenue, with its potholes and broken macadam. Small stores lined the north side of the street. A hairdressing salon with darkened windows abutted a grungy restaurant next door to a storefront church. Beyond that, and next to a shop that sold used appliances, a grimy front had laundry scrawled on it.

Turning south on Northwest Twenty-Ninth Street they drove between small warehouses. Each aged and mildew-streaked building had an overhead garage door alongside an entrance door to a cubicle-sized office, with all doors open for ventilation. Mustiness emanated from them. Cars and trucks parked helter skelter, many double-parked, which decreased the roadway passage to barely sufficient for larger vehicles to pass. Dust and trash flitted about in the breeze.

Olecki found the address of the dingy warehouse given them by the woman, and parked behind a battered minivan with a broken passenger window. The heat of the day combined with the pathetic functioning of their air-conditioner had induced them to remove their jackets while riding. So they left them in the car, exposing their holstered pistols when they trudged around the minivan to approach the open doorway, where Latin music pulsated from within.

Bravo peered into the dimly lit cavern to make out men working at benches. He and Olecki glanced to each other, both reluctant to penetrate that dark pit. When a man working at a nearby bench turned to them Bravo said: "We need to speak with Juan Batista Perez."

The swarthy man scowled at the two intruders and demanded: "Who want him?"

"Sheriff's Office," Olecki said, gesturing toward his badge pinned on his gunbelt.

The man yelled into the interior: "Policía aquí para Juan Batista Perez."

From deep in the dark hole of the shop they heard the clatter of dropped tools and running feet. Bravo charged into the shop while drawing his gun. But darkness prevented him from telling anyone apart, so he stopped at the first bench.

Assuming the man bolted for the rear door, Olecki ran back to the car and gunned the sputtering vehicle around the row of buildings. He turned into the dirt alley separating the backs of attached warehouses and spotted the man in the dirt-streaked and sweaty undershirt running away from the building. Squealing to a stop, he swung open the door and drew his pistol while climbing out and yelling: "Halt! Police!"

The fugitive scurried behind a huge trash container. "Come out of there with your hands in the air," Olecki yelled. "Manos ariba!"

He jerked back behind the car door when the guy popped up and fired a revolver at him. After gasping a breath to suppress surprise and fear, he squatted behind his car door and aimed his weapon, all the while shouting *ten-seventy-eight* into his radio. "Need assistance! Under fire!" He hoped to hell while giving his location that the mook didn't blow out a window of the Ford; not all that eager to report another shot-up vehicle.

Reacting to the sound of gunfire, Bravo ventured deeper into the shop to duck behind a greasy bench short of the rear door. With gun grasped in both hands, thrust before him, he glanced around at the three workers in the dark shop. Seeing that they backed away while holding their hands exposed to telegraph their lack of intention to get involved, he pulled out his cellphone to report the situation to Daggler.

That done, he crouched with his semi-automatic pistol thrust out in both hands and edged toward the open rear doorway. Peeking out he yelled repeatedly in both English and Spanish to the man to put down his weapon. A bullet pinged into the metal doorbuck.

Flinching, Bravo flattened himself against the concrete block wall. He glanced back at the workers, who had distanced themselves and knotted together at the opened garage door in front. Hoping they were smart enough not to get involved, he returned his attention to the shooter beyond the rear door and again yelled in both English and Spanish for the man to surrender. Another shot smacked into the doorbuck.

Olecki opened up with his forty-caliber Glock, his bullets pinging off the huge metal garbage container. He knew he didn't hit the man but derived pleasure from knowing the hump cringed from bullets pinging around him.

Then it surprised him to see Perez bolt out from behind the container to race down the alley in a crouch. Olecki aimed as he yelled, "Halt!" But before he got off a shot the guy ducked into the open back door of a building adjacent to and a few doors down from the one he'd fled. Olecki fired three shots that pocked cement near the fugitive a second after he'd disappeared.

"Som'bitch ducked into the building two doorways down," Olecki yelled to Bravo.

"I'll cover the front," Bravo yelled as he ran back through the dingy shop and out front to cover all of the buildings, hoping to block Perez from escaping from whichever he'd entered.

He breathed gratitude when a cruiser with screaming siren arrived and Mac and Mac jumped out. Despite panting he brought them up to speed. Then they conferred with Olecki by radio and agreed that the fugitive enjoyed an advantage, since they weren't certain whether he remained in the warehouse he'd ducked into or fled out of it somehow.

They had no idea if any of those buildings were interconnected, or had access to the roof from inside. None of the officers relished the prospect of a crazy with a gun having a height advantage. So they called in more back-up, after which Mac and Mac took up positions to support Bravo in covering the front of the building. Another cruiser arrived with two more sheriff's deputies.

Leaving them with Mac and Mac, Bravo ran around the row of buildings to station himself at the opposite rear corner of Olecki, with six abutting buildings separating them. They waved acknowledgement to each other.

Loscalzo and Epps arrived in their bucar, followed moments later by Baggler and Pedrazo. All four took up positions in the rear of the buildings, two to bolster Bravo and the other two backing up Olecki. Additional Broward deputies screeched to a halt in their cruisers and bolstered Mac and Mac and the other deputies covering the fronts of the buildings. Red lights atop police cruisers swirled continuously, injecting the trauma of crisis into the area.

Workers fled buildings and sought cover. Two informed the police in broken English that the man with the gun remained in the building they evacuated. Both assured that only two means of egress existed—at front and back. Mac and Mac conveyed that information to Olecki by radio.

Two other cars arrived with sirens screaming to take up positions, one at the end of the alley with Olecki, and the other with Bravo. And minutes later Cleo and Danly Coombs screech to a halt and joined Bravo.

"We're going to storm the building," the deputies in front radioed to Olecki. He transmitted that information to all others at the back of the buildings. Their concern was to avoid injuring each other. With weapons at the ready those in front advanced on the wide opening of the overhead door of the building the fugitive hid in.

Suddenly Perez darted out of the rear door and raced for warehouses across the narrow alley. He fired his revolver in both directions, inducing the police to duck for cover. He grabbed a door handle, only to be frustrated when he couldn't budge the door. Apparently many of the occupants in nearby buildings closed and locked all their rear doors when the shooting started.

Regaining composure, the police returned fire. Perez opened up wildly on them as he raced for another door, assailed by a withering fusillade from the police. One deputy on each side of the buildings fired shotguns that spread projectiles choked to cover an area too wide to miss.

The acrid smell of cordite hung like a suffocating mist over the area. Perez jerked and twitched before falling back against the building. Propped there and bleeding, he aimed his revolver at the police. But he'd spent all his bullets. Unaware of that, the police deluged him with their salvos.

The fugitive jerked backwards to bounce off the building, then toppled onto the dusty roadway. The police rushed to him and kicked away his weapon. One of them knelt at his side and put a finger on his neck, then shook his head when he felt no pulse.

TWENTY-SIX

Bravo and Olecki, along with Mac and Mac, questioned the workers from all of the shops, including the one Perez had worked in. None of those people apparently knew him all that well and hadn't a clue as to why he resisted. The boss of the shop he'd worked in commented that he might be loco. Two of his workers nodded agreement.

Other police searched the warehouse but found nothing that could be classified as contraband or illegal. The FBI agents and Pedrazo poked around as much as legally acceptable in the cars and trucks parked helter-skelter in the area. Workers emerged from surrounding factories and warehouses to object to the search of their vehicles. Fearing retribution if they declined to cooperate some submitted to an examination of their cars and trucks, as well as their persons.

McGee and Maguire inquired of regions of origin from all of the Hispanic workers, but encountered only three other Puerto Ricans. Those three adamantly denied involvement with radicals. And none of the many questioned were aware of a green pick-up truck with a cracked windshield.

The cops decided not to waste time with Salvadorans, Hondurans, and Dominicans, as well as Nicaraguans, Colombians, Guatemalans, and Mexicans, aware that those people formed groups with their own nationals and weren't disposed toward the political participation of the others. As a matter of fact, most immigrants from those countries distanced themselves from the politics of the countries they'd left, making every effort to assimilate in their newly adopted nation.

An emergency squad ambulance arrived with siren screaming. A moment later the morgue wagon pulled up. None of the factory and warehouse workers or any of the law enforcement people had sustained injury so didn't need treatment, though a few shook their heads to dispel residual trauma. The fugitive had passed the need for medical attention, so the two morgue attendants zipped him up in a black bag and thrust him into their wagon. The police concurred that continued rummaging was futile since they hadn't uncovered anything incriminating. Most of the deputies returned to their cruisers and regular duties.

"Now I gotta' submit one long-assed report detailing everything transpired," Olecki complained. "Could take a damn hour or more."

"Think you can convince the sheriff's department to assign people to stake out the house of Perez?" Bravo asked. "His wife likely will have a wake and a funereal. Other Independistas might attend, giving us a line on this guy's cohorts."

"Good thinking. My guys will likely cooperate but will want the cost reimbursed, or at least shared."

"I'll impose on the FBI or the US Attorney's office for that. When it comes to budgets my bureau squeaks."

Heading back to their car, Bravo passed a dazed-looking Danly Coombs. When asked if he was alright Coombs nodded while exhaling a deep breath. "Never been anywhere near anything like that before—with a barrage of bullets whizzing past my head. Looking back, I wonder what would happen to my wife and daughter had I been killed."

"I understand, buddy. Legal beagles don't usually experience something like that. Sorry I got you involved."

"Got a new respect for y'all . . . for how you earn your pay."

"Incidentally, where the hell were you two that you arrived so late?"

Coombs averted his eyes and flailed his hands. "Thank God we received that call. Was the only thing kept that horny broad from climbing all over me."

Bravo guffawed.

"Not funny, man. That gal is a predator. Had to yell at her to get her concentration back on the job and respond to the call. Never before came so close to getting raped."

Bravo related that to Olecki and neither could stop laughing as they strode to their car. It felt good to relieve pent-up emotion.

After returning to their headquarters building Bravo dropped into an empty office, but not Maylene's. He preferred not having her happening in on him and taunting him about his lack of success with his marital problems.

Aware of the time as five-thirty, he nevertheless called Yzabel's office since she often worked late. She and Fabienne Argonne were two ambitious people who'd established a successful business by determined application. The voice on the answering machine advised that the office hours were from 9:00 AM to 5:00 PM. If the caller wished to leave a message, please do so after the tone.

Jiggling the hook flash, he called their home, but the phone droned monotonously four times before that goddam answering machine responded. No, he didn't want to talk to that either, so hung up.

Where in hell was Yzabel? And why wasn't she at the office or at home? Screw it! He refused to concern himself with whether it disturbed her during a meeting, and dialed her cellphone, but got the voice mail. He spurned leaving a message. Could she possibly be in transit, maybe stopped to shop? Voices sniggered in the recesses of his mind, where the name Nando reverberated.

Abandoning that quest he joined the others in the conference room and grimaced when invited to go with the bunch for drinks. About to decline, he reconsidered, deciding he gained more by being one of the boys rather than aloof and antisocial, especially after that scary escapade. And no question he needed to blow off steam as much as they did.

He'd long ago accepted that until residual fear fades into remote cortical fibers of memory it keeps law enforcement officers hyper . . . for hours, even days. No matter how they try to shut their minds to it, they relive the stunning events again and again—shivering whenever they recalled those incidents all too vividly. The military referred to it as PTSD . . . Post-Traumatic Stress Disorder.

Programmed by intensive training, the police like the military generally performed fearlessly under fire. However, the brain persists in reminding how close someone skirted injury or death. Post-traumatic Stress Disorder affects cops just as it does combat soldiers. Most apply effort not to expose the lingering fear they must overcome before he or she can again make that split-second decision to put themselves in harm's way.

Also, having survived, and with the immediacy of peril diminished, they experience remorse if they'd killed a human being . . . wasted a bad guy . . . an *estúpido* in the recent case. Why in hell had the dumb bastard left them without alternatives? He had to know he'd end up dead if he turned his gun on them. Why did he make them all go to the brink of sanity, especially since they'd only wanted to question him—had nothing to charge him with?

Had terrorist credo been so deeply ingrained in fanatics like Perez that they sacrificed their lives by resisting to the death? Or had that lobo been fearful of being associated with crimes he'd committed, unaware he was only sought for questioning?

Yes, and it riled Bravo when after the shooting some of those from nearby shops criticized the use of extreme force. How would they react if their lives were threatened? Would they still be bleeding hearts if the police arrived to curtail bullets assailing them?

Okay, breathe deeply to evacuate the anger and the misgivings, especially the residual fear. He tried to grin, only managed to sigh as the booze nipped his tongue, warmed his throat, and expanded within him. The mellowing effects permeated his being, with that loud country music of Murphy's Saloon throbbing in his ears. It made him want to dance and romp, exhaust himself in a sexual tangle.

His eyes lingered on Maylene and the goodies he knew resided below the conservative folds of that dark green suit with a white blouse buttoned to the neck. Of all the women he had known in his life—white, black, blue, or green—none of them exuded sensuality like this gal.

But he had reservations about anyone learning that he letched for her. He had enough problems with the FBI agents resenting his command position, and didn't need Archison lecturing him on the negative aspects of office romances. Puerto Rican pride insisted he be seen as ethical. So he determined to avoid public awareness of anything that questioned his status as the taskforce leader.

It made him chuckle when he considered that despite having bounced around in bed with Maylene only two nights ago he yearned for her like he'd never had her. Funny, that's how it had been in Atlanta, and the reason he resolved not to respond to her telephone calls, e-mails and snail-mail after being whisked off to Kansas City. He'd realized he'd been infatuated and needed to prevent the blossoming of an all-consuming craving for that ecstasy. He had an obligation to maintain a stable family for his kids to grow up in, and refused to waver from preserving his marriage.

Many times through the years he'd rejected the alternative of divorce because of his kids. Yes, being catholic also influenced his thinking. But his and Yzabel's problems had intensified beyond anything experienced hitherto, amplifying doubts of resolving them this time. Thankfully the boys had matured to where they can understand. Last thing he wanted was to alienate them.

And there hadn't been a Nando during past rough patches . . . to his knowledge!

"You left that bucar at the garage and came here in mine." Olecki said. His voice jolted Bravo back to the hilarity of the barroom. "Time for me to get home to my family. You want, I'll drop you off at the garage or at your motel. Or you can get a lift from one of those boozers."

Bravo wavered, reluctant to leave Maylene, but concerned that any sign of yearning might start tongues wagging.

"Cleo will be willing as hell," Olecki said, "to get you into her car."

"I'll go with you," Bravo said. "Fact is, I really don't need to toss down any more booze." He and Olecki waved as they yelled to be heard over the blaring music and the merriment of their leave-taking to the others,. Yes, he accepted that as his best course, because the more he drank the more he'd letch for Maylene. Hell, he could end up in a mooning contest with Boisey Epps.

Poor sap. For a reasonably bright guy Epps couldn't accept that he didn't have a chance in hell with Maylene. Doubt it was his marital status turning her off, considering Bravo being married didn't deter her from trysting with him. Okay, she knew the shaky nature of his marital situation. What difference did it make anyway?

While driving away Olecki jerked him out of his introspection by asking if he'd take dinner at his house. Bravo bobbed his head about, ready to demur. If he had his druthers he'd opt to spend the evening with Maylene. But he didn't know how long she'd celebrate with the guys and what time she'd get home. They hadn't discussed getting together.

"It'll be the first time either of my wives cooked for and served an Hispanic," Olecki said, chuckling.

"You saying that's a problem in your house?"

"Hell no. Just fooling around. Never ever heard Stephi demean anybody's ethnic background and like that. Fact is, there's two black couples we socialize with every once in a while. And we raised the kids to get along with everybody in school no matter what their race. They bring home friends of every kind of color, even children of those immigrant Mexicans and such."

"Sounds real nice. Yeah, I'd like to meet your wife and the kids."

"Great." Olecki called home on his cellphone and prepared his wife for a visitor. "See you in a little," he told her and clicked off.

After a block or so he turned to Bravo. "Is there a lot of political activism among Puerto Rican folks?"

"Not among those born here on the mainland, being as their destiny is tied to the same wagon as yours. But those in Puerto Rico as well as those who migrated here are political because it's heaped on them every day."

"With respect, I suppose, to the future of Puerto Rico."

"Survival with the local economy being what it is, which is abysmal at best."

"That'll make anybody political. But why do some go off the deep end and take the road to revolution?"

"Actually, the majority prefers continuance of the commonwealth status since it's easier to deal with familiar things than to grope around in change. Quite a few, however, would like Puerto Rico to become the fifty-first state. Both of those groups differ with the extremists who want independence from uncle."

"Where are you on that?"

"Pragmatically I see Puerto Rico benefiting most from commonwealth status. But my pride makes me wish the island becomes a state, an integral part of the United States of America."

"I got no problem with any of those choices," Olecki said. "However, I'm committed to preventing madmen of any affiliation from wreaking havoc. Believe that I'm ready and willing to come down hard on every skel threatens this community."

"Count me in, buddy. We're both on the same page when it comes to taking criminals off the streets. While I grant the pro-independence people their right to political aspirations I don't condone outrageous acts to promote their cause."

TWENTY-SEVEN

Bravo thanked Olecki for that enjoyable evening with a really tasty dinner as he climbed out of the car at his motel. Entering his room Bravo hung up his suit jacket and slipped off his necktie before sitting on the bed. Then he stared at the phone for long minutes before dialing Yzabel. But he got the machine, which ate his gut that the thing informed him that no one was available to receive his call, but at the tone. . . .

Screw her. Let her romp in the sack with that Spanish Lothario. She'd get her serving of pain when the libertine dumped her, as he probably had before, and returned to Spain. Then let her beg to be taken back. No way. No fucking way! She wanted to stray, let her fucking stray. Damned if he couldn't stray as well, so picked up the phone and dialed.

"Maylene? Wondered if you'd be home yet? Well, you might still be hanging out at that bar. Me? Yeah, I had dinner with Olecki and his family. He just dropped me off. Sure, we can get together tonight but I don't have a car. Left it at the office—rode with Olecki. Sure, come on over."

# # #

Emerging from the tunnel of sleep Bravo peeked at the clock, wasn't surprised to see the time since he awoke by rote at six. Sensing something out of the ordinary he frowned while searching around. It took a nanosecond to realize Maylene's head was not on the pillow next to him. He climbed out of bed, expecting to find her in the bathroom, the door of which stood ajar.

Shit! He realized that none of her clothing remained. Exhaling his disappointment, he accepted she'd gone home. Okay, she'd clawed her way up the ladder to enjoy that level of luxury, and refused to retrogress . . . even overnight.

Conceding her right to her pride he shrugged off that disappointment and called Olecki's cellphone to remind that man that he had no car. Olecki assured him he'd pick him up within the hour. Flicking the hook-switch, Bravo dialed his home. He really wasn't that anxious to speak to Yzabel, but something deep inside needed to know that she would be home at that hour of the morning, had not stayed out all night. He refused to dote on where or with whom.

"Hello." Her sleepy voice cracked with the waking-up process.
"It's me. Needed to see how everything was."
"Or are you checking to see whether I shacked up with Nando."
"Hey, I didn't say that."
"Deny that's why you called."
"I called to speak to my wife."
"Okay, you're speaking to her. What is it you want?"
"You're making me sorry I called."
"If you have nothing important to say, I need another hour of sleep before having to get ready for work."

Ray sputtered, unsure how to respond, then winced when he heard the click.

Sonofabitch! But at least she hadn't spent the night with Nando. Actually, how would he know that? She could have screwed that Catalonian bastard and then gone home . . . or the hump could be in the bed beside her while she spoke to him.

Goddammit, he needed to have better answers, needed to know if he could salvage his marriage. But did he want to if she was screwing that Iberian hump? It wasn't for the boys any longer. They were mature enough to be informed of their parents' deteriorating relationship. Broken families weren't unusual these days.

Okay, her behavior justified his having an affair with Maylene. But how would the boys accept his alliance with the black woman. He recalled incidents when one or the other of them indicated displeasure with African-Americans. They weren't expressing bias, just indicating their awareness of racial differences. And on occasion those encounters hadn't encouraged fraternal sentiments, in spite of his teaching them to treat everyone on an individual basis without regard to race, creed or gender.

Back in high school Romero complained about the black bullies in his classes, bussed in from the ghetto, who picked on him and a few of the others—with impunity. Why, the boy entreated, do the teachers make excuses for them and pussyfoot around at chastising those ruffians?

Yzabel had the deepest-rooted aversion to blacks, which resulted from an incident one night when Ray was in Omaha on a case. She'd awakened during the night to a noise in their apartment in a midrise building in Georgetown. When she switched on the nighttable-lamp, she saw a hulking black intruder at the foot of her bed. Her breath caught when she realized he'd removed his pants and stood there with a throbbing erection.

She started to scream, but remembered the boys and didn't want them rushing into the room. They were only ten and seven then and she feared endangering them. But he frightened her when he moved toward her and ordered her to *cop his dick*. She gagged, all but puked, at the thought of that thing entering her mouth.

Bolting upright, she grabbed the clock on the nighttable and flung it at him. The sight of the missile headed toward his genitals impelled him to recoil and cover them. But its cord prevented it from hitting him. In that instant she scrambled across the bed and jumped out the other side. Having recovered from flinching from the thrown missile that dropped harmlessly to the floor he grinned as he shuffled around the bed to box her.

Denied any escape, she grabbed a ladderback chair, but realized the futility of using it against that brute, so threw it at the window. The shattering glass froze him in place. A yell from outside spurred him to grab his pants off the floor and flee. She ran to the phone and dialed 911.

The police responded, but didn't find the intruder. However, they reassured her they'd stake out the building. It took months for her to feel safe at night, even with Ray there with her.

He took her to a psychologist to deal with the trauma. Once the shrink had primed her to talk about it, she gushed out descriptions. Ray remembered the vitriol in her voice when she referred to what she characterized as animals that lacked respect for people. They rape and kill, steal and despoil, victimizing their own people as well as everyone else. Thank God, she uttered, our families are not contaminated with their accursed blood like many Latinos Criollos.

TWENTY-EIGHT

Bravo climbed out of the bucar in the sixth-floor garage to trod with head bowed, having suffered two more frustrating days of failing to make any headway in learning the whereabouts of those stolen weapons and explosives. He worried that his lack of success induce Archison to change taskforce leadership.

Hell, he didn't even know if those weapons and explosives remained in the area or had been transported on America's wide-open highways to Washington or somewhere. Damn right he knew he'd be considered at fault if they caused havoc somewhere. It would wound his pride to be demoted in the presence of those gringos.

Entering the conference room he encountered sheriff's deputies McGee and Maguire sipping coffee and chatting with Olecki and Cleo. Both wore chino slacks and polo shirts, their gunbelts exposed, complete with thirty pounds of equipment.

"Yep," McGee responded to Bravo's question, "we pulled stakeout duty at the wake and funereal of that Lopez guy what got his ass shot off. More than a dozen people paid their respects."

Other staff-members ambled in and became attentive to McGee reporting that they'd picked up on two could-be extremists. A few still need to be investigated, but two stood out, with long yellow sheets. Maguire dropped two mug-shots on the table while announcing that Emillano Veracruz and Sebastiano Melendez were the center of attention. Everybody buzzed around and sucked up to them like they were the goombahs of the Puerto Rican mafia.

Bravo nodded as he poured coffee into a Styrofoam cup. "Any chance Abdulo was there?"

"Nobody resembled that photograph," Maguire said.

"Not that the thing is clear enough," McGee said, "to match anyone to."

"You'd have known if Abdulo showed," Baggler said, "with folks flocking to him like flies to a dung hill."

"Kissing his ring," Epps quipped. "Hear what—?"

"I take it you didn't pick up those two who stood out," Bravo said to McGee.

"We didn't want to blow the surveillance," McGee said, "by busting folks."

"Besides," Maguire said, "swilling liquor and stuffing your face at a wake ain't illegal last time I looked, so don't serve as probable cause."

"Got any idea where to find them?" Olecki asked.

"No," Maguire said, "but we've distributed those photos among county and city cops to keep an eye out for them and to report any sightings."

"Like as not," Olecki said, "we'll find them in those same grungy warehouses where we took down Lopez."

"Be real nice," Cleo said, "if we run into them and recover those guns and explosives before they get to using that stuff to terrorize folks."

"Pass out those mug-shots to my guys," Bravo said, "and we'll get back out there and sweep those neighborhoods. What are you two guys up to today?"

"We're yours, you want us," McGee said as he hitched up his gunbelt.

"Hell yeah! That'll give us one more team out there. Okay folks, we're going hunting again. Coombs, you still with us?"

When that man nodded assurance Epps addressed Maylene: "You need to come out with us, to get you some street smarts."

She glanced side-eyed at him and sucked her teeth before turning away.

"It might teach you to be less conceited," Epps said.

"What is your problem?" she snapped at him.

"Okay, people," Bravo cut in. "Let's hit the streets and find those two mooks, with the hope that they'll lead us to other terrorists and that cache."

While the others quipped, quibbled and taunted each other en route to the garage, Danly Coombs sidled up to Bravo and whispered: "Any chance I can be reassigned to a different partner."

Bravo chuckled as he remembered the guy's complaint of the day before and put Coombs with Olecki. As a consequence, Bravo had to partner up with Cleo, and they rode in the borrowed bucar.

"What'd he say about me?" Cleo asked as they turned onto Broward Boulevard.

"I put the tenderfoot with an experienced cop for his own protection," Bravo said. Then he grimaced, knowing that lame excuse wouldn't appease her.

"I'm not experienced?"

Breathing deeply, he said: "More than most I know." Squirming while anticipating her angry retort he added: "It's just that I didn't want him to feel like he was mothered."

"Why you bullshitting me?"

"Let's concentrate on our mission, not on peripheral matters. You're one of the most dependable cops on this taskforce and I want you focused on catching mooks."

He drove east on Broward Boulevard to Federal Highway and then north to Oakland Park Boulevard. And he silently thanked an unnamed deity that she didn't continue that contentious discussion. Turning east after crossing the railroad tracks, he swung north onto Dixie Highway.

"We keep on going east," Cleo said, "we'll get us down to the beach."

"Doubt we'd find terrorists tanning themselves by the ocean," Bravo said.

"They just might you know. Folks take a break now and again to give themselves some recreation."

"Next thing you'll say you brought a bathing suit."

"Spot I know, darlin', don't need none."

"I'd rather not know about it."

"You see me naked you won't turn me away."

"Are you forgetting why we're out here?"

"I'm suggesting a tumble in the hay wouldn't be all that bad for either of us. Take the edge off."

"Forget it, Cleo. That's not why I'm out here. And I'd appreciate your not coming onto me again."

"Don't tell me you're not horny after being away from home all these weeks? And don't tell me you're so married you don't never have yourself a little side action."

"I'm telling you I don't have sex with partners."

"Lord, you are sticky."

He scanned the buildings they passed, to avert his eyes for fear that they'd glint with guilt for trysting with Maylene . . . expose him as a hypocrite.

Both focused on dusty streets separating small warehouses and factories. Cars and trucks parked helter-skelter narrowed those passages. Many of the workers in dirt-streaked and sweaty clothing looked Hispanic, but weren't distinguishable as Puerto Ricans as opposed to other Latinos. Despite careful scrutiny for two hours of cruising they saw nothing to construe as probable cause allowing them to examine in an invasive way.

TWENTY-NINE

Bravo stifled yawning to conceal boredom from endless combing of the area without success. He perked when Cleo's radio crackled, followed by an excited voice: "Think we spotted that green pick-up truck."

"Sounds like McGee," she said breathlessly

"Find out where," Bravo said—sucking in anticipation.

"Location," Cleo demanded into the radio.

"Northeast Forty-Second Street north of Dixie Highway near Northeast Eighth Avenue. Behind a chainlink fence and piles of cartons and crates."

Bravo wheeled a wide u-turn, having to maneuver around and between parked vehicles, then revved it up. Meanwhile Cleo got on her cellphone to alert the others. Within minutes Cleo pointed out the dirt-streaked pick-up truck of Mac and Mac, which they'd used in the stake-out of the Lopez wake so as not to attract attention.

When Bravo pulled alongside them the two deputies directed his attention to the jumbled stacks of crates beyond which the green pick-up truck was barely visible. "We been waiting for back-up before approaching it," Maguire said.

Sounds of industry emanated from beyond the fence and the weathered building, distinctive in that neighborhood since it wasn't connected to any other structures. Bravo gritted his teeth at his inability to see enough of that vehicle to confirm that it fit the description of the one they sought . . . not that they had specifics to guide them.

A few moments later Olecki pulled into the street with his Chevy Impala, its windshield replaced. He and Coombs joined the others in taking positions that allowed them to spot anyone who tried to flee from the tumbledown workshop. The two Macs and Bravo cautiously approached debris piled around the green pick-up truck. Cleo stood behind the bucar with her Glock semi-automatic pistol trained on the building entrance. Olecki and Coombs, with guns drawn, sneaked along the side of the building to cover the rear.

Two other cars pulled up and the FBI men along with Pedrazo poured out to bolster the ring of police in surrounding the building. Maguire pointed to the spidery crack in the upper right corner of the windshield, then climbed onto the jumble of crates to wiggle deep enough into them to ascertain that it had no front bumper.

"Hey!" an irate voice called from the doorway of the factory. "Why you poke around in that boxes?"

The law enforcement people aimed their pistols at the belligerent man in sweat-stained and dirt-streaked undershirt.

"Don't move!" Cleo shouted to him.

"Hands on your head!" Loscalzo yelled.

The surprised look on the man's face obviated his not having seen the police surrounding the building. Nor had he identified those rooting around in the jumble of boxes and crates as police. None of the police wore uniforms and none of their vehicles were marked. He probably hadn't heard them arrive because of industrial noises.

"Step into the open," Cleo yelled to him.

The man postured stubbornly while remaining half in and half out of the overhead doorway, scowling as he rubbed his unshaven face. "Who the hell you are?"

"Police," Cleo replied, holding up her badge.

The guy sneered his contempt. "Why you poking there?"

McGee leaned toward Bravo and whispered: "He's the one called Melendez we told you about."

"You own this truck?" Bravo called to the guy.

"Truck? What truck?"

"This damned truck," McGee said, slapping his palm on its cab roof while teetering on cartons in its bed.

The man shrugged. "Never saw that thing before. People in this place, they park all over."

"That's not parked," McGee retorted. "It's hidden."

"Took effort to pile all those crates around it," Cleo added. "Now get your ass out here 'fore I put a bullet in it."

The guy shrugged again, posturing bravado while shuffling into the open.

"What's your name?" Bravo asked.

"Melendez," he answered, glowering defiantly at them. "Sebastiano Melendez."

"Turn around and put your hands behind your head," Bravo said.

"Why for?" he retorted defiantly.

"Because," Cleo barked at him, "we told you to."

Bravo and the two sheriff's deputies sidled toward Melendez, their pistols at the ready, alert for danger—especially from inside the building.

When the guy obeyed, while continuing to glare at them, Maguire cuffed him.

"You can no arrest me for work here."

"You have ID?" McGee asked.

The man jerked his head to indicate he kept it inside the building. Mac and Mac went in, flashing their badges at three workers, and asked which jacket belonged to Sebastiano Melendez. When one of the workers pointed to it, Maguire searched it and removed a wallet. Then they directed the other workers to present identification.

Cleo informed Olecki by radio what was transpiring, then called in for a flatbed truck to take the pick-up truck into the police garage. Meanwhile McGee ran all the names through the laptop in his pick-up truck. He smiled triumphantly as he approached Bravo. "This Melendez guy and one more is out on parole." He tapped the photo with the name printed on it.

"Which one of you is Emillano Veracruz?" Bravo yelled into the warehouse.

A tall, skinny man in a tee shirt bolted for the back door. Mac and Mac gave chase. The man pushed through the rear door to stare into the muzzles of the pistols of Olecki, Coombs, Baggler and Loscalzo. They'd been alerted by cellphone to expect him. The would-be fugitive meekly surrendered. They handcuffed him and brought him out front, where he and chunky Melendez scowled at their captors.

"This vehicle proves to be the one we're looking for," Olecki said, "you two are going to be in a world of hurt."

"How that can be?" Melendez asked. "We no break law."

"How 'bout parole violations?" McGee asked.

"We do nothing to violate parole," Veracruz said, his voice and attitude as surly as that of Melendez.

"Except you're in possession of a truck connected to that raid on the airport," Olecki said. "Your testy asses going to face murder charges."

Melendez continued to sneer. "Who we murder?"

"That no we truck," Veracruz said, also scowling. "You have nothing on we."

"We lift your fingerprints out of that truck," Bravo said, "we'll damn sure connect you two *malhechores* to terrorism and murder."

Melendez sneered at their being referred to as *malefactors*.

"Plus murdering your old buddy, Elizondo," Cleo added.

"As well as two US marshals and a deputy assistant US attorney," Olecki added.

"You never prove we do that," Veracruz said.

"We do if we find your prints in that truck," Olecki said.

"*A veces*—sometimes—we sit in cars and trucks around here to eat lunch because is too hot in *chabola*," Melendez said. He gestured to the building he referred to as a shanty. "That why we fingerprint they can be in many vehiculos. We no break law."

"We'll decide that," Olecki said. "When we do, your asses going to be headed for a maximum security prison to wait for that needle to get stuck up your asses."

"We do nothing," Veracruz said. "We innocence."

"What country y'all from?" Cleo asked.

"This one," Melendez answered in his surly manner.

"You were born here," Maguire asked, "and speak with that much accent?"

"I am born in San Juan in Puerto Rico," Veracruz said. "Where you born?"

"We ask the damn questions," Olecki said. "You damn well answer them."

"How 'bout you?" Maguire asked Melendez. "You have you a green card?"

"No need green card," Veracruz snarled. "I am born in Ponce in Puerto Rico and have right for live here."

"Then act like a good American," McGee said, "by telling us how that damn truck got there."

Veracruz shrugged. "We have no information for give."

"On your way to the lock-up," Bravo said, "you'd better think about the benefit derived from cooperation."

THIRTY

Olecki instructed sheriff department deputies to take the prisoners to the county jail in separate cruisers and to request the jailers to keep them apart to deny them conferring. Then he joined McGee in wriggling down among the crates and empty cartons to search the truck bed. They rifled through paper and plastic bags, as well as discarded fast-food wrappers and other debris. Two others searched the cab.

Some of the law enforcement people combed the small warehouse-factory while others interviewed workers. But no one uncovered anything incriminating, rankling Bravo to have nothing to use as evidence against Melendez and Veracruz. Still, he continued to question curious workers who wandered over from nearby buildings. No one admitted knowing anything, and a follow-up search of the shack-like workshop turned up nothing to substantiate charges against the two they'd taken into custody. But undeterred, the lawmen went through the building again.

After half an hour McGee wandered to the door to catch a breeze to relieve the stifling of dark, dank and airless indoors. "Hey!" he yelled, "somebody's stealing that truck."

Bravo and Olecki raced to the doorway, along with Maguire to gawk at two heads in the truck, barely visible behind the piled crates. They heard its motor grinding.

McGee bolted toward it, yelling: "Hey! Whatta' you think you're doing?"

A stream of bullets from the truck stimulated him to dive behind one of the haphazardly parked cars. That barrage of machine gun fire induced the others to duck inside the door or behind vehicles, crates, barrels, or whatever cover they found. Cleo hunkered inside the doorjamb, clutching her pistol while seeking a target. Pedrazo and the three FBI agents hugged the sides of the building. Most of the uniformed deputies had already left the area.

Olecki, and Maguire scampered to positions from which to return fire. Bravo ducked behind a car parked close to the target truck, aware that one of those yahoos sprayed them with bursts from a TEC-9 machinegun pistol. Piles of cartons and boxes denied the police a target to return fire at the green pick-up.

The crates and boxes surrounding the truck tumbled away as its tires clawed at the loose soil and sand. The dirt-streaked truck with its motor roaring darted among the haphazardly parked vehicles which shielded it from police firepower as it sped away. Bravo glimpsed a male and female, both with ponytails, though the woman's was bushier and longer than the man's. The guy sported a Fu Manchu mustache.

Yelling to each other, the law enforcement people scrambled to their vehicles to pursue. By the time they got onto the roadway the fugitive truck had disappeared—frustrating them. Olecki yelled into his radio for everyone to spread out and assigned each areas in different directions to search. Coombs contacted everyone on the taskforce by cellphone to inform them of Olecki's intent.

Then Olecki called for back-up and a helicopter, shouting the description and probable location of the hunted vehicle, as well as the imperative to locate it. All the while he wheeled his car up and down the roads between warehouse-factories, narrowed by haphazardly parked vehicles.

Bravo darted up and down other streets narrowed by recklessly parked vehicles while he and Cleo scanned for a sign of the quarry. He grated from pending failure after getting so close. Damned if he didn't need to corral that truck, a definite connection to the extremists. He needed to wallow in the pride of clearing this case.

"Got him!" came over the radio. The excited voice gave the location where he'd spotted the green pick-up. All pursuers converged on the area. But the fugitive sped at full-tilt into the open garage door of a warehouse, scattering workers as it knocked over benches and crates before crashing through the rear entrance, splintering the narrow door and jamb and crumbling surrounding blocks. Then it disappeared before the police circled the warehouse—hesitant to pursue through the building and further damage private property—possibly injuring civilians.

They spread out again, with lights flashing and sirens screaming, combing the roads and yards and storage sheds. Additional cruisers joined the pursuit, to be directed by Olecki in attempting to block off escape routes. A sheriff's department helicopter arrived to circle overhead with its turbine-driven rotors grinding. Olecki contacted it, but received no promising information.

"There it is!" someone yelled into the radio. "Headed for the alley behind buildings off Twenty-first and Fifty-sixth!" Bravo spun his car around on the gravelly roadway and headed in a direction he hoped would cut them off. The helicopter announced that they had the culprit in sight. When they gave the coordinates all cars converged on it.

"They're in a dead-end!" someone yelled, shouting the location. "Hurry and help us bottle them!"

All of the cars raced to barricade the green pick-up truck hemmed in between buildings and a tall chain-link fence topped with razor wire. Two cruisers screeched up to a hundred feet beyond the far side of that fence, to deny the fugitives escaping by bursting through that stout wire barrier. The man and woman scrambled out of the target truck to squat behind their vehicle and spray bullets that held the cops at bay.

The police returned fire, ripping the truck apart with pistol, rifle and shotgun fire. The woman rose to her knee and fired repeatedly to cover her cohort who spurted toward an entrance to one of the buildings, his braid flopping behind him. He tugged at the door, which refused to yield. Spinning around, he fired at the police, who rained salvos on him. Bullets tore into his body, knocking him backwards until he collapsed. Then they fired at the woman.

A bullet tore through her shoulder, knocking her backwards. Her weapon tumbled to the asphalt. The police rushed up to her and stomped on the machinegun pistol to deny her regaining possession of it. Others flipped her over onto her stomach and cuffed her hands behind her, unmindful of her shrieks of pain and angry curses.

Other police hurried to her cohort and declared him dead. They exhibited no sympathy for the woman they roughly shoved into the back of one of their cruisers. "Take her to the lock-up," Olecki directed. "They can treat her wound there."

"Shouldn't she be taken to a hospital?" Danly Coombs asked.

"We'd need to secure the hospital first," Bravo replied. "No telling how many more of these wild-heads will come out of the woodwork. We can't put those people in the hospital at risk."

He glanced at her slumped in the back seat of a cruiser, surprised that he found her comely in spite of her scowl and her disheveled hair braided into a bushy pony tail.

"Wouldn't put it past those lobos," McGee said, "to stage a raid to free her."

"Putting the hospital at risk," Cleo added, "along with everyone in it."

"Reason we need to put her ass in a secure place," Olecki said, "and bring medical attention to her."

THIRTY-ONE

Bravo nodded, as did other taskforce members to Baggler's grouchy remark: "Wildass som'bitches." They leaned against their cars breathing heavily to evacuate the hypertension while waiting for the flatbed truck to take away the green pick-up truck. Most shook their heads in disbelief as they watched the cruiser leave with the female prisoner, then the morgue wagon haul away her dead partner in a body bag.

"Brainless," Loscalzo said. His receding panting indicated he was recovering from that reckless chase and scary shoot-out.

"Anybody else wonder why they did something that dumb?" Bravo asked as he scratched his head and searched the faces of those around him.

"That wreck sure ain't worth dying for," McGee said.

They stared at each other, with one after the other's eyes sparking revelations. Almost in a single motion all approached the truck to probe in different parts of the vehicle. Some popped the hood while others pulled apart the door panels. Bravo and Olecki explored its underside.

Maguire ambled to the back and dropped the cargo-bed hatch. He and McGee climbed in and pushed out the remaining empty crates and cartons.

"Hey!" McGee yelled. "Thing's got a false bottom."

Everyone probed the floor panel, searching for a way to open it. McGee succeeded in finding a concealed handle and pulled it up. And they gawked at sixteen sections of bangalore torpedoes, packed long-ways, along with a radio-controlled remote activation device.

"Holy shit!" Olecki said. "One bullet could have blown this thing sky-high."

"They tried to pull off that desperate stunt," Bravo said, "to retain this stuff."

"To make a statement by blowing up a building," Olecki said. "Damn good thing we recovered it."

"Too bad it's not big enough to hold all those carbines and ammo," Epps said. "Hear what—"

"We found these," Loscalzo said. "Ought to be able to find the other stuff."

"Damn sure better," Cleo said, "before those wildasses shoot up this town."

# # #

Bravo poured a coffee for Olecki when that man strode into the conference room to report that the two wise guys taken into custody had been deposited in separate cells. The woman had been placed in the prison hospital under guard. The three FBI agents and Pedrazo, along with Danly Coombs and Cleo, ambled in to join them, closely followed by Archison, and Maylene Brown.

"Just got off the phone with the lieutenant who heads up the gang squad in Chicago," Loscalzo said. "He identified the woman by her description as one of the queen bees of the Macheteros, a group of Puerto Rican extremists and gangbangers."

"Macheteros are not all gangbangers," Bravo said.

"Hell they're not!" erupted from Baggler. "They're trying to overthrow the government."

"Many legitimate political activists advocate independence for Puerto Rico," Bravo said.

"Anyway" Loscalzo said, "she is known as María Blanquita. But the lieutenant warned that it might not be her real name, as many gangbangers adopt monikers to sound like rock or movie stars."

"Not surprised," Bravo said. "More than a few Puerto Ricans born on the island don't have birth certificates, don't need passports because they, like other Americans, aren't required to carry that identification. Consequently they don't need green cards and they can obtain as many social security numbers as they apply for, using a different name each time."

"Which makes that wild'o gal a damn mystery," Baggler said.

"From everything the police know about her," Loscalzo said, "they estimate her age as about thirty. Said they believe she was born in a dismal slum of San Juan, in Puerto Rico, and is believed to have two brothers serving time there. They have limited information regarding her parents, both of whom are believed dead."

"Another damn ghost infiltrating society," Olecki said.

"They said she fled indictment in a gang killing in San Juan when sixteen," Loscalzo continued, "along with her twenty-something boyfriend. They're believed to have ended up in the barrios of New York, where they immersed themselves in gang activities."

"Not no whole lot different than a bunch of runaways," Cleo said.

"Two years later," Loscalzo went on, "the New York City Police arrested that boyfriend for holding up a convenience store. She slipped away—to Chicago they believe, where she ran with the gangs."

"Predictable," came from Maylene Brown.

"A year or so later," Loscalzo continued, "the Chicago police arrested her and a few other members of the Macheteros for armed robbery. She did six of ten. They believe that after her release, a few months ago, she joined the gang run by Abdulo."

"Why doesn't that surprise me?" Cleo asked.

"Confidential informants of the Chicago police," Loscalzo said, "say that Abdulo really fell for her."

"Think we'll get her to tell us where to find that Abdulo?" Maylene asked.

"Doubtful," Loscalzo said. "According to Chicago police she's harder than nails and less likely to cave than any guy."

"Any info about the mook was with her?" Bravo asked.

"Not much," Loscalzo replied. "They say the description sounds like a lobo called Pancho."

"At least we've succeeded in recovering those explosives," Archison said. "Kudos to Bravo."

"Stumbled on them," Baggler commented, sneering.

"Even blind squirrels find them some acorns now and again," Boisey Epps added, also snickering. "Hear what—"

"Still got those carbines out there," Olecki said, "with a slew of pistols."

"And enough damn ammo," Cleo added, "to shoot up South Florida."

"Job isn't done," Baggler said, "by no long shot. Don't rest on your—"

"Damn dumb when you think about it," Epps said. When puzzled faces turned to him, he explained: "Suckers used that pickup to rob that Amos truck, then took it along when they raided the airfield. In spite of that they stupidly cached explosives in the same damn truck. Had to know we searched for it. Hear what I'm saying?"

Olecki snapped his fingers, revelation brightening his face. "The reason they dodged through town a couple days ago like maniacs when spotted by that cruiser—to avoid being pulled over, searched and busted."

"With those explosives," Cleo added.

"Why in hell didn't they stash them in a more secure place?" Bravo wondered aloud.

"For lack of one," Cleo reasoned.

"Having used all available space for the guns and munitions," Coombs said.

"We've been putting a whole lot more heat on them than they needed," Cleo said. "Don't be surprised if they do something desperate now."

"Making it imperative," Archison said, "to get them off the street—pronto!"

That Spanish word initiated chuckling by all except Baggler, who commented in his surly way: "Only thing we're lacking is direction."

"Let's go over to the jail and interrogate those two hard cases," Bravo said. "They may not be that tough and maybe will aid us in putting an end to this madness." "What if they refuse to talk?" Baggler asked. "You got you some alternatives?"

"We'll go back to pounding the bricks," Bravo said, trying to conceal being nettled by Baggler's criticism, and of his own awareness of being at a dead-end in spite of the day's achievements.

"We beat that rough half a dozen times already," Cleo said.

"Concealment is limitless there," Loscalzo said.

"Sure makes me wonder how they live in that squalor," Baggler said. "And don't nobody tell me they don't have a choice, 'cause everybody's got some kind of damn choice."

"Not true," Cleo said. "Lived in a dismal trailer camp growing up, 'til I got on the cops and earned me enough to move to a decent place."

"I grew up in an urban slum among a bunch of immigrants," Olecki said. "Mostly Pollacks and Ukranians, with a sprinkling of Hunkies. Everybody did the best they could."

"Folks need to live somewhere," Epps said. "Hear—"

"Until they can work their way out," Loscalzo said, "like my grandfather."

"Think case," Archison growled, "not sociology."

"Agreed," Bravo said. "Before we go back to trash-kicking, let's see if we can't get a heads-up from one of those prisoners."

# # #

Bravo trod with slumped shoulders as he led the others out of the interrogation cubicle and into a club room for guards and other prison personnel. All dropped wearily into chairs. Boisey Epps bowed his head in dejection. "Stubborn sucker. Hear what—"

"We have any number of charges against that gal," Archison growled, at Bravo, "but how long do you intend to hold those other two without definitive charges?"

"We tie them to that green pick-up truck," Olecki said, "we can hold them for violating their parole."

"Plus connect them to those terrorists that robbed the airport," Loscalzo said.

"However," Archison said, "without a basis for indictment we need to set them free."

"Last damn thing we can do," Olecki said, his face twisted with angst, "is let them loose to get back with their pack-rats."

"Sure ought to charge them with parole violations," Cleo said, "and ask the court to hold them without bail."

"Ridiculous," Maylene Brown said. "Any lawyer in the county can get those frivolous allegations dismissed."

"The longer we keep them off the streets," Bravo said, "the safer the populace." "I don't like those kinds of tactics." Archison said. "But then, Bravo has a way of distorting the law."

"To break the damn case," Bravo retorted, "and take that so-called red cell off the streets." He choked back adding: *And getting your ass off the hook so they won't deny you that appointment to the next US Attorney's post.*

"Cell?" Baggler scoffed. "We dealing with a bunch of gangbangers. Let's not hang no pretty titles on those lowlifes."

"An FBI agent I worked a case with," Bravo said, "told me that the dedicated agents make the bureau look good by applying themselves to learning as much about the quarry as possible. They never take anything for granted or underrate it and always give the bad guys the credit they're due so they'll understand them and be able to anticipate and outwit them."

"Hey!" Baggler growled. "If that's aimed at me it's a crock. I'm as dedicated as any man in the bureau."

"Let's concentrate on the job," Bravo said. "We need to break those mooks."

"Best way," Olecki suggested, "is we do it in shifts, with two of us at a time grilling each of them, and keeping it up without respite until they're too brain-dead to deny that they're members of that Vasillo Rojo, as well as confessing to associating with known criminals and violating their parole."

"Why not let me and the lady prosecutor lean on that gal?" Cleo asked. "Female to female, we just might have a whole bunch more success than you apes."

"Worth a try," Maylene said.

Bravo hunched concession. "Okay, everybody expect to be here half the night, until we crack one of them."

"My old man is due any time now," Cleo said. "Hope to hell we won't be here too damn late. He's going to be hot to trot."

"You hope," Olecki said. Bravo chuckled with him.

THIRTY-TWO

Bravo yawned as he wheeled the bucar across the intracoastal bridge on Southeast Seventeenth Street, then turned onto A1A, the coast road flanked by impressive apartment buildings and luxury hotels. Profusions of palm trees flanked both sides of the roadway, interspersed with the disc-like leaves of sea grape punctuated by blazing red bougainvillea and the fern-like leaves of poinciana.

Damned if he'd expected to get away so early, having anticipated a long and grueling night with those two hard-cases. But those two wiseguys lawyered up after two hours of stonewalling and reminded their interrogators that they could no longer be questioned. That she-devil gave no hope of cracking. Hell, she even disdained calling a lawyer, seemingly unaffected by detention. She bore her bullet wound like a Spartan warrior.

It baffled Bravo that those two lobos held out and then opted for lawyers at the same time, in spite of having been detained and interrogated separately. Shrewd leadership prompted the name, Galbos, to tumble around in his head. Who was that guy? Having the same family name didn't mean they were related. The preponderance of Latinos had similar names, which influenced the practice of adding the family name of the mother to the father's family name to distinguish which Gonzalez, Perez, or Lopez was referred to: the family of Gonzalez Perez, Gonzalez Lopez, Lopez Perez, or Perez Lopez.

Bravo anguished with the possibility that he and Galbos were related. Believe that it made him squirm. No way did he want to be known as having a familial connection with that mad-ass terrorist . . . a mulatto.

Since he was denied the right to continue questioning those two skels after they asked for lawyers he recalled the taskforce members from the two interrogation rooms. When all agreed to call it a night Pedrazo and the FBI agents concurred to meet at Murphy's on Las Olas Street. Cleo begged off, needing to be home in case Butch showed up, hoping to hell he'd already arrived. Olecki opted to spend that free time with his family.

Bravo sidled over to Maylene, who'd hung around to render legal advice. "I'm going back to the motel to shower," he said. "Then how 'bout I pick you up at your place to go someplace for a late snack?"

The glimmer in her dark eyes was all the answer he needed.

Now he checked for the number to identify her building among the array of luxury digs hugging the coast. Finding the one he sought he parked, then strolled into the sumptuously furnished lobby, whistling his appreciation of it. And his breath caught when he entered her impressively decorated apartment, with a terrace overlooking the blue expanse.

She poured Grand Marnier into two snifters and handed him one. Taking hers, she lounged on a large sofa and patted the seat next to her. He took a long sip of the liqueur then sat so close they touched. Placing the snifter down on a glass-topped table he took hers from her hand and set it down to clink against his.

She unbuttoned his Hawaiian-design sport shirt and kissed his neck and his chest. "I take it we're not going to dinner right away," he said.

# # #

Bravo stretched out in his motel bed and sighed contentment. Conyo, that woman filled him with joy. He appreciated that she wasn't the cloying type that whined for you to stay and snuggle. She understood that he went back to his own place because he'd forgotten to bring his cellphone, his base camp while on a case.

Yeah, he chuckled at her audacity of setting her staff, claiming him as her man, unconcerned for his marital status, confident of her ability to become the dominant woman in his life. The thought of spending the rest of his life with her scintillated him.

Still, it disturbed him. How would his sons react? Yzabel came to mind and he thought of phoning her but vacillated and drifted off.

# # #

He flinched. Something disquieted him—invaded his sleep. He couldn't immediately define what disturbed him—whether a sound or a movement. His reasoning ability registered intruder. He remained still, with his eyes closed and listened with his ears as well as with the pores in his skin. Unable to characterize any specific sound, he slitted open his eyes to search the surrounding blackness.

While unable to see anything, his sixth-sense-alarm continued to clang. Blinking to clear his eyes, he searched for the abnormality in the veil of night that cloaked him. Then he made out the vague outline of a shadowy form as his eyes became accustomed to the darkness, then a second form, and identified them as humans.

One burglar was upsetting—two or three working as a team was scary, especially in that dingy motel. If they were burglars they had to be lowlifes—probably local hoodlums hungry for whatever they could scrounge up. Easing over on his side he inched closer to the nighttable and the drawer where he'd deposited his gun.

"No, man! You do that foolish thing and we have to kill you."

The voice froze him. It had the harsh quality and street-slangy accent of barrio-badboys. Okay, since those intruders detected that he no longer slept, he decided to be aggressive rather than timid and not let a bunch of audacious burglars assume they had an advantage.

He sat up—postured belligerently. "Who the hell are you? What the hell do you want?"

The shadowy figures stepped back—startled. But they continued to aim guns at him. Then that harsh voice commanded: "¡No se preocupe, primo! Todavía no."

Those words reverberated in Bravo's translation chamber. *No reason to worry, cousin. Not yet.* He probed the darkness with eyes that flashed anger for that person to have the audacity to assume familial status . . . or was the cheeky bastard mouthing an expression used by ghetto rats, without necessarily suggesting relational ties?

"When you breathing change, primo, I know you wake up."

Bravo clenched his teeth, irritated at himself for having exposed that. It further aggravated him that the sonofabitch persisted in referring to him with that familial term.

"We wait a long time for you to come home, primo. You here only a few days and already stay out late. Got you a *novia* already in this place, hunh?"

Bravo blinked, but refrained from admitting he had a *girlfriend*, though stunned to hear that they surveilled him.

"It impress me, primo," the voice said. "Yeah! Why not? That shit run in the family. How they say it: pro-miz-cuz?"

"What the hell is it you want?" Bravo demanded, angered by the gangbanger continuously alluding to a family relationship. He squirmed, anxious to rise from the bed, but concerned with whether they'd let him. He damn sure wasn't anxious to provoke one of them into putting a bullet in him.

"We got things to get straight, primo."

Bravo glared into the darkness, aware of at least three shadowy figures. He nodded to his decision not to attempt going for his pistol . . . and get shot two or three times before he reached it. He'd play along until an opportunity presented itself.

Scowling, he conceded that those thugs had been there long enough for their eyes to adjust to the darkness, leaving him at a disadvantage. Not that it mattered, when he thought about it, since the visitors didn't appear intent on harming him, though they continued to level guns at him. It grated his gut to sit there, vulnerable. He needed to know what he dealt with to devise a defense.

"Who the hell are you?" No way he'd appear meek. "Have the courage to identify yourselves."

A stinging laugh rang out of the darkness. "I am the nightmare to visit you each night, primo, until you release my lady and those two *compatriotos* you busted today."

"Not my call." Anger caused Bravo to flex his muscles as he retorted, expressing defiance. But he remained in place, acutely aware of those pistols aimed at him.

"Make it your call then," the harsh voice said. "Tell you people to give up hunting everywhere to recover those weapons. Sí, you stumble upon the explosives, which cause me to change my plans. But I soon have a new idea to bring glory to the Vasillo Rojo."

Bravo blinked, stung by the realization that the braggadocios bastard he hunted held him at bay. Just maybe he could turn the table and take this mook into custody. First though, he needed to formulate a survival strategy. It didn't mystify him that they'd gotten in, since picking that door lock didn't require expertise. He should have applied some security measure. Too late now.

"We already make for us a reputation for the daring," the harsh voice said. "TV and newspapers glorify how we raid that army post and take those weapons. We soon strike again in that daring way, and again become the main subject of the media. You hear what I tell you, primo?"

That continuing of familial reference galled him, but he refrained from openly objecting; tried to accept it as simply gangbanger usage. Besides, it made sense not to rile the bastard. Doubtful the wise-ass intended to harm him, since he sought to gain some end. If he'd intended to kill it would have been easier with the victim sleeping.

"In the morning," the grating voice said, "you do what you have to in getting my lady and those two faithfuls released."

"What makes you think I would do that?" Bravo asked. He snickered to intimidate the bastard, belittle him in the presence of his cohorts, hoping for impertinence to unsettle the crude bastard and erode his confidence. He now plainly saw two of them and a shadowy third.

"You do it because you one of us, bro'. Yeah, you wear that suit and tie, have a government badge, and work with those honkies, but you not one of them. Look in the mirror, hombre."

"I know who I am."

"Sure, primo, you Puertoriqueño like us . . . El Boricua."

Bravo scoffed at that terminology. He concentrated on irritating the lobo, see how he reacted. So he said: "Don't delude yourself into believing every Puerto Rican supports your mad-ass scheme of revolution. The fact is that you extremists are a minority among those advocating independence. Most are law-abiding and supportive of government both here and in Puerto Rico,"

"*Boriquén,* hombre. Boriquén is the name of our island home. Only those Yankee exploiters call it Puerto Rico, the rich port. You been there, cousin, visiting your fat-cat uncle, who struts around Mayaguez like those motherfucking Yankees with their slave factories."

Bravo blinked, stunned that the guy knew of his uncle, and had awareness of his having visited.

"Most of our people live poor-assed," the coarse voice continued. "So don't call it Puerto Rico in the way of those fucking gringo exploiters."

Bravo clenched his jaws to keep from retorting that all Puerto Ricans weren't poor-assed. But it defied reason to go off on that tangent. Besides, he needed to be circumspect and not goad the guy into harming him.

"Boriquén is the true name of our beloved island," the growly voice said, "given it by its natives, the Taíno Indians. It mean the land of the valiant. The valiant, bro' be those of us sacrifices ourselves for independence. We wants those honkie motherfuckers out of there."

"Then why don't you go back to fight your war there where it counts?"

"Wrong, bro'. We don't going to bring destruction to our homeland. No, man, we going to wreak havoc on the Yankee turf."

"What's the point?" Bravo asked in contemptuous tones to antagonize the guy.

"Open you eyes, primo, it's the way of wise men who revolt. The IRA robs banks and blows up buildings in England, on the enemy's turf, not in Ireland. Palestinians don't blow up they asses on the West Bank. No, man, they do it in Israel where it has effect. El-Qaida bomb high-rises in New York and Washington, using airplanes of the Yankee oppressors. And they blow up buildings in Saudi Arabia and other countries, punish the British in Turkey, turn the political tide in Spain, then explode bombs in the subway those London honkies calls tubes. That ISIS send death squads to operate in different countries."

"What is this?" Bravo asked, "a commentary on current events?"

"A warning, primo, of what I am capable of. I study that shit, have learn how to wage war on the other guy's turf. No way I cause devastation in our barrios."

When Bravo scoffed the intruder growled: "We getting off the subject, primo. I want my lady and my two compatriotos turned lose."

"You're dreaming."

"Don't fucking diss me, motherfucker. I do your ass before you blinks again, even though you a blood relative."

"Bullshit!" blurted out of Bravo, impelled by aversion to being linked relationally to the despicable character.

Abdulo laughed. "Me and you is family, primo, whether you admit it or not."

"That's your claim. I deny any kind of ties to some mad-ass terrorist like you."

"Liberator, primo. And you can't deny blood. But that's not the reason for my visit."

"You mean invasion. You have to be invited to visit."

"Like those people invited you guys in Iraq?"

Bravo scowled as he waved that off. "I'm not arranging the release of some fanatical woman who opened fire on the police."

"Show respect, hombre. You talking about my lady . . . a queen among our people."

"I'm talking about a trigger-happy female who had the bad judgment to shoot at the police."

"In self-defense. You boys chase her and kill Pancho. How you expect she react?"

"Before or after she decided to steal that truck with those explosives?"

"And the two working in the factory—you say they had guns and shoot at you?"

"No, but they violated their parole by aiding and abetting those two fanatics that tried to whisk away those explosives."

"Hurts my heart, man, to lose those bombs. I have big plans for those suckers.

Now I need to make a new strategy—do something to make the world aware of the capabilities of Abdulo."

"You won't have the time or opportunity. We'll have the bunch of you in custody before you can pull off any more capers. We'll have—"

A harsh laugh cut him off. Then a growly voice demanded: "Why you shoot Perez the other day? What he do to deserve that?"

"He fired on the police, didn't leave anyone any alternative."

"That piss me off, man. I should kill you for that, but I got other things I need you to do for me."

"You got the wrong guy." Then he inhaled while reproaching himself for not putting a halter on his emotions. Yes, he needed to avoid intimidating the braggart and getting himself killed.

"You best prepare you proud ass to do what I tell you." Abdulo thrust his pistol close to Bravo's face.

Bravo glared defiantly at it, in spite of quaking inside. "No way I free terrorists."

Ay Dios! Again! Get a hold on your emotions, hombre. Don't lose control and get your ass shot. Keep your mouth shut and wheedle yourself out of this predicament.

"You has no proof against them, primo. You know that and I know that. You using phony shit to hold them, causing me one big-ass problem."

"You saying those two are that important to you?"

"All my people important to me, primo. I pledge to all my brothers and sisters who fight this war with me that I never leave them in the gringo's jail."

"Then why'd you murder Elizondo when you had the chance to spring him?"

"That pandejo betray me, man, by try to make a deal with the G-men."

"How do you know that?"

"Because I have ears in every corner. But you don't have to worry about that shit, primo. All you needs to do is free my brothers in revolution. And I wants my woman back. I miss that lady in my bed."

Bravo snickered as Loscalzo's report flashed in mind. How 'bout that? They had taken into custody the reigning queen of the Vasillo Rojo. Was Abdulo so naïve he really believed he could effect her release?

"You send her back to me, primo, I hold no grudge."

"What makes you think I would go against the bureau?"

"You don't be the first. A whole bunch of you boys, and I mean white boys, have sold out to the dopers—in Miami, Houston, New York, Chicago—you name it. Hell, man, a few of you true-blue wonder-boys sold out to the Russians. That's rank, man. That's betraying you own world. Nobody can't get no lower."

"One dirty agent or one dirty cop doesn't vilify the entire agency or force."

"Save that philosophy shit for you Sunday school class. And don't feed me no bullshit about agency scruples and all. That queer-ass boss of the FBI sold out to the ginny mob. Yeah, I know you going to deny it. Just tell me why Hoover the only person in the whole goddam country in those days deny that organized racketeers sucking the economy dry."

"I'm not in the FBI and don't need to defend Hoover. Besides, he's dead. I can tell you that I won't betray my bureau. And I damn sure won't betray my country. I'm talking about the United States of America."

"I don't want to hear no bullshit like that."

Bravo held his breath, alarmed by the wrath reverberating in the guy's tone. Yes, he needed to back off before he provoked that fanatic to do something in a fit of rage. After a short silence the guy said, in tempered voice: "I ask only that you release those Puertoriqueños, bro'. I mean Boricuas, man. Our people. Cut them loose and I stop haunting you ass."

Bravo swallowed—suppressing a retort:

"It is my exploits, primo, that popularizes Abdulo, el caudillo del Vasillo Rojo, the liberator of Boriquén and one baddass terrorist."

"Don't you have the courage to use your real name: Clemente Galbos?"

"Bravo, Bravo. So you have already traced me, know who you pursue . . . and know we are related. That don't be important—not to me, primo. I wants my lady and my compatriotos released."

"Why? You can't recruit new cohorts?"

"We the same like you Special Forces, primo—don't leave none of our own behind. My success comes from being thorough. I leave no witnesses, and I leave no trail for follow me. No one knows where to find me tomorrow. So cut those people loose and we'll split and give you back this tropic burg."

"Split to where?"

Abdulo chuckled. "No need to worry where we go and what we do next. Just cut them loose. That be you contribution to the resurrection of Boriquén."

"You've got a better chance getting snakebit."

"So then will your wife, Yzabel in Washington, that snooty one who moon half the night for that Lothario from Spain. Don't it bother you, bro', that you wife has hots for another man?"

"That's none of your goddam business!"

"Punched you anger button, eh?"

"Keep my wife out of this."

"Okay, since it changes nothing in my life if you high-born bitch from España screws around. Believe that we have people on her, ready to strike at my signal. And don't think we can't reach Romero in that private school, nuns or no nuns. We badasses, primo, will kill those bitches as well if they gets in the way. Reaching into Duke for Esteban is easy as pie—American apple pie."

"You touch any of them, you sonofabitch—"

"Tranquilo, primo. Be cool. Nobody need for be hurt. If my lady and my aces back on the street within twenty-four hours then I vanish. No más problemas, primo."

"Knock off that primo bullshit." Bravo could see him clearly now, laughing tauntingly. He wished he had his gun in his fist so he could blast that bearded mulatto out of his life and eliminate anyone learning he is related to a half-black terrorist.

"Do what I ask, primo, and I don't fuck up you life by tell everybody we cousins. Then you never need to admit you don't be *blanco de pura cepa*."

Bravo winced as he remembered his uncle, Tio Rico, use that phrase, boasting while describing the family tree as: *pure white to the core*.

Bravo blinked—because of something affecting his eyesight. Those three figures became fuzzy? Then he realized that all three had backed into the darkness. He could barely see them, especially Galbos.

Abdulo, my ass!

Dim light momentarily bathed the room, making him blink again. It took only a second to realize it came from the hallway—that they'd opened the door. The shadowy forms slipped out and clunked the door closed behind them, shutting off the light.

Bravo rolled out of bed and dropped to the floor, instinctively cautious, despite believing they left him alone. Pulling open the middle drawer of the night table he groped for his semi-automatic pistol, removed it from the holster and flicked off the safety before aiming it in the direction of the door.

His eyes had adjusted to the darkness so he rose to a crouch and flicked on the lamp, bathing the room in light that permitted him to probe every shadowy corner to be certain that no unwanted visitors remained. After exhaling a huge breath of relief he hurried to the door and flung it open. Flattened against its jamb he peered up and down the dimly lit hallway, his gun gripped in both hands—at the ready. Nobody!

Deciding against pursuit, since he was naked, he went back inside and closed the door then locked it. Locked it! That was a joke. A stumblebum could pick that poor excuse for security—not that he found it any better or any worse than locks in most hotels and motels.

Picking up the phone, he called his Washington office, with intent to have his wife and kids moved to a safe house. Even as the phone droned, he knew it wouldn't work. The kids needed to go to school. Yzabel wouldn't be amenable to restriction in a safe house, denied the freedom to tend to her business. But he demanded they put a round-the-clock security on them. He knew she'd object to that too, but determined to force it on her. Yeah, she'd be bitching about it before morning dawned.

THIRTY-THREE

Bravo started to climb out of his car in the sixth floor garage when his cellphone trilled. He answered it while rising to his feet. "Hello."

"Is it your intention to ruin my life?"

"My concern is to protect my family from terrorists."

"What have we to do with your police work?"

"There are killers out there who will harm you and the boys to divert my attention from their activities."

"Sorry, I don't believe that."

"Then you're being foolish."

"Why makes us pawns in that game?"

"The bad guys are doing that. I'm trying hard as I can to protect you."

"Get out of law enforcement."

"Please, Yzabel, be practical."

"Practicality is not disrupting my life and that of the boys."

"Is it isolating you from that Spaniard that's sparking your anger?"

"That's a disgusting accusation."

"What other reason do you have for objecting to protective custody?"

"I have a business, consequently a clientele to be available to."

"They won't interfere with your work, only keep an eye on you until we round up those terrorists."

"I'd think your terrorists have more to do than bother with me and the boys."

"Think again. They have you and the boys under surveillance. Why do you think I ordered protection?"

After a gasp and a second of silence she asked: "Are you telling me that the terrorist are aware of us?"

"Yes, they described your activities as well as the boys. Believe that they are capable of harming the family." He blinked, concerned with saying anything that revealed his familial relationship with that mulatto.

"Are you telling me the terrorist speak to you?"

"That's exactly what I'm telling you. They held me at bay in my motel room last night while goading me about your attending that ball and chatting with the don."

"Ay Dios! Are you all right?"

"Yes, but accept that terrorists also attended that ball."

She gasped again. "But how could *they* get invited?"

"Why couldn't they have been among the help—waiters, porters—whatever?"

"Dios mio! Could one of those servers have been a terrorist? How frightening!"

"I'm glad you're waking up to the threat of terrorism in the United States, much less the rest of the world . . . such as in Spain and London. Look what happened recently in Paris. We're even more at risk because terrorists of all persuasions have no problem infiltrating our polyglot populations, especially with the tens of millions of undocumented foreigners wandering around the country."

When she only gasped but didn't reply, he said: "It's a war that demands alertness and the willingness to make sacrifices. At the least, we have to stop being complacent and accept that danger lurks in every shadow."

"But I can't close down my business."

"You don't have to. Just accept the protection. I'll feel better knowing that your back is covered, as well as that of the boys."

"Yes, Ray, it makes sense. I'll check with the boys. You take care of yourself and be safe. Bye bye."

He breathed relief as he traipsed to the elevator. Getting anyone as stubborn as Yzabel to cave had to be considered an achievement. Still, he smarted with the awareness of her infatuation for Nando.

Should he have realized the inevitability of these past days when he first met her? Actually, he had no clue of her romantic involvement with the Spaniard back then. From the moment he saw her he bcame enveloped in that aura of fantasy and blinded to everything else. He'd never, in his wildest dreams, expected to hobnob with the *hidalgo*, the nobility of Spain at an embassy ball.

Fact is, he hadn't anticipated getting closer to that society than viewing them on the glossy pages of expensive magazines. Nor would he have dreamed of that lovely black-haired lady being attentive to him. He'd never anticipated the entrancement of dancing waltzes and the intoxication of sipping champagne from the same crystal goblet. He'd never before even bothered to fantasize experiencing that ambiance of culture and wealth.

And while falling helplessly in love, he ignored rumors that popped up through the years inferring that she had chased after Fernando Guijón Montoros. Hell, he knew Don Fernando was married, so dismissed those cackles as malicious gossip. No way he'd let anything impede his pursuit of her.

Sure, she could have had a schoolgirl crush on the guy. He only knew the first princess he met in his young life responded favorably to his attentiveness. No, it never occurred to him that he competed with a rich and pampered nobleman of Catalonia.

Dios en cielo, he felt like a conquering hero that day when a Puerto Rican born in Spanish Harlem married the daughter of the Sevilliano upper crust, a society in which he never before coveted acceptance. In no way did he expect it to haunt and torture him twenty-two years later.

The discord that punctuated ensuing years should have prepared him, but didn't. Nothing soothes a man's pride wounded he suspects his wife is consorting with another man. Most men seethed with anger. The Latino psyche churns with rage.

Upon entering the conference room Bravo noted the irritability on the faces of his staff for having been called in that Saturday morning. He hoped that attitude didn't result from their not taking the business as seriously as they should. Yes, he knew it was partly because of their disdain for Puerto Rican gangbangers, disbelieving they were as capable of terrorism as others. If the bad guys had been Muslims they'd have more readily accepted the gravity of that imminent harm to their society.

Before nine-eleven most Americans scorned the camel-herders and sluffed them off as ragheads—incapable of harming the U. S. of A. Then the crushing loss of the World Trade Center and the damage sustained by the Pentagon shook Americans out of that apathy. Still, even that horrendous experience couldn't bring them to accept a handful of Caribbean Hispanics from a tiny island as menacing . . . heretofore a bunch of servants and laborers they'd disparaged.

Besides, they'd retrieved the explosives, the most threatening portion of the ordnance taken from the Nininger US Army Reserve Center. True, those yahoos still had a large supply of rifles and pistols, with an abundance of ammunition, but that didn't make them equal to law enforcement in a gunfight . . . especially with fed-power backing up the locals. Doubtful they'd have the courage to engage in battle, their defeat being a foregone conclusion.

But the bad guys didn't always intend to win the battle . . . but rather to make a statement. The screw-ups at Ruby Ridge sure demonstrated that, ending up with the unnecessary killing of a man, his wife and their dog. The siege of the Branch Davidians at Waco, Texas was far worse, ending with six Davidians and four ATF agents dead. Talk about losing the propaganda war.

Bravo slapped the table with his palm to get everyone's attention. Then he spellbound them by relating his experience of last night. They gawked, impressed by the daring and guile of those gangbangers and the determination of those terrorists to hurt America. No, he did not share with them his family ties to Abdulo.

"Why in hell didn't you call us last night to back you up?" Olecki asked.

"No point. Bye the time I had an opportunity to call anyone the danger had passed."

"Then why not call for psychological support," Danly Coombs asked. "Considering how scary an experience it must have been," Boisey Epps added. "Hear what I'm saying?"

"Had no problem dealing with it after the danger passed. Won't deny I wasn't all that confident while those mooks stood over me with guns in my face. But that's past and I'm now sharing that experience so you'll appreciate the ruthlessness of those militants.

We need to take that threat seriously and remain alert to possible attacks on our persons as well as on our families."

Shocked into realization of danger impelled them to think proactive. They nodded concurrence to Bravo that more intense efforts were demanded to penetrate the secret cell and get a line on those miscreants. Yes, they needed to prevent those desperadoes from raining terror on America.

"Even though they can no longer blow up a building," Olecki said, "they still have those guns and munitions and can leave bodies strewn across the landscape."

"Or use them in a desperate raid to acquire new explosives," Bravo added. "No question in my mind that Abdulo is an unstable egotist who plans to pull off an horrific act to publicize his name."

"Maybe against you as an example," Loscalzo said.

"You need to change residences," Olecki said. The others concurred.

Bravo shook his head. "Doubtful they'll kill me since they're using me as a duct into the system and won't want to erase that connection. Just possibly they'll leak enough so we'll be able to lay a trap for Abdulo."

"We need to bandy this business around to decide how to approach it," Baggler said.

"We need action, not further discussion," Bravo said. "So we're going to form teams to again comb the slums for a lead to Abdulo, and to hopefully recover those weapons." He reconnected with Olecki by pairing Cleo with Baggler, hopeful that those two managed to get along. At worst, Baggler might accept the bounty offered. Sure as hell, there wouldn't be repercussions.

And he sent Danly Coombs out with Boisey Epps, to avoid further discord by having two African-Americans together. That left Loscalzo and Pedrazo to team up. Olecki got the Sheriff's Department to loan them Mac and Mac again.

Within minutes all cruised the factory-warehouse area where they'd happened on that green pick-up truck. The first couple of hours passed without incident. At midmorning Olecki stopped at a lunch-wagon to get coffee for both, while Bravo cellphoned his wife.

It relieved him when she assured: "I'm fine and the kids are fine. But everywhere I go federal agents trail along, denying me privacy."

It took effort not to shout that she wouldn't require privacy if she didn't tryst with that Spaniard. But he didn't want Olecki to overhear that condemnation. God, he didn't want the guy to know he suspected his wife of infidelity.

"We seem to be so much at odds this time," Yzabel said, "that we should certainly consider divorce."

"What about the boys?"

"They're essentially grown. And divorced parents are more the norm than the unusual these days."

"Are you forgetting we're Catholic?" He swallowed to choke off adding that the church condemned promiscuous behavior. Hell, he hadn't exactly been saintly lately, consequently would be the proverbial pot condemning the kettle.

"Let's put off those decisions until I get home," he said. "Hopefully it'll be within a few days."

After clicking off he accepted the container of coffee from Olecki, who asked: "Repercussions for not attending that embassy affair?"

He grimaced while nodding, but didn't enlarge on it. No, he couldn't share marital discord with the man. Nor did he dare inform the man of his relationship with Maylene. God—he still had hours before meeting her at her place.

THIRTY-FOUR

Bravo exhilarated as he drove back to his motel, his mind dancing to melodic memories of the hours he'd spent with Maylene. He'd reluctantly agreed with her that they needed to keep their relationship secret to avoid it affecting their professional alliance. God, no denying she satisfied him in every way a man desired—certainly injected more joy in his life than Yzabel has of late.

Yzabel's threats to divorce him diminished hope of saving their marriage. Besides, obviously both he and Yzabel strayed. Their problems had expanded over the years and left them with no alternative but to dissolve their marriage.

Then a momentary depression clouded those thoughts. He had to protect her and the boys from the peril of terrorism. Remembrance of last night made him wonder if he might be surveilled. So he utilized the rearview and the two sideview mirrors but failed to pick up a tail.

With light traffic at half past one in the morning he knew he should be able to spot a shadow. And he feared the tail knew where he came from and might target

Maylene. He hoped he hadn't compromised her—wondered if he shouldn't call and warn her to be alert.

But should he frighten her if it wasn't necessary? Hell, he hadn't spotted anyone tailing him. It made him wonder if he'd become paranoid. Of course, two or three cars can pass him off, deny him awareness of surveillance. However, he doubted this bunch of gangbangers had the resources or the smarts to utilize that system.

He studied the few cars around and tried to remember if he'd seen any of them before . . . a difficulty since he hadn't paid particular attention to his surroundings. So he turned off Southeast

Seventeenth Street and circled three or four blocks. Upon passing behind a dark and silent shopping plaza he pulled to the curb and doused his lights.

Since no vehicles passed for five full minutes he returned to Southeast Seventeenth Street. Still, he continued to scrutinize other vehicles, checking his mirrors without identifying any as concerned with him. But hell, why would they need to dog his tail? All they had to do was wait for him at the motel, with no more difficulty picking the lock tonight than last night.

Arriving at his room, he threw open the door, his hand on his gun, but found the room empty, so relaxed. After locking the door he wedged a chair under the doorknob to increase the difficulty of entering uninvited. And after undressing he tucked his pistol under his pillow.

Anyone tried to get in would get a bullet up their ass. He determined that he wouldn't waste time conversing with shadows but rather shoot the hell out of any mook that invaded his room. Yes, especially Abdullo.

Abdulo, my ass. Believe that he'd delight in blowing the lights out of Clemente Galbos—to terminate that embarrassment. Sure he knew an officer of the law shouldn't contemplate that sort of misdeed. And he berated himself for harboring that prejudice. But he obsessed with the desire to erase the sneering mulatto from his life. Fact is, he dreaded the thought of capturing that motor-mouth and having the hump publicize familial ties. He bit the inside of his mouth to repress anger and shame for entertaining small-mindedness.

An alarm resonating in his brain extracted him from a deep sleep, making him realize he'd dozed off. Sparked by memories of last night he kept his eyes slitted while searching the darkness, to deny anyone awareness that he'd awakened. He replicated the same breathing rhythm as when sleeping. But hard as he peered around he saw only a black void. There! His ears identified the soft sound as the sliding of a window.

With as little movement as possible, he withdrew the pistol from under his pillow, and slid it down to his side, concealed by the covers. It mystified him that anyone opened the window without breaking the glass. He'd checked before going to bed, certain the lock had been secured.

Of course, they could cut away a piece of glass and hold it with a suction tool, then pull it away, reach in and release the latch. Okay, when they got halfway in he'd blow that sonofabitch out of the goddam window. Damn right he hoped that sonofabitch was Abdullo.

Oh shit! Detection of footsteps indicated someone had already entered. The hairs on his neck bristled. But he remained as still as he was able to. And he forced himself to continue breathing rhythmically while clutching his pistol beneath the covers.

Then he flinched—from the scathing voice from the dark. "You fail, primo, to release my woman and two compatriotos. Those Puerto Ricans—Boricuas that is —people of Boriquén, deserve my efforts to keep them from be victimized by the gringos."

Bravo didn't respond, denied himself the slightest movement. Peeking through slitted eyes to conceal being awake, he tried to accustom them to the dark. He wanted to see the forms clearly before he began a gunfight, not put himself at a disadvantage.

"Pretend to sleep, primo, but I know that you are not. Do not think me a fool. I am wiser than those US attorney people and FBI agents at your office."

Bravo decided to annoy the bastard, so snickered. He opened his eyes fully then to speed up the process of accustoming them to the dark.

"What the hell you laugh at?"

"You—for your conceited bullshit."

"No bullshit. I am the Puerto Rican Che. All the world will recognize in time that Abdulo will precede Che Guevara in the hierarchy of Latino liberators and heroes. Your cousin will bring glory to the family name."

"God forbid!"

"Why you shamed of me, primo? I going to be famous, and make the family known throughout the world."

"Only thing you're going to do is get shot down like a dog to bleed out your useless life in the gutter, then be remembered as a *payaso*."

"You offend me by call me a *clown*. And you deny me credit I deserve as a master strategist. You know how many books I read on the subject—by Che Guevara, by Schwartzkopf, and that Chinese genius, Sun Tzu. I even read books about the FBI and how they and other government agents fuck up so much."

Bravo snorted to antagonize the boasting bastard.

"Believe, primo, that I will eat you mothers for supper. You know why? Because I take advantage of things, don't burden myself with stuff. I access resources, like that which I took from that military base. And I move around constantly so can't be traced. I too shrewd for you dumb asses."

"Like you stored those explosives."

"One setback, because I try to keep them mobile, to use wherever I decide. It hard, man, to keep all those guns and bullets ready to move. But I score without the bombs. I soon make a name for myself that never be forgotten."

"You'll be shot down and be remembered for trying something stupid."

"Is it stupid if I force you and your Yankee buddies to fight me on my terms and on my turf, in the way Hezbollah mess with those Israelis in Lebanon? I study strategy, primo, and learn how to sucker you mothers into fighting when it is to my advantage."

"Give me a break."

"A break, primo? Think about what I have done to date. I acquire weapons from you National Guard, then create chaos, deceiving my enemy by isolating and menacing them."

"Not for too much longer."

"You deny that I menace you, primo."

"Not as much as you think. And you sure as hell won't outsmart the government."

Abdulo laughed shrilly. "We will launch multiple attacks, switching between this place and another faster than you people can respond and adapt. We kill so many of you police and government agents that the populace be terrified."

"In your dreams."

"Let me tell you, primo, we will utilize the orthodox spiced with the unorthodox, mix the expected with the unexpected, keeping you fools guessing."

"Don't underestimate us," Bravo said.

"Nor will we overestimate you."

"In the final analysis we'll blast you and all terrorists out of this world . . . put an end to your boastful bullshit."

"Everything ends. Life has limits. No one lives forever. But when I die, primo, I become the most celebrated of all Latino heroes."

Dios en cielo! Bravo hadn't realized the guy had a martyr complex—that he justified sacrificing his life for mention in a history book.

As Bravo's eyes became accustomed to the darkness, he saw the small square cut out of the window, it now the only part not fazed by age and dirt. It annoyed him to realize that those mooks had the advantage. And it rankled his gut that Abdulo could, and probably would make front-page news with some maniacal enterprise, resulting in publicizing their family relationship.

"Wait—you will see, when I trick you gringo police into a battle of my choosing and in a place that I select. It will be written about in newspapers and spouted on TV so often it will cause amazement world-wide."

"You really think you can outshoot the police?" How, he wondered, could he talk this kook out of some insane attempt . . . prevent his lunacy from being publicized . . . along with their familial connection?

"Not important, primo. To engage them on my terms and damage their ranks will be an achievement to be talked about throughout the world."

"Meanwhile you and your gangbanger cohorts will be wiped out."

"Patriots, not gangbangers. This is not about gang turf, but about the liberation of Boriquén."

"Call it what you like. You'll still end up dead."

"But that sacrifice will motivate every Boricua to stand up and fight for freedom in Boriquén. And I, primo, will forever be known as the one who inspired our people to cast the invaders from our homeland. Perhaps they will honor me by changing the name of

San Juan to Ciudad Abdulo, or Galbos, to make that family name widely known."

God forbid! Clenching his teeth, Bravo aimed the pistol, still under the covers, at the middle of three shadowy figures in the dark. He assessed that the voice emanated from that one—ringing like a clarion in his ears and blinding him with rage—fueling the compelling need to quiet it.

"You going to be famous, primo—interviewed on those TV talk shows as a blood relative of Abdulo."

Bravo winced as anger squeezed the trigger—three successive times in an inverted vee pattern. Tat, tat, tat. Flames flashed from his light-weight blanket. He heard the expulsion of breath, saw the shadowy form stumble backward, then collapse.

At the same instant he rolled off onto the floor, tangled in the bed covers . . . nanoseconds before a barrage of bullets tore up the bed. Flinching, he hugged the floor, knew instinctively that they fired three guns. How many of them, he wondered, had entered his room. Bullets tearing through the bed pinged the floor around him.

Then he winced at Abdulo's vitriolic voice. "Bastardo! You have kill a Puerto Rican freedom fighter—a Boricua—so must now die."

Shit! Bravo gritted his teeth in disappointment having been desperate to kill that braggart and rid his life of that menace. He shrunk into his shoulders, hugging the floor as bullets ripped up the bed. By some miracle none of the bullets hit him. Shaking lose of the bed covers he slithered to the end of the bed, where he could peek past it and get a shot at that brag-ass sonofabitch.

He saw a muzzle flash and fired two quick shots at it, then quickly rolled away to bounce off the wall. He knew he'd soon be in jeopardy, since at least three remained, unless he just eliminated another one. So he fired two quick shots at where he saw another muzzle flash. Someone screamed, then thumped to the floor.

Bullets tore into the wall around him. He fired repeatedly in the direction of the muzzle flashes, desperate to fend them off. But after three shots the hammer clicked on an empty chamber.

His breath caught with the realization that he'd expelled all ten bullets. His head jerked to the direction of the nighttable—to the middle drawer—where he kept his extra clip. Without it he'd be unable to defend against being shot to death. But how much chance did he have of reaching that clip? Would they shoot his life out before he managed to reload? He didn't even know how many of them survived . . . whether he'd gotten lucky and taken out Abdulo.

Accepting that he had to try, he poised in a crouch to leap to the nighttable, only a few feet away. But he froze when light bathed the room. He instinctively recoiled from it and flattened himself against the wall. Blinking because of the unexpected flash of light, he realized that someone had swung open the door to the hallway. Two or three figures hurried out of the room while emptying their guns into the room to cover their retreat.

In retrospect he remembered hearing the chair tossed aside. He wasn't certain but thought they half-carried and half-dragged a body or two with them. Again he twinged with disappointment as he heard Abdulo curse him for an idiot and a traitor—condemn him as having forfeited his life—and that of his family. They fired a number of shots into the room before the door closed and plunged the room back into blackness.

He gritted his teeth in anger as he accepted that the bastard survived— threatening his family. So he scampered on all fours to the nighttable—to grope the drawer open and grasp his other clip of bullets. He held his breath as he ejected the spent clip and inserted the full one, then shot the bolt. Without thinking about it, he wheeled and fired at the closed door, splintering it.

No way he could tell if he hit anyone. As much as he wished to kill Abdulo, he had to hold himself back from charging after them, reasoning that they waited for him to open the door. He'd surely be shot down. So he reached up for the telephone to call the police, careful not to silhouette himself in the window and end up being shot by one of them posted outside. It took only a moment to be assured of immediate response.

As he hung up he recognized the acrid smell of smoke. He snapped on the light, to see one body on the floor, and smoke curling under his door. The body didn't move, but he crawled to it and felt for a pulse. Finding none, he accepted that the guy was dead, so picked up the dead guy's pistol and hurried to the door to yank it open. A wall of flames almost devoured him.

The heat forced him to step back and swing the door closed. Then he rushed back to the phone to call for the fire department, his mind racing with how to alert all of the others staying at the motel. Hopefully some had been alarmed by the gunfire, maybe seen the smoke if not the flames, and alerted others.

He heard sirens, knew that was the police, giving him a sense of relief that they'd get everyone out safely. He poised to jump out the window, but hesitated, aware of being naked.

Gritting his teeth he pulled on pants and slipped into shoes. Estimating that he had two or three minutes before the flames engulfed his room, he gathered up his clothing and toilet articles and stuffed them in his luggage, which he threw out the window before leaping out.

THIRTY-FIVE

Police cars with flashing lights screeched to the scene with one braking only inches from Bravo. Two deputies with guns drawn leapt from the cruiser, training flashlights and pistols on him as he struggled to his feet.

"Hands on top of head!"

"I'm a federal officer. "

"Down on your belly! Hands on your head!"

"I'm a federal officer," he yelled again—but complied. In spite of being incensed he understood their guardedness, so opted for safety over polity. "I'm with ATF."

"Let's see your ID!"

"It's in the inside pocket of my suit jacket over there. Jesus H, there's real bad guys running around here, and you're wasting time hassling a federal officer."

They ignored his tirade as one cop perused his credentials and the other shuffled through his belongings, strewing it around. The one with his ID asked: "What the hell you doing on these cheap-ass premises?"

"Staying here at the motel." It came out in an angry burst, increasing the adrenalin pumping within him from residual fear and excitement. He started to get up but the cop thrust his pistol closer, cowing him into submission.

The other one trained a flashlight on his face and studied his features. "You saying you're a federal cop?"

"Yes, I am. The feds hire spics, even if you cracker bastards don't."

"Keep a civil tongue," the other one barked at him.

"It'll be less than civil when I report this shit to Detective Olecki."

"You know Peter Olecki?" the second one asked.

"We're partners on a taskforce."

"Why didn't you say so?" the other officer said. They helped him to his feet, then to gather up his clothing and luggage and put it in the trunk of his car. Fire engines pulled up with sirens screaming and lights flashing.

Motel guests streamed out into the parking lot, many half-dressed and most in a state of hyper-excitement. The two deputies excused themselves to care for those people. Bravo called Olecki on his cellphone.

While it rang he watched people stream out of the building passing the firemen rolling out hoses to extinguish the flames. After informing Olecki of what transpired he called his office in Washington to demand they increase the security on his wife and two sons, concerned that the terrorists retaliate against them.

Olecki arrived, and soon after Baggler and Loscalzo did also. A Ford Mustang screeched up to the motel and Cleo bounded out. His concerned taskforce cohorts gathered around him, prodding him to share every detail with them.

"Any idea where to find those mad-asses?" Baggler asked.

"Or where they intend to strike?" Loscalzo asked.

"Sounded like he's planning something bordering on a suicide attack," Bravo said. "And he's insane enough to do something wild-assed."

"We'll put an end to his madness," Baggler said.

"Don't play him short," Bravo said. "He's determined to make a strike that'll live in the annals of history."

"Something in Washington," Loscalzo said, "according to what Elizondo allegedly told that guard."

"Elizondo may have been using that threat to get attention," Bravo said, "believing he'd survive if taken to Washington . . . distanced from those yahoos in South Florida."

"Why else would they need those Bangalore Torpedoes?" Loscalzo asked.

"What's the difference?" Olecki asked. "We recovered them. Whatever he'd planned with them won't work now."

"But he'll think of something else," Bravo said. "That guy is devious, besides being psychotic, and will pull off some kind of wild caper."

"Transporting all those weapons and munitions to somewhere without being intercepted will take doing," Olecki said.

"He sure as hell can find a target hereabouts," Cleo said. "Why would he need to go anywhere else?"

"He can cause a lot of hysteria in this heavily populated area," Loscalzo said.

"To reverberate around the country," Baggler added as he shuffled impatiently on the lawn, apparently vexed by feeling inept since they lacked any idea what to do next.

"Let's not let him lead us around in circles," Bravo said. "Tomorrow morning we need to concentrate on taking his rotten ass into custody."

"Or blow it away," Baggler said.

"Got no problem with that," Bravo said, then winced, uncomfortable for having endorsed that utterance . . . admitting his eagerness to kill the man.

"Why wait for morning to get after the sonofabitch?" Loscalzo asked.

"Because we're bone-tired," Olecki said. "Let's us all get us some shut-eye and be ready to hunt in the morning, when we're bushy-tailed."

"Meanwhile I have to find a place to crash for the night," Bravo said.

"I'll check with the management," Olecki said, "and see if they have any undamaged rooms available."

"Forget about it. I sure wouldn't get any sleep here. Those door locks won't deny entry to an aggressive bulldog."

"It's four in the morning," Olecki said, "late for finding a room somewhere. Wish I could take you in, but barely have enough space for my family."

Bravo nodded, remembering the neat little house he'd had dinner in.

"Come on over to my house," Cleo said. "We have a spare bedroom you can use as long as you like."

He studied her with squinted eyes. "Butch come home?"

Cleo grinned. "Not an hour ago. Hadn't received this call, we'd be hot and heavy at it."

"One night," Bravo said, "to get a little shuteye."

# # #

Bravo pressed the pedal of the bucar to keep up with Cleo's light blue Mustang. She didn't dawdle. Meanwhile he remained alert for the possibility of being tailed and ambushed by the terrorists. He wouldn't put it past Abdulo to finish the job. He hoped Cleo realized that possibility. He thought of calling her on her cellphone, but knowing her she'd take offense at not being considered a consummate cop and smart enough to remain alert to the possibility of danger.

He followed her west on Davie Boulevard, a major thoroughfare with little traffic at that hour of the morning, making it easy to ascertain if anyone followed them. Continuing west of Interstate 95 and the Florida Turnpike, even west of US Highway 441, they barreled through residential and commercial areas draped in the quiet of night.

She led the way into an area called Jacaranda. He hoped to hell they hadn't led any of those heartless terrorists in there, to bring harm to innocents. Middle-income homes in pastel colors, surrounded by tropic flora, were fronted by moderately-priced cars, vans, and pick-up trucks. When Cleo pulled into one of the garages, Bravo parked in that driveway.

She waited for him to gather up his things, then led him into the House. He glanced back, still not secure that they hadn't been followed, weren't safe from attack. Then he had all he could do not to pull back and gawk at sight of Butch, a huge, robust guy in undershirt, with tufts of chest hair protruding from the neckline as well from under his arms. Slouched in a kitchen chair, he clutched a stubby glass on the round table and scowled at the visitor while Cleo timidly introduced them, all but stuttering while explaining why she brought him home.

In spite of not being warmly welcomed, Bravo endowed the man with a smile while stepping up to the table to proffer a handshake. Butch scrutinized him for a few seconds before extending a veritable bear paw, inducing Bravo to anticipate a vise-like grip. So he thrust his hand between the guy's thumb and forefinger to prevent getting squeezed too hard.

Butch waved them to sit, then picked up the bottle of rye whiskey from the laminated table and poured into two stubby glasses with thick bottoms. Bravo accepted the one pushed to him, raised it to clink against Cleo's and her husband's, then took a sip. When Butch asked what happened, Bravo related his scary experience, truncated to avoid boring the man. Besides he was tired and didn't want to extend the time before getting in the sack.

Butch nodded, then rattled on endlessly about his adventures as an overland truck driver—living on the edge endless times. Bravo accepted that the gruff guy didn't want to be overshadowed by someone else's exploits. Or maybe he resented another guy posturing heroically in his wife's presence. Whatever. Bravo resigned himself to listening to Butch's adventures.

Bravo sipped his one shot while the bruiser knocked off three. Cleo knocked down two. Bravo would have preferred scotch, but Butch didn't offer anything except that rye whiskey, which Bravo assumed was all he had in the house. So, finishing his drink, he begged them to understand that he needed shuteye.

Acknowledging his state of exhaustion, they put him up in the spare room, which had been their daughters. Nobody explained why she wasn't in the house, and he didn't ask. Beat after a trying night, he put his curiosity on hold to avoid having to suffer through a long story. And he wasn't in a mood to be sympathetic . . . or celebratory if their daughter had gone off to college or gotten married.

Stripping down he climbed into the lumpy bed with posts at each corner. He felt awkward, sleeping nude in a girl's bed in a strange house. But he never packed pajamas since he traveled as light as possible. And he hadn't donned his skivvies before escaping from the fire at the motel. He'd worn them a whole day, so rejected putting them back on now, and didn't want to sleep in clean ones. He even postponed showering until the morning.

THIRTY-SIX

Strange sensations disrupted Bravo's sleep—had him breathing jerkily. He twisted and turned as he emerged from soporific depths. Jeezus! He gaped at the silhouette bending over his lower body. "Hey! What the hell you doing?" he yelled as he jerked away.

"Sshh! Christ, don't wake up Butch." Cleo twisted around and he saw that she was naked. Giggling, she pressed herself against him. He tried to wriggle away but she lay atop him and when he exerted effort to dislodge her the bed squealed. He gasped, concerned with awakening that muscle-bound brute . . . to come in here and find him hugging up to the guy's naked wife.

It dawned on him that Cleo had orally stimulated his erection, creating the sensation that invaded his sleep. Now she pinned him with her bulk while straddling him and maneuvering her lower body to slide his throbbing penus into her moist and warm portal.

"What the hell you doing?" He tried to pull away, to resist.

"What's wrong?" she demanded in a hoarse and angry whisper. She locked her strong legs around him. "Come on! You're hard." She pressed her upper body down to pin him. A big woman, in top physical shape from intensive exercise in the police gym, she restrained him.

Light bathed the room—freezing both to stare wide-eyed at Butch in his boxer shorts and hairy chest, hulking in the doorway. "What the hell y'all doing?"

Bravo lurched sideways, dislodging Cleo, who'd gone lax. He hopped out of bed across from the brutishly-built truck driver. Waving his hands about, he groped for an explanation. Could he claim innocence—claim he'd been unaware of her—was being raped?

Cleo clawed the bedding as she crawled toward where Bravo had jumped out, desperate to distance herself from Butch, her big body clumsily bouncing on the lumpy mattress. Fear expanded her eyes when Butch lunged around to that side of the bed.

Bravo leapt back onto the bed and trampolined across it to jump down to the floor on the other side. Cleo floundered as she tried to change direction, her efforts retarded by the springiness of the mattress. Butch grabbed her ankles and wrenched her off the bed, slamming her into the wall. While struggling to regain balance, she managed to dodge his fist so that it glanced off the side of her head.

She pulled her legs back to tightly flex her knees against her chest, then thrust her feet outward to thud into Butch's midsection. His breath exploded from him as he fell backward, knocking his head against one of the bedposts. He collapsed to his knees but struggled to regain his footing while snarling like a ferocious dog.

Bravo gathered his clothing off a nearby chair and extracted his pistol, which he trained on the man, temporarily freezing him. Then Bravo grabbed his shoes off the floor and fled from the room. Finding himself in the kitchen, he bolted through the back door into the yard.

Since Butch didn't pursue him he paused to catch his breath and take note of where he was so he could decide what to do next. What in hell had he gotten himself into? Aware of being naked, he stumbled about while donning his pants—difficult while clutching the pistol—but refused to release it even for a second. After slipping into his shoes he pulled on his shirt, but didn't bother to button it.

Glancing back at the house he wondered if he had any chance of retrieving his suitcase with the rest of his clothes and his toilet articles. Shaking his head he conceded he'd never see them again, so decided to jump into his car and get the hell out of there. Thank goodness he'd been too tired to empty his pockets, so had his car keys and wallet as well as his creds.

The sound of fists on flesh jerked his attention to the house. Having no doubt that Butch beat-up on Cleo had him vacillating whether to intercede. Hell, he didn't feel like he had the right to, but felt partly responsible. And yes, it pierced his soul when Cleo screamed. Could he stand by and do nothing if the brute tried to kill her? After a loud crash he heard Butch shout that she broke the goddam lamp on him and cut him—that he was bleeding. His whimpering was followed by a moment of silence, then of Butch angrily shouting.

Lights snapped on in surrounding houses, the hullabaloo apparently attracting the neighbors . . . but no one emerged. Bravo never doubted that the curious peeked out of their windows from behind blinds, probably having heard those two boisterously attacking each other more than a few times. Behavior is characteristic, typical and predictable.

"I'll hit you with another lamp if you don't stop walloping me," Cleo screeched. "Got a goddam right to—catching you doing it with him!"

"Wouldn't need to if you screwed me—especially on your first night off the road. Why in hell ain't you horny?"

"Was drunk. Passed out."

A few more moments of shrill yelling by both and then Bravo heard doors slamming so loudly they sounded like they were being shattered. He surmised that Butch chased her through the house. Holy shit! It occurred to him that they may have left the room he'd slept in. He peeked through windows until he found that room, then forced open the window and climbed inside. After gathering up his belongings and stuffing them haphazardly into his luggage cases, he threw them out the window and jumped out after them.

More and more lights clicked on in neighboring houses, illuminating the back yard. Anxious not to be identified, concerned that it jeopardize his federal position, he gathered up his things and ran around the house, where he tossed everything into the bucar while clambering in.

Aware of people peeking at him, he backed out of the driveway without snapping on headlights and taillights to give anyone a chance to note the license plate number. Turning into the street, he gunned the motor to get the hell out of there.

Goddammit! he worried about Cleo. Hell, that ole' gal ought to be able to take care of herself. She sure as hell had more ability at hand-to-hand combat than Butch. So he needed to focus on finding his way out of that area. After turning a corner he snapped on the lights.

After a few exploratory turns he happened onto Broward Boulevard, so sped east through light traffic at five in the morning. And he continually ground his teeth in vexation because of concern for Cleo. Okay, too late to intercede. Anyway, he doubted Butch would seriously harm her. Sure, he'd punch her a couple of time. But the brazen hussy knew how to survive . . . maybe sustain only a few lumps . . . he hoped.

Last thing he needed was to be publicized as the other man in a murder charge brought against the jealous husband. Not only would it affect his marital situation but probably stymie that promotion. Oh shit! How in hell would he explain it to Maylene? Would she accept that Cleo overwhelmed him and forced him to almost fuck her?

At Federal Highway he turned south toward the motel. But as he neared Seventeenth Street he decided against returning to that place, so hung a left at the corner and headed east. Spotting the Hotel Embassy he shrugged concession to take a room there, on whatever floor and despite the time required to wait for elevators. At least he'd feel relatively secure . . . and have an opportunity to get some shut-eye . . . if that was possible after everything that had happened.

THIRTY-SEVEN

Bravo peeked at the digital clock on the lamp table and grimaced at having slept past nine. Hell, he considered it justified, based on all he'd experienced last night. Besides, he believed he deserved to take Sunday off, in spite of the terrorist threat. The brain and the body craved rejuvenation. Yes, he remembered how gung-ho he and the others had been last night outside that burning motel, but believed the others were as willing as he to postpone the hunt for Abdulo, being as beat-up as he.

He chuckled when Cleo flashed in mind, then guffawed. Holy shit! That was something! No, he refused to believe he'd been innocent—refused to accept he'd resisted enough. Hell, she had him pinned with her husky body and almost stuffed his pecker up to her kidney. Believe that it was her doing rather than his. But he'd been halfway receptive, once she got his mojo going.

He couldn't stop thinking he ought to call her, concerned that she survived intact. But prudence inhibited him doing that. Besides, what in hell would he say if Butch answered?

More of a concern was Maylene learning about that escapade. He knew damn well he'd have a hard time convincing her he'd been the innocent victim. And he had no idea how Cleo intends to explain being battered and bruised when she shows up at the office. Conyo, he sure hoped that brazen broad didn't open up to the world and embarrass the hell out of him. No way he'd convince Maylene of any kind of blamelessness. What would his bosses believe? How would they react?

The sound of rain pelting his window brought his eyes to the closed drapes. Somewhere in the recesses of his mind he'd been aware of the downpour for quite a long time, possibly an hour. Exhausted, he'd dismissed it. But this downpour threatened to be unlike those fifteen-minute tropical showers or squalls characteristic to South Florida. It assaulted the world in an endless deluge, with no indication of letting up any time soon.

He sat up and dropped his feet out of the bed before calling the US Attorney's office. Receiving a taped message instructing the available days and hours of the office relieved him that his group hadn't assembled and waited for him. He called each of the people in the taskforce on their cellphones to suggest that everyone rest over the weekend and he rejoiced when all agreed.

His last call was to Olecki, who he invited to breakfast. No, he didn't have breakfast with Cleo and her husband. He left there hours ago. They needed to talk.

He'd decided to garner support of someone who was able to explain her antics in case that business went public. Boy, Archison would have a field day with that scandal.

Olecki chuckled as he said he'd already had breakfast but would take coffee while Bravo ate. Yep, he'd sure as hell like to hear about it. So he directed Bravo to meet in half an hour in a diner on State Road 84, west of Federal Highway. Bravo accepted and hurried to dress then drove to the diner.

They sat across from each other in a vinyl-upholstered booth in a diner decorated in the art-deco of the nineteen sixties. Olecki chortled at what Bravo told him. "I don't doubt for a minute that Cleo is that crazy. And, yes, I'm confident the gal survives Butch's rage. Like as not she'll settle the guy down, give him the bang of the week, and they'll go on like nothing happened."

"Needless to say, I can't afford for that business to be publicized."

"I sure as hell won't say anything. However, there's no guessing whether that brazen gal spreads the word. Don't do or say anything to piss her off."

"Can you talk to her?" Before Bravo received an assurance from Olecki, his cellphone buzzed. He answered it, and his jaws ground in vexation when he heard Yzabel's voice.

"When will we be free to live our lives?"

He fiddled with his nearly empty coffee mug. The breakfast he'd just eaten threatened to gurgle up on him. Wrong time for marital discord and its accompanying stomach-churning aggravation. Still, he accepted that he needed to mollify her, so said: "I need you to do me the very big favor of being patient."

"Patient! Our lives are interrupted. Call your office to end this nuisance."

"It will end really soon, Yzabel. I promise. We'll be rounding up those terrorists and then our lives can return to normal." He decided against mentioning last night when the Vasillo Rojo attempted to kill him and dispose of his body in a pyre.

"Our lives will never return to normal, as you call it, Ramón."

He winced, stung by her irate tone and her addressing him formally. "Just hold out a couple of days, Yzabel. This will be over and I'll return home."

"Think different home. I'm planning to talk to the boys today, to inform them of my intention to divorce you."

"Can't we do that together when I return?" He had been purposefully cryptic, not anxious to share his marital problems with Olecki . . . or anyone else.

Click! Her hang-up was her reply.

He clenched his jaws, remembering how unreasonable she'd been for weeks, since learning about that Spaniard's intended visit. Did she really carry that torch for twenty-odd years? When will she let it go? Has she been trysting with him these past few days . . . these many years?

If so, why is she so cantankerous? You'd think she'd have mellowed after enjoying a burst of passion. Hell, that's how he felt—enthralled, reborn—his spirits lifted by amorous interaction with Maylene.

Had Nando frustrated her and fueled that distemper? My God! She hadn't enjoyed the balm of ecstasy that might have soothed her, as it had him. Smiling at memories of Maylene, he decided to spend the day with her. Yes, he'd let all of the angst of terrorists and a failed marriage drain away in the enthrallment of passion.

Ay Dios, hopefully she didn't find out about that escapade with Cleo.

THIRTY-EIGHT

Bravo scowled annoyance for failing to extricate Galbos—Abdulo—from his thinking as he shaved in preparation for Monday morning meetings with the taskforce. At least he had a full-sized bathroom at the Hotel Embassy. He cringed at memory of that brazen mulatto threatening to divulge the family relationship. Dammit! Why did he have to shoot the wrong guy? Why couldn't he have gotten lucky and eliminated that hump?

The trill of his cellphone jolted him to check his watch before answering it, concerned with being delayed getting to the conference room. Hell, he'd only gotten back to his room on the sixth floor a half hour ago. A smile lingered from memories of that long day and wonderful night spent with Maylene. Yes, they violated their agreement to sleep apart so as not reveal their relationship. But their ecstasy last night denied them parting.

He answered without checking his caller ID, having assumed it to be the US Attorney's office or his bureau in Washington. His eyebrows arched at the sound of Yzabel's voice; she being the last person he expected. "I called you a few times yesterday. You apparently didn't have your phone with you, which worried me, considering that you and that thing are inseparable."

He blinked, remembering he'd left it at the hotel when he went to Maylene's. Fatigued by everything that happened the last couple of days, he'd decided to separate himself from it and the job, take a break, and reward himself with respite. No, he hadn't expected Yzabel to call.

"I won't ask where you were and why you didn't have your cellphone with you." Yzabel said.

He swallowed—his lips moved but no words emerged.

"For a time there I worried whether you might have been harmed, but hearing your voice relieves that anxiety."

"I'm happy to hear you're concerned, Yzabel."

"I'm calling to apologize for my hysteria yesterday."

He tilted his head to listen, disbelieving the contriteness in her voice—a softness he hadn't heard this past week . . . or a few weeks preceding that, for that matter.

"I've been distraught these last few days," she said, "mostly disappointed by you not being here to escort me to that ball."

He didn't respond, not sure how to.

"Yes, I know, your office assigned you there in Fort Lauderdale and you had no choice, considering the present terrorist problems. So I'm trying to hold myself together until you return. Then we need to talk face-to-face, as you suggested."

He clenched his teeth as he asked: "What about Nando?"

Silence. "I asked you a question."

Another few seconds of silence. "That ended twenty-four years ago."

He swallowed, stunned by that unexpected pronouncement.

"Yes," she said, "Nando and I talked briefly. That's about it. We both accepted our long-ago adventure as a delightful memory."

"Then why the hell were you so testy?"

Again a few seconds of silence. "Frustration, I suppose. I'd wanted him to flatter me. And, yes, I had hoped to recapture something of the enchantment we once enjoyed. But it wasn't to be. And in the final analysis I've come to the realization that family has more value than revisiting an old romance, which should have been forgotten when you and I married. Please come home, Ray, and talk about it."

"Okay, like I said yesterday: have a little patience. Hopefully within a few more days we'll wrap things up here. Then you and I can sort all that other stuff out."

"Thank you, Ray. Good luck."

After she'd clicked off he stared at the wall. Had she finally come to her senses? Was it true that she hadn't cheated with that Spaniard? Did their marriage have a chance of weathering that storm? Storm hell! That had been a raging hurricane.

But how could he go backwards, considering the thing with Maylene? Half a dozen times yesterday he'd been on the verge of avowing devotion by assuring Maylene he'd dissolve his marriage.

How does he deal with that now? Would Yzabel understand that during those torrents of disagreements he'd found solace in the arms of another woman—adoration that expanded into devotion? How will his boys accept a black stepmother?

THIRTY-NINE

Bravo winced when Cleo entered the conference room.

"What in hell you run into?" Joe Lee Baggler blurted out.

The others flinched at Baggler's insensitivity. But the way they stared at her intimated that they were as eager as he to share the revelation of how Cleo got that shiner, a split lip and numerous other bruises.

Bravo held his breath, dreading her explanation. But Cleo only smiled as she appeared to disregard the question.

"Sure looks like Butch did a number on you," Baggler said.

"No big thing," Cleo said. "Wasn't the first fight we've had and more'n likely won't be the last."

"But this one must have been a doozy," Baggler said.

Bravo wished the blow-hard would shut-up. He assumed by the expressions on the others that they also disapproved of his continued insensitivity.

"What you should ask about," Cleo said, "was our making up. Man, you wish you had you a volcano like that."

"Talk about it!" Baggler said. "And I mean blow by blow."

Ay Dios! Bravo shrunk inside. Sure made him question the effectiveness of the FBI psychological profiling of applicants.

Archison strode into the conference room and gaped at Cleo, as did Coombs and Maylene who accompanied him and took seats around the long table. The growly demeanor on the Assistant US Attorney's solemn-face with his bristling mustache ended the repartee. At intervals all glanced at Cleo's bruises but no one commented.

Archison turned to address Bravo. "How long do you intend holding those two prisoners you brought in with the female devil?"

"We're hoping to milk them for info," Bravo said. He glanced at Maylene, hoping she didn't question Cleo about those bruises.

"You can't hold people indefinitely without arraigning them," Archison said.

Bravo nodded. "I'd like to grill them once more."

"Be prepared to charge or release them by noon," Archison said. "Everybody else hear me?"

"By noon," Bravo assured before turning to his staff. "Let's go over to the jail and intensely interrogate those two hardcases."

"You forgetting they lawyered up?" Epps reminded.

Bravo shrunk into his collar, aware that Archison glowered at him. "We'll let them know they're free to go," Bravo said meekly, "while offering rewards for information." Then he turned to Olecki. "Hope you can arrange with the jailers to accommodate us with separate rooms for interrogation?"

Olecki nodded. "I'll call over there but I can't accompany you. Been summoned to my lieutenant's office for a review to justify assets assigned to this case."

"Come over," Bravo said "soon as you can."

"Yeah," Baggler said, "we sure need us all the help we can get."

"No denying," Loscalzo said, "this investigation is floundering."

"We flailing around without knowing what our next step is," Epps added. "Hear what I'm saying?"

Bravo clenched his jaws to deny them the awareness that they'd rankled him. Most irritating was the realization that they'd correctly appraised that the case had hit a dead end. He breathed deeply while hoping Archison didn't make any managerial changes, giving him time to show progress and avoid being superseded . . . a circumstance that could make waves in his agency and negatively affect his promotion.

# # #

Bravo glared across the small table at Sebastiano Melendez, as did Cleo and Coombs. The man slumped in a straight back chair, wearing orange coveralls stenciled with the Broward County Retention Facility. His scoffing attitude indicated his awareness that he intimidated them with his surly replies. That lack of compliance etched lines of vexation in the faces of his inquisitors.

"You're not helping yourself," Coombs said, leaning pugnaciously across the table. Huddled together, they crowded the interrogation room, made it feel even smaller.

"Why I need help? You have no case for hold me. Any lawyer I get will make fools of you in court."

"We've talked to your parole officer," Bravo said, "and he's agreed to cooperate with us by sending you back to finish up that three years if you don't tell us every damn thing we want to know."

"My lawyer he fix that too."

"Not likely," Bravo said, "considering we have six or seven witnesses who saw you aiding and abetting those two by helping them conceal that truckload of explosives."

Melendez scowled. "What people can say that thing?"

"A whole bunch in the area of your shop," Cleo said, "who got caught with narcotics on their persons."

"You plant that shit on people to make them say lies," Melendez said. "I bet that how you get you face busted—messing with potheads."

"You just need to answer the damn questions," Bravo said. Damn right he diverted conversation away from the subject of Cleo's bruises.

"Just keep in mind," Coombs said, "that we have a number of witnesses willing to testify against you."

"And we can double that," Cleo said. "We go back there and shake down all those folks in the area of your shop and we'll have us a dozen witnesses."

"My lawyer prove they lie to save they asses."

"No question about it," Bravo said. "But it serves our purpose."

"That wrong, man," Melendez said.

"Right, wrong, or lop-sided," Coombs said, "you have only one way to save your dumb ass from finishing those three years on the inside."

"Maybe he likes prison life," Cleo said.

Melendez scowled at her. "Okay, what benefit I have for talk?"

"How about being able to walk out of here and go home?" Coombs asked.

"Spend the next three years," Cleo said, "with family and friends, instead of with goons in a prison."

"Free to walk to the store when you want," Coombs added, "and hang with your amigos . . . have a beer with your lunch, or a glass of wine with dinner."

"What I have to tell you?"

"Where we can find Abdulo," Bravo said.

"You crazy? I do that I kiss my ass goodbye."

"He'll be taken into custody," Coombs said, "and no longer able to hurt you." Melendez chuckled as he glanced around at the stern faces focused on him. "You say I tell you about Abdulo and I get out, go home, no go back to *cárcel*—how you say, slam?"

"That's the deal," Bravo said. "Tell us where to find Abdulo and you're free as a big-assed bird."

"Until tomorrow," Melendez said. "Then you bust again. I want clean record with no more parole, or I have no reason for talk."

"I'm with the sheriff's department," Cleo said, "and can speak to the parole officer and get you wiped clean."

"This clean, it mean I never get pick up again with threat to finish sentence?"

"You got that right," Cleo said. "But you need to give us accurate information."

"I want guarantee in writing."

Bravo flinched—knowing they couldn't do that. Still, he stared hard into the man's eyes to instill confidence. "I need that information and will be too grateful not to grant that concession."

"Believe this man," Coombs said. "His word is his bond."

"I never believe the gringo—never trust."

"Then believe a Puerto Rican," Bravo said. "I'm a federal officer and will write you a guarantee here and now. Let's help each other." He knew damned well whatever he wrote wouldn't be worth the paper he wrote it on. But he desperately needed a heads-up—a direction to nail Abdulo and the rest of those hoods—justification to save him from being replaced as taskforce primary.

Melendez laughed raucously. "You people a joke."

The law enforcement officers gaped at him, their faces fraught with frustration.

"You playing us?" Bravo demanded, leaning menacingly across the small table.

Melendez chcuckled. "You play you'self with you lies and bullshit."

"You'd better cooperate," Coombs said, "or spend the next three years in stir."

"It don't going happen. Any way I do that standing on the head."

Bravo jumped up, sending his chair sliding away as he glowered at the prisoner. "Last chance. Talk or finish those three years in stir."

Melendez continued to chuckle, further irritating Bravo, who turned and headed for the door. Coombs and Cleo reluctantly followed him, and the door closed behind them.

"Sonofabitch yanked our chains," Bravo grumbled as he and the others slumped in chairs in a small conference chamber.

"Worse thing," Cleo said, "is we got nothing on that hardcase to continue holding his ass."

"And no basis to revoke his parole," Bravo said.

"Hopefully," Coombs said, "the FBI guys and Pedrazo get something out of the other one."

"Don't bet the farm on it," Bravo said. He looked about to enlarge on that when the door opened and Peter Olecki ambled in.

"Glum is the only word comes to mind looking at the lot of you," Olecki said, chuckling.

"Humor isn't appreciated at this moment," Bravo said.

"Then let me inject sunshine," Olecki said.

They stared at him with brows furrowed by skepticism. Olecki grinned as he explained that they had him hanging around the cop house cooling his heels while waiting for that meeting to begin, with none of the bosses in an all-fired hurry. Being restless, he dug into the file they had there to see if he couldn't uncover something useful . . . something that'd been overlooked.

Impatience lined the faces of his listeners as they waited for him to relieve their angst. Olecki sat and leaned back in the chair. "Read that damn report twice before I realized that green pick-up truck hadn't been stolen, as assumed. Those lobos had actually purchased that cheap piece of shit."

"Why is that important?" Bravo asked.

"They registered it," Olecki said, "in the name of Celia Melendez, the wife of that skel."

The faces of his listeners brightened. "Got her!" Coombs exclaimed. "She's the owner of a vehicle used in the commission of a felony."

"Accessory," Bravo said, "to everything that truck was used in."

"Time to see how cocky Melendez is now," Cleo said. "Doubt that laughing cowboy is all that willing to send his old lady to the slammer."

Nodding to each other, they returned to the interrogation room accompanied by Olecki in time to intercept the guards taking away the prisoner.

"Give us another minute with him," Bravo requested of the guards.

"Why you come back?" Melendez asked, sneering.

"To talk about your wife," Bravo said.

"What Celia have to do with anything?"

"That truck used in the robbery at the airfield," Coombs said, "as well as used to store those explosives, is registered in your wife's name."

Melendez stared dumbly at them and shrugged, obviously unsure how that affected him.

"Her owning that vehicle," Cleo said, "makes her an accessory to every crime it was used in."

"Somebody they steal that truck," Melendez said.

"Yeah, yeah," Bravo said. "And stashed it outside of that shack you work in,"

"Besides you smart-asses never reported it stolen," Cleo added.

"Your wife's going to do some hard time," Coombs said.

"Hope you don't have young children," Cleo said.

"What niños have to do with this?"

"Knowledge of your wife's allowing that truck to be used in a felony," Bravo said, "affects your parole. With you back in jail for violating your parole and your wife doing hard time for the next ten years, as an accessory in a whole lot of things, your kids will become wards of the state."

"Like orphans," Cleo said, "made to live in foster homes."

"No! You no can punish niños."

"Only thing that'll prevent that," Bravo said, "is your cooperation."

"I do that and Abdulo and the vasillo, they kill me."

"It's the only way," Cleo said, "to save your family."

"We'll protect you," Olecki said.

"My wife no have charges if I talk?"

"Can't promise that," Coombs said. "But I can assure you she'll get paroled—won't spend time in prison."

"Be free to tend to the young'uns," Cleo added.

"Okay, I take chance, because *mis compatriotos* maybe never get me out. They call me *hermano*—how you say—brother—but leave me here to serve three more years. Maybe they kill me like they do that Elizondo. That is their way. They have no—how you say—*no sentimiento*."

"Which is why we'll help you," Olecki said, "and turn you loose if you tell us where to find them."

"We'll take them off the street," Cleo said, "so they can't ever threaten you or anybody else."

"Best damn chance," Bravo said, "you have of surviving."

Melendez dropped his eyes and wagged his head in defeat. "They stay in factory is *vacío*—how you say?—empty—behind chain fence at end of Forty-eight Court, near the Ten Avenue."

Bravo repeated the location. Melendez nodded. "You have to promise no to tell them I send you there."

"If you're telling the truth," Bravo said, "you won't have to worry any more about Abdulo."

"Is true. You find him in that place, with his vasillo."

"Where'd they store all those guns and ammo from that robbery?" Olecki asked.

"Guns and bullets in truck," Melendez said.

"What truck?" Bravo demanded.

"He buy cheap truck for store them."

"Where is that truck now?" Olecki asked.

Melendez shrugged. "He move it every day to keep police from find it. Only Dios and Abdulo know where he park it today."

Bravo rose and directed a guard to return the prisoner to his cell.

"¡ Icy! You promise I go free."

"After we check out that location," Bravo said.

"You guys crazy. I dead meat here."

"We'll put you in solitary," Olecki said. He talked to the guard on the way out about keeping Melendez out of the general population.

"We're not supposed to hold him any longer," the guard said in lowered voice, "according to a directive from the US Attorney."

"Do us a favor," Bravo said, "by holding him one more hour. If you don't hear from us by then you can kick him loose with his compadre."

FORTY

Bravo breathed deeply to suppress excitedness while summoning the FBI agents and Pedrazo from the other interrogation room to relate what occurred. Collaring Baggler he said: "Got a location for Abdulo and need a SWAT team in a hurry. Can you get your outfit to supply it?"

Excited by the news, Baggler went into the nearest office and telephoned FBI headquarters in Miami. After a few minutes he returned with head hung. "Sorry, guy, but the bureau is presently bogged down with more cases than they can handle. They say they can't deploy a fast-strike team for two or three days—if then."

Bravo groaned. "I've got Abdulo in my sights and can't pull the damn trigger."

"I'll call my office," Olecki said, "and see if they can't get one organized."

#

Bravo, along with Cleo, and Maylene, rode in the Chevy with Olecki driving to the Twelfth District Sheriff's Office. Located on Northeast Thirty-eighth Street off Third Avenue in Oakland Park, it was in an area of low-rise apartment buildings whose facades indicated they were in an area of moderate rents. The rest of the staff had been instructed to meet them in that sprawling one-story pink building with a faded green fascia. Maylene accompanied them since she had to prepare the indictments against the terrorists when apprehended.

Lieutenant Frisch of the Sheriff's Department assembled a dozen men to form a Special Weapons and Tactics Team. The lieutenant acted as intelligence officer as well as SWAT commander, and requested two snipers and a paramedic. A dozen deputies who had been vigorously trained and rigorously tested to qualify composed the team. But because many were off-duty and had to be called in it took most of the afternoon to mobilize. Darkness threatened to settle over the area by the time they were ready to move out.

Bravo had all he could do to contain himself for those long hours. He at least enjoyed the reassurance of two cruisers having been sent out by the sheriff's office to surveil the designated area. They reported by radio the lay of the land while scrutinizing the target building, which they described as a weather-worn barn-like structure with rusted and unused conveyers, plus lifting devices and paint sprayers. Wedged between two buildings it had restricted access. A tall gate in a rusted chainlink fence fronted the property about forty feet from a wide overhead door, with a single door alongside it. All windows and the rear door had been blocked up.

No activity had been sighted in the vicinity of the building, raising questions of finding Abdulo and his gang there. But with no other leads they concentrated on taking that building, hoping it panned out as their needed bonanza. They needed it to at least yield a store of arms and munitions, since it provided ample space to garage a good-sized truck.

Everyone studied every aspect of information about the structure as they prepared to assault it. They practiced rigid security in the event the bad guys waited to ambush them. Nothing could be taken for granted when dealing with Abdulo. Bravo remembered his boasting of confronting the police on his terms. And he'd learned of this place from that prisoner Melendez.

Bravo and his taskforce members had donned black combat fatigues and body armor as well as Kevlar helmets. Besides they carried goggles around their necks to protect their eyes if that became necessary. Lieutenant Frisch advised of his intent to apply *dynamic entry*: speed and surprise to overwhelm occupants of the building before the bad guys had time to regroup and put the police at risk.

Since Danly Coombs volunteered to go along, the guys goaded Maylene into joining them. She capitulated and donned the ninja-like uniform with a flak jacket and strapped on a Beretta nine-millimeter semi-automatic handgun supplied by one of the deputies. Only Bravo had reservations about taking her along. But since Cleo accompanied them, as well as two women on the assault team, he didn't have the right to exclude her from her possible initiation into violence.

Bravo stole glances at Cleo in the tightly fitting ninja outfit that accented her ample figure. He remained uneasy even though not one word passed between them about the incident. So far it saved him from explaining that fiasco to Marlene.

FORTY-ONE

Lieutenant Frisch assembled the taskforce and addressed it. "We've reviewed all information and briefed everyone on their duties. It's time to proceed to the next step so let's board the vans and get the show on the road."

Bravo nodded and instructed his team to climb onto the bus-like vehicles for conveyance to the target site. Night settled fully over the area as the convoy of three vehicles made their way east on Thirty-Eighth Street to Dixie Highway, then north to Forty-Eighth Court, into an area of weathered warehouses and tired-looking factories. Finally the target site loomed out of the night, foreboding and impregnable.

They split up at Tenth Avenue, with Pedrazo, Loscalzo, and Baggler, along with two deputies, taking up positions that prevented anyone escaping by the narrow alley at the rear of the building. True, there didn't appear to be any means of egress with all the windows and doors blocked up, but why take a chance? Epps elected to stay near Maylene, insisting that it was incumbent upon FBI personnel to protect US attorneys.

Since most of the buildings in the vicinity had been locked up for the night few people remained in the area, reducing the time and involvement of evacuation to prevent injury of innocents. None of the trucks and cars that usually parked helter skelter remained, leaving wide-open and unobstructed space in front and behind the target building.

To obtain additional information regarding the lay of the land before deploying, Baggler contacted the Miami FBI office and arranged for air reconnaissance. They sent out a single-engine

Cessna 182RG with the wing mounted atop the cockpit where it didn't obstruct observation. The plane flew without lights so as not to alert those in the warehouse—an exemption from Federal Aviation Administration rules the FBI enjoys. They had, of course, equipped that plane with infrared night-vision capability.

Heat-detection and imaging equipment had been removed to send to a lab for upgrading, so it lacked ability to ascertain whether any people were in the building. After ten or fifteen minutes the operators of the plane reported the same lack of activity as the deputies in the Sheriff's Department cruisers.

Based on the lack of activity in and around the target building the assault team doubted they'd encounter anyone. Nevertheless one SWAT truck parked with its broadside at the chained gate in front of the building. Its occupants scrambled out to take positions behind it to cover the two front entrances from every angle. The two snipers climbed to the top of nearby buildings to acquire advantages.

When their van stopped fifty feet behind the SWAT truck, Bravo, Olecki, Cleo, and Maylene, joined by Epps, crouched to lessen themselves as targets while hurrying to take cover behind the SWAT vehicle close to the gate. Bravo and Olecki elected to carry pump-action shotguns, besides sidearms. Bravo gritted his teeth to squelch exposing anticipation of cutting that bearded bastard in half with a choked load of buckshot.

He, like the others, peered at the cement-faced concrete blocks streaked with mildew, a surface that hadn't been cleaned or painted in years. Unlike the many flat-roofed buildings around it, it had a peaked roof, which breadth suggested a heavy timber frame, more than likely supported by columns.

A sign with faded letters above the single door advertised it as FURNITURE REFURBISHING. Lieutenant Frisch had obtained information that the company went bankrupt some seven months ago and that the building remained vacant.

"Damn lack of activity worries me," Lieutenant Frisch confided in Bravo.

Both men scrutinized the building without defining anything to indicate whether their quarry was inside. Exhaling his impatience, the lieutenant hailed the warehouse with a portable loudspeaker.

"Hello inside Furniture Refurbishing. This is the police. The building is surrounded. Open the door!"

Nothing stirred. The doors remained closed and quiet prevailed. The lieutenant repeated the advisory.

"Let me try," Bravo said. When the lieutenant handed him the bullhorn he loud-hailed the building. "Hola en el edificio de Restauración de Mueblas. Ésta es la policía. Hemos rodeado el edificio. Abran la puerta!"

Still no sound or movement.

"Maybe we got a hummer from that Melendez guy," Olecki said.

"Hard to believe he'd pull something that stupid," Bravo said, "considering his wife's freedom is at stake."

Cleo snuffled. "Can't depend on anything extracted from a skel."

"Guy played us," Olecki said, "knowing it'd be too late to do anything about it once we realized we'd been scammed."

"Yeah," Cleo said, "y'all left direction for the jailers to turn them loose an hour after we left. That sucker hurried home, snatched up his family, and is in Georgia by now."

"Or Puerto Rico," Olecki added.

Bravo ground his jaws, incensed for having let himself be played by that mook. Dammit, he'd been susceptible because of his eagerness to take out Galbos—Abdulo—and save himself the embarrassment of exposure of familial connection.

"Can we get that door opened?" he asked the lieutenant.

"Doubtful with a battering ram," Lieutenant Frisch said while signaling over one of his men. "Think you can blow that door, Leo?"

"Piece of cake." Leo's grin indicated he relished the chore. He returned to the second SWAT vehicle and obtained what resembled a backpack, then loped back to the barricading van. Two SWAT team members accompanied him to the chain link gate, their rifles at the ready. One used huge chain-cutters to slice through the lock's chain.

Disdainfully pushing the creaking gate inward, Leo stooped forward to reduce himself as a target as he scampered to the overhead door. His two cohorts remained at the gate, down on one knee with their assault rifles aimed to cover him and blow away anyone who appeared from that dark building.

Everyone watched, taut with anticipation and with weapons at the ready, while Leo placed the claymore-like mine. He fumbled around with something in it, then hurried back to take cover behind the barricading van, accompanied by the two who had backed him up.

"Fire in the hold!" Leo yelled. And everyone drew in their heads.

The door blew down with a resounding explosion that erupted billows of smoke. Air pressure expanded. Debris and smoke suffused in every direction. Spotlights focused on the dark building with its cavernous opening.

Lieutenant Frisch and a couple of his men made their way toward the opening with plastic see-thru shields held in front of them and their weapons at the ready. Four others followed a few feet behind, crouched to stay in the protection of the shields.

Bravo and Olecki gestured to each other then darted to one side of the gaping opening as soon as the SWAT cops reached that position. A moment later Mac and Mac dashed to the other side of the door. Two of the ninjas shone flashlights into the darkness to halo a cavernous emptiness interrupted only by massive timbers supporting the ceiling beams.

"Nothing and nobody," one of the deputies said, shaking his head.

Still, they employed caution. One man with a flashlight mounted on his assault rifle darted into the doorway and crouched against the closest wooden column that supported the huge wooden beams criss-crossing the building twenty feet above them. After scanning the area around him he waved to those behind him.

Another deputy sprinted past the first to flatten himself against the next column. Then another and another until half a dozen had penetrated the vast space. Their searchlights probed every corner of the darkness.

"Clear," yelled the one furthest inside.

One ran his light across the area of the massive beams above them. Another traced his along a block wall, then yelled that he'd discovered a door—attracting all attention to that area. Two deputies sprinted to it and took positions at each side of it. One of them tried the door handle. It yielded and he swung it inward. Both probed the small room with flashlight beams, their rifles at the ready.

"Clear," one of them called.

"So much for that tip," Lieutenant Frisch said, grimacing as he glanced around at the assembled force that had been wasted in a futile exercise. Nevertheless he yelled to the half dozen or so officers in the dark cavern: "Hold your positions."

They remained in place, in the partial cover of the huge wooden columns that held up the massive beams. However, relieved by the lack of activity none of them appeared as attentive as before.

"We got snookered," Olecki grumbled as he and others wandered into the wide doorway and peered around.

Bravo clenched his teeth in frustration. Cleo and Maylene, followed him into the cavern, with Epps ambling behind. All probed the silence and darkness with their flashlight beams while venturing deeper. Dead air and humidity engrossed them. Cleo snickered at their disappointment before she and Olecki hunched acceptance of frustration and returned to the gaping doorway, both shaking their heads to wordlessly commiserate with each other.

Lieutenant Frisch ordered the SWAT team members to retreat to the doorway, abandoning positions with the same caution they had used to attain them, as if performing an exercise. When all of the SWAT officers had exited the building, the lieutenant shrugged capitulation to circumstances, frustrated by the waste of energy, caution and apprehension.

FORTY-TWO

Bravo remained in the warehouse, along with Maylene and Epps, probing every corner of the dark grotto with their flashlights. He kept shaking his head. "That mook steered us here for a reason. Somethings not right."

"Played our asses," Epps said. "Hear what I'm saying?"

Bravo nodded, his face distorted by the questions swirling in his head. "Abdulo has a devious reason for wanting us here."

"Never knew you to be paranoid," Maylene said.

"Might be intuition," Epps said. "Hear what—"

"Check with headquarters," Bravo yelled to Olecki, "to see if anything broke out somewhere while we're distracted to this out-of-the-way place."

"Good idea," Cleo said. "The mook may be occupying us out here while pulling a caper somewhere else."

"We'd have been advised by radio," the lieutenant replied.

"Messed with our heads," Epps said. "Hear what I'm saying?"

"Why?" Bravo asked, more deliberative than questioning while strolling deeper into the dark interior. Maylene and Epps followed, in spite of everyone else having wandered back to the doorway.

"When are you going to accept," Maylene asked, "that there's nothing here?"

"The guy is a psycho egocentric," Bravo said, "on the verge of madness. I'm convinced that Melendez was told to steer us out here. Why?"

"To waste our damn time," Epps said, searching around while passing his flashlight over the hefty columns then along the broad beams above him. He gawked. "Holy shit! Look at—"

A rifle barked. Epps pressed himself against a column as a bullet split the concrete an inch from his foot. A second shot, then a third, pinged the floor around him.

Bravo fired a shotgun blast at the gunflash from the beams above them as he herded Maylene toward the doorway. But a fusillade of rifle fire dissuaded them from fleeing in that direction. Realizing they were too far from it, with bullets pelting the concrete floor at their feet, the three of them flattened themselves against the massive columns.

Another fusillade from above scattered those at the door. Two officers just inside the door went down, while the rest scurried to crouch beyond its jamb. The two wounded dragged themselves to cover, indicating that their flak jackets had saved them from serious injury.

The SWAT team members near the entrance went down on their knees and aimed their weapons at the darkness, but withheld fire for fear of hitting their own. Besides, they were unable to define a bad guy to shoot at.

Bravo pointed to pits in the floor as bullets peppered the cement floor around the three of them. But as Maylene moved toward one she gasped and collapsed to her knees. Bravo fired at the beams as cover while stooping to attend to her. He dropped his shotgun to cradle her.

Epps had already leaped into a concrete-lined pit with valves in the floor, bullets chopping up the cement around him. He fired his pistol at the flashes of gunfire above, only to imbed bullets in the thick beams. But he continued shooting to cover Maylene and Bravo.

That cover-fire allowed Bravo a minute to pull Maylene into a different pit—one that housed a pump needed during the rainy season. He huddled with her as close to the edge as he could while shielding her. Bullets assailed them but didn't penetrate the concrete at the rim of the pit.

Inspecting the wound in her shoulder, he consoled her by assuring her it wasn't life-threatening—certainly not fatal—and that he'd get her out to medical attention. She groaned so he gathered her into his arms. He knew by the sounds of the bullets that pinged all around him that they fired those M-4 carbines they stole from the airfield. It gratified him that they only had carbines rather than longer-barreled and more accurate rifles. But the rat bastards had the vantage point of those beams.

He clenched his teeth to keep from howling how Abdulo set this up to ambush the police, exactly as that psycho bragged he'd do. And the conniving sonofabitch had somehow gotten word to Melendez to pass on to the police the location to set them up for this ambush. He'd probably even anticipated the time of preparation, expecting them to arrive after dark, giving him that added advantage.

But why hadn't they held fire until they had more victims in their sights? Then he remembered Epps spotting one of them, which apparently triggered the shooting. Thank God! Had a few more minutes passed everyone might have become complacent, causing many to wander around . . . to be slaughtered en masse.

When one of the terrorists fired he triggered the others to follow suit. They had probably been drilled in the rudiments of guerilla warfare, but hadn't acquired the discipline of soldiers. Bravo assumed that the police outside didn't return fire for fear of hitting their own, so he called Olecki on his cellphone. "We're in pits below the level of the floor. Those lobos are on the beams supporting the upper part of the building."

"Copy that. We'll put a hurting on their asses."

"Normal bullets won't penetrate those thick structures."

"We've got one of those anti-materiel rifles that can penetrate concrete and thick wooden beams," Olecki said. "Stay in those pits and keep your heads down."

Two rounds of the M82 tore through the beams, knocking a terrorist off his perch. A third and fourth round each knocked another terrorist down as those missives shredded the beams. After the fifth and sixth rounds others panicked and shimmied down the huge columns to run for that small door in the back. Abdulo yelled for them to hold their positions. But others panicked and abandoned the beams.

Bravo yelled into the phone that the shooters scattered. He rose from his concealment, his semi-automatic held in both hands as he aimed and fired, knocking over two more.

Then he froze at the sound of the voice behind him. "*¡Ahora morirás, primo!*"

The rasping voice of Abdulo rang in his head with the words: *Now you will die, cousin!* Bravo froze at sight of the pistol aimed at his head, only a few feet away and knew he wouldn't have time to bring his weapon to bear on the man.

"You defy me for the last time," Abdulo snarled at him. "I kill you now, and that lady with you. After I escape this place, I kill you wife, then you two boys."

Distressed by that threat, Bravo crouched lower as he reeled about with intent to bring his pistol to bear. Abdulo's gun already sparked at him—sending two bullets whizzing past his head. Nevertheless he sought to bring his gun into play, accepting he'd die, but cared only that he killed Abdulo to save his family and Maylene.

Abdulo stumbled forward, his eyes wide with disbelief, his pistol dangling from his hand. Then he pitched forward, dropping his weapon to clatter into the pit. He fell on his stomach with his head hanging over the edge. Boisy Epps stood behind him, holding a smoking nine-millimeter SIG Sauer semi-automatic pistol.

Bravo gaped at the dead body. Breathing deeply to reduce hypertension he reached over and felt for a pulse in the terrorist's neck. He nodded to Epps, indicating that Abdulo was dead, then breathed relief for ending the terrorist threat . . . as well as squelching information damaging to him personally.

Turning back to Maylene, he frowned dismay at her limpness. She'd only been shot in the shoulder. Beaming his flashlight on her, he gulped when he saw the hole in her temple. Oh, God! When did that happen? He remembered Abdulo's shots that missed him. No, God! He clamped his eyes shut. Pain shot through his brain. *Please, God, not those shots! . . . meant for me! Let it be from one of the shooters on the beams.*

"Oh no!" Epps wailed as he leapt into the pit.

Deputies armed with rifles and shotguns rushed in to take positions that permitted them cover while firing into the beams. But no one remained there.

"That small door in the rear," Bravo and Epps yelled to them.

They barged through it, weapons at the ready, to find the room empty. Then one spotted the hole in the floor, a sewer into which they assumed the terrorists fled, since they saw no other way out.

Spreading the word by radio, men hurriedly searched outside in the dark, their searchlights lancing patterns on the landscape. Finding a manhole cover, they removed it and crouched around it with weapons at the ready. The terrorists emerged one at a time to find themselves surrounded. Denied alternatives they meekly surrendered, handing their automatic carbines to their captors.

Bravo stayed behind and cradled Maylene. Olecki and Cleo helped him and Epps gently lift her out of the pit. The paramedic wheeled in a gurney to take her away. Bravo watched as it disappeared beyond the doorway. Then he spun about and kicked the sprawled body of Abdulo.

Olecki grabbed his arm and pulled him away. "It doesn't solve anything, Ray, doesn't change anything."

FORTY-THREE

Still disheveled and smeared with the black grease under their eyes, applied to deaden reflections, Bravo and the other members of the taskforce huddled morosely around the conference table at the office of the Assistant US Attorney. "Why," Epps asked, shaking his head. "Why'd I have to flap my big mouth and goad that woman into going along."

"It's on me," Bravo said. "I let her go in there . . . led her, in fact. It was my responsibility to make her wait until we secured the area."

"How could you know?" Olecki asked. "We all thought the building was empty. None of us knew they were hiding up on those beams . . . intending to ambush us."

"Nobody's to blame," Archison said, "for a terrorist's bullet."

"I buy that," Loscalzo said. "Any of us could have bought it."

"We know going in," Baggler said, "that it's a dangerous game."

"It's over," Archison said, "and no one has the right to claim responsibility for that death. It happened. Let's mourn her passing and leave it at that. Then let's all thank God we apprehended all of the terrorists and recovered the rest of the weapons, ending that threat to the American people."

"Thank God a couple of those mooks gave up where they hid the truck with the rest of the guns and ammo," Olecki said. "I'll remember forever," Bravo said, "that I let her accompany us."

"Don't beat up on yourself like that, man," Baggler said. "Considering the ambush they had planned, thank God it isn't all of us."

"Might have been," Loscalzo said, "if Epps hadn't spooked them."

"That Abdulo sonofabitch guy had a warped mind," Bravo said. "Probably thinks he died a martyr and will get some kind of recognition for something that ridiculous."

"Got to admit that the slick bastard really played us," Loscalzo said.

"So did that Melendez at the jail," Olecki said.

"More'n' likely with his compadre in on it," Cleo added.

"Like to get my hands around their throats," Bravo said. "Any idea where those deceiving bastards went after the guards released them?"

"They'll show up," Olecki said. "Small-time punks always do."

"Thanks to Epps," Bravo said, "for shooting that sneaky bastard, who had the drop on me. Fact is, didn't think I'd make it."

"Wish I could have gotten Abdulo quicker, man," Epps said, his head still hung forlornly. "I'd've saved Maylene and wouldn't feel so low. Hear what I'm saying?"

"It may not have been his bullet," Bravo said, hoping he was correct. He knew he'd never check, never want to know for certain . . . avoid seeing that ballistic report. Yes, he assumed Epps didn't want to know either whether it could have been one of the shots he fired at Abdulo.

"Now that this is over," Baggler said, "we need to get back to Miami."

"Need to check on flights and get back to Washington," Bravo said. Archison's gesture invited Bravo to use any of the offices surrounding the conference room. Bravo avoided using Maylene's. While all personnel prepared to leave, Epps approached Pedrazo. "I don't know more than a few words in Spanish, but I heard that som'bitchen terrorist chief address Bravo as number one just before he shot at him. That's high praise."

Pedrazo's eyes narrowed as he asked: "What did he say?"

Epps thought for a moment. "Sounded like primo. That's number one, right?"

"Did he say primo or primero?"

Epps shrugged as he and Pedrazo watched Bravo reenter the room and announce intention to catch a flight in a little under three hours, so had to get back to the hotel and gather his stuff.

"You can't have the bucar," Baggler said. "We have to take it back to Miami."

"Oh shit," Bravo said.

"I'll give you a lift," Olecki said.

"Let me do that," Pedrazo said. "Two Latinos should talk as they leave town."

Olecki shrugged. "Got to get back to headquarters and make out one long-ass report. Then he and Bravo shook hands and briefly embraced. They looked like they had a lot to say to each other but neither managed to find the words. Cleo thrust out a hand to Bravo, which he shook. She scoffed as she squeezed his hand but refrained from saying anything. Bravo turned away to exchange goodbyes with the others.

#

Pedrazo smirked, relishing the moment as he steered his black SUV onto Federal Highway. "Epps told me Abdulo called you primo."

Bravo's head jerked around. He stammered but failed to say anything intelligible.

"Epps misunderstood it," Pedrazo said. "Confused it with primero, so doesn't realize what he heard."

Bravo gnashed his teeth but didn't respond. He'd hoped to survive having that relationship publicized. And he damn sure lacked faith in Pedrazo keeping his secret.

"Remember that woman who approached me," Pedrazo asked, "the mulatto wife of my cousin? They marry into our families and cast a bad light on all of the members."

"What are you trying to say?" Bravo asked.

"That he can be your cousin because of someone in your family marrying one of them. It is amazing how they affect our lives."

"How does that affect your life?"

"If someone hears that a Negro is related to you in some way, people suspect that you have that blood in your veins as well. If you stand next to one, people study you because your complexion is dark, as if seeking to see in you an infusion of that race."

"His family name is Galbos," Bravo said. "My mother is from that family."

Pedrazo waved that off. "Many of *nuestra gente*—our people—have similar names without being related by blood."

"But I believe that Abdulo is from the same family as my mother."

"*¿Es pariente de suyo negrito?*" Pedrazo asked. He appeared to struggle to deny his face contorting with distaste.

"She didn't appear to have Negro blood. But I need to find out, to tell my sons who they are."

"Let that sleeping dog lie, amigo."

Bravo wagged his head in uncertainty. Having arrived at the hotel he went to check out and get his luggage. While riding the elevator up, then down he contemplated Pedrazo's advice. No, he decided, he would not let that dog lie; would seek the truth. Perhaps as Pedrazo said: someone in the Galbos family married a black person, or one of mixed blood, not unusual in Latino families from the Caribbean. Perhaps it didn't affect Ray's mother. But he vowed to learn that truth.

On the ride to the airport Pedrazo remarked that having dark people in the family is a thing they must deal with. *Estúpidos* in their families marry with *them*. It does not create a problem in Latino societies, but it does among the gringos. If they see you with one of *them* they disdain you as also of that race.

"Rather not talk about it," Bravo said.

"Then you are not sure," Pedrazo said.

"Are you certain of your blood-lines?" Bravo asked. Then he waved that off. "Let's not get carried away with demeaning each other. That's not what this is about. The truth is: I don't know for sure if there are black people in my mother's family. But it's what I need to learn."

"Why? What purpose will it serve?"

"It'll put to rest in my mind who I am. I need also to inform my wife and my boys if that's the case."

"Better they do not learn what they do not presently know, amigo," Pedrazo said as he pulled up to the front of the terminal and parked. "Believe that I know it is better to live without those things to torture the mind."

Bravo wagged his head at that as he thanked Pedrazo for the ride, grasped his luggage and entered the terminal. While shuffling along in the line boarding the plane he bobbed his head first pro then con as he considered going to Puerto Rico to research his family trees. It wouldn't surprise him to learn that he had some strains of blood from the Moros that were driven out of Spain six hundred years ago. And he'd have no problem reconciling that with his wife and his children.

More than likely the intermarriage occurred in Puerto Rico, rather than Spain. As hard as he conjured up the face of his mother and examined that memory, he could not discern a Negroid feature. Probably a close relative intermarried with a black, which didn't directly affect his mother.

Then the question exploded in his mind: What is wrong with infusions of black blood? . . . or any other kind?

The End

www.ingramcontent.com/pod-product-compliance
Ingram Content Group UK Ltd.
Pitfield, Milton Keynes, MK11 3LW, UK
UKHW041945230426
12048UKWH00008B/151

9 781639 451081